To Jeff

Best of luck

John Mac

MW01155719

QUESTION AUTHORITY

John William Macdonald II

⁇

Text Copyright 2012 John William Macdonald II
All Rights Reserved

⁇

This story is a work of fiction. Any events or similarities to people alive or dead depicted in this book are purely coincidental.

As Joel Goodson once said to Bill Rutherford, "Sometimes you gotta say, 'What the fuck! Make your move.'" Risky Business (1983)

⁇

⁇

Chapter 1

The endless waves roll onto shore. The sky is overcast and there is a misty chill in the air which is usual for this time of year along the Southern California coast. The temperature is in the seventies. Behind me sits the Hotel Del Coronado in Coronado, California, and in front of me, across the entrance to San Diego Bay, lays Point Loma. I'm treating myself to a few days of luxury at the Hotel Del before heading off for Europe with Jim for a summer of backpacking, and then we are moving into an apartment in Santa Monica, a few miles from the UCLA campus. When the Navy SEALs passed by on their morning run I got a hearty hoo-yah. I consider myself one of the boys, but I don't run with them. This will make sense as the story unfolds. My name is Susan England.

Just to keep the record straight, all charges against Jim and me have been cleared or dropped. Well, maybe that's not completely accurate, but at least we aren't going to be prosecuted. I am waiting for Jim to be discharged from the Navy, honorably I might add.

Mesmerized by the waves I reflected on how my life had been transformed the past five months and how a lady as naïve and innocent as me could be charged with the heinous crime of murder. Five months ago I was a straight laced bureaucratic staffer in Washington, D.C. My life goal was to marry the man of my dreams (rich), settle down in a suburban colonial house, with the dog de rigueur (Labrador or Setter), have two children (one of each) while maintaining a youthful figure, private schools for the kiddos of course, join the country club, play golf on lady's day, tennis, bridge, lunch on the terrace, cocktails at six, dinner with the 'correct' friends, always invited to the 'right' parties (popular), jewelry galore, clothes (never to be seen in the same outfit twice), big station wagon, travel, second home (can't decide between Nantucket or Florida), and whatever else I felt entitled to as a lady of my stature. Could anyone argue with that?

Never in my wildest dreams could I have imagined living in California with their hippies, drugs, and sex crazed culture. But here I was and now all I craved was a beach life. Was I right in what I did? I believed so or I wouldn't have done it. And I'm sure plenty of people thought that what I did was wrong, maybe to the point of treason. Some of those people are now in prison and for good reason. I questioned authority and did what I thought best, and now I have to live with the consequences. I know I was responsible for others' deaths. Isn't that punishment enough? After I tell my story others can judge as they please.

The escapade started innocently enough when I skipped into work fashionably late on a Monday morning in early October 1967, ready to tackle another boring week in the President's budget office. That's correct; I worked for the President of the United States. Sound impressive? It really wasn't. I was scheduled for a 10 o'clock meeting with the budget director, Mr. Bob Williams, along with several others. I don't recall what the meeting was about, so much had happened since. Randy Finkland not being present was the first sign something was amiss. That was uncharacteristic of Randy who was always punctual and dependable.

I was decked out in my work uniform, an A-line blue wool skirt, white blouse, low pumps, my auburn hair slightly askew, pulled into a bun. I owned nice clothes and dressed according to the occasion, but for work I didn't want to draw attention to myself. Some of the girls in the office dressed for the kill every day. To be frank I was pretty plain, five foot seven, 125 pounds (115 on my driver's license), and no bust to speak of, if it really must be known. I was a good athlete, having played varsity tennis at Smith College in Northampton, Massachusetts. Not number one singles mind you, but good enough to make the team. I'd been called a tomboy which I hated. And nobody mistook me for Natalie Wood, which I also hated.

I was confident with my sexuality. I had a boyfriend (i.e., lover, soon to be his fiancé, so I thought) so I didn't feel compelled to flaunt it. I hate to disparage the other girls in the office, but most of them were on the prowl to upgrade their socioeconomic status, present marital situation notwithstanding. As they say, 'all's fair in love and war.' As I mentioned, this was Washington, D.C., the nation's capital where hard working taxpayers sent millions upon millions of dollars to the government which, in return, was supposed to govern. Governing did go on, but there were a lot of other shenanigans that went on as well. The citizens were to blame. They voted the clowns into office.

When I arrived at the Monday morning meeting I expected to see Randy. We worked in the Executive Office building adjacent to the west wing of the White House. Randy worked as a cost analyst in the administration's budget office, but his real duty was to keep track of the President's re-election finances. I worked as an administrative assistant to the budget director, the before mentioned Mr. Bob Williams. The job title sounded impressive, but I simply scheduled his appointments, travel, dry cleaning, and official entertainment. I didn't need a degree from a prestigious women's college to pick up laundry and I was never going to tell my father that after the exorbitant tuition he'd paid.

Mr. Williams was the prime target of many women. It wasn't difficult to understand, and why not? He was handsome with jet black hair, about six foot one with an athletic build, and alluring mannerisms. He dressed impeccably. Harvard MBA, Colgate undergrad, private prep school, New England social connections, and family money made him a very desirable catch. To the disappointment of many, he was married with two little girls, but that didn't stop the sharks in the secretarial pool from circling. To Mr. Williams I was a know-nothing employee who was there to make his day run smoothly. He and his family lived on a 'gentleman's farm,' near Charlottesville, Virginia. He also owned a townhouse in Georgetown where he stayed during the week.

After I left the meeting I went to Randy's office to see if he'd arrived. The stereotypical geek would be an accurate description of Randy. He wore thick glasses and was slight of build. His hair was too long for the high and tight administration types. He wore retrograde clothing and was shy in demeanor, but it was all an act. Randy was super smart having

5

graduated magnum cum laude from Princeton with a double major in economics and finance. Randy befriended me when I first started working for the executive branch. He was the outcast geek and I was the outcast tomboy. We didn't fit in with the swell, ultra-competitive, overachieving, and glamorous types of the administration. We became fast friends. There was never a sexual attraction between us. We enjoyed one another's company and lambasted anybody wearing a tie or girdle, and we were sure they ridiculed us for being so not-with-it.

Randy and I would go to hippie counter culture coffee houses, listen to jazz and poetry, and get into long, deep discussions about the meaning of life. There may have been some recreational drug use which made the discussions more profound. Randy was against the Vietnam War, as was I, but we would never bring that up at work as we wanted to keep our jobs. On the other hand, we supported the President's war on poverty and affirmative action.

Although I was against the war, I didn't side with the hippies either. No group advocated violence more than those peace loving jerks. Hypocritical doesn't begin to describe those sickos. The typical waitress at a hippie café would be an emaciated waif. She would exhibit the unhealthy complexion of a vegetarian. I imagined the waitress was on a strict diet of granola and hashish. She'd slur, 'hey, man,' which in hippie speak meant, 'may I take your order or do you need a few minutes?' I would get the glare. The hippie people wanted to be accepted as being liberated from all hang-ups, like people shouldn't be judgmental of the way they dressed, or conducted themselves, and normal people should be tolerant of the hippie's weirdness. Everyone should just chill out. So why weren't they tolerant of me? Did I represent the dreaded establishment by the way I dressed? Did they think I was going to be judgmental about them being underachieving, hygienically challenged, drugged out, ne'er-do-well jerks hiding behind a veil of enlightenment? Give me a break.

I called Randy's apartment on the chance he was sick and stayed home, but there was no answer. I asked around the office on the chance somebody had seen or heard from him. Nobody had a clue. I was concerned because this was so unlike Randy. At the meeting I'd made excuses for him.

That evening I called his sister thinking maybe a family emergency called Randy away, even though I knew he would have called his office notifying them that he would not be into work.

Randy's sister, Emily, lived in the SoHo district of Manhattan. She and her husband worked for Goldman Sachs, and made a gazillion dollars a year. They met at work and started a relationship which was taboo, but they convinced their supervisors it would not interfere with their duties. Emily was three months along with their first baby and so excited, and I was so envious.

Conceiving was a struggle for the couple in their mid-thirties. Emily and her husband tried for several years, and then resorted to all sorts of experts including quacks who prescribed herbs and potions. Not being able to conceive seemed to be common among high stressed professionals who'd put off having children until they were 'ready.' My personal belief as to why they couldn't conceive was because they ate only organically grown foods which left them without enough energy or oomph to perform the job properly.

"Emily, have you heard from Randy? He wasn't in his office today, and we had a meeting scheduled."

"No, I talked to him this weekend, but not today," replied Emily.

Emily and I both knew Randy's secret, but we never revealed it to one another. Emily and I were acquaintances via Randy and not confiding friends, but I felt this was important enough to bridge the gap, "Do you think he ran off with his friend? Randy was always talking of chucking it all and moving to Tahiti."

There was hesitation on Emily's end of the line, "I doubt it, though anything is possible."

"Okay, if you hear from him give me a call." I was ready to end the conversation.

"Wait, before you go there is something." I was all ears. "Randy has been acting depressed for the past few weeks. When I talked to him Saturday he told me something disturbing about his work. I don't want to repeat it over the phone."

I was at a loss, but my curiosity peaked. "Listen, I'm going home to St. Louis Friday for my mother's fiftieth. I could change my plans and fly to New York Friday morning. I need to get her a decent present. I can't find anything I like in D.C. I could then fly on to St. Louis. Could we do lunch? Besides, I need an excuse to do some shopping for myself."

"Okay, sounds good," Emily's voice sounded more positive. "Give my office a call when you get in and we'll go from there."

After I hung up I sat on my bed for several minutes contemplating. I shared a two bedroom, two level, townhouse in Georgetown with Mary Jo, a secretary for New York's junior senator. One of my college friends introduced us when I moved to the nation's capital. Mary Jo and I had been living together for over three years, and were not close which I found strange. I knew D.C. wasn't rah, rah college, but still two girls living together should confide somewhat. I tried, but Mary Jo was very guarded to the point of being an introvert. I thought Mary Jo was weird, though harmless, but nonetheless weird. I knew I wasn't. I was the last normal woman on the planet.

Incidentally, the senator Mary Jo worked for was the brother of the President who was assassinated in 1963. Not that it mattered, but in my opinion Mary Jo was a country girl from Pennsylvania, who went to a small college, and was socially in over her head in D.C. Mary Jo tried to look fashionable, but just didn't have the knack. Her brown hair was homely, her figure average. In fact, everything about her was average, from her make-up, to her clothes, to her presentation, everything. I thought Mary Jo was secretive, conniving, and possessed unrealistic ambitions by the way she talked, but who was I to judge? We both agreed not to bring men back to the townhouse, so what Mary Jo was doing or who she was doing was none of my business. And I really didn't care.

When Mary Jo didn't come home at night I didn't inquire the next day. What Mary Jo did with her time was her business. And to be truthful, a few nights I didn't come home. Mary Jo and I girl talked about men we met at work or socially, but never on an intimate level. We didn't speak about our relationships.

Around 9:30 p.m. that evening my boyfriend called. He called every night he wasn't in a late meeting or he wasn't traveling, which seemed to be all the time. We didn't cohabitate which was all the rage in the liberated sixties. His schedule and other factors prevented us from being a high profile couple. The deciding factor was he also worked for the administration and if our relationship became public one of us would have to go. He being senior and a male you can guess which one of us would get the boot.

We were working through this difficult period of our relationship. We were committed to each other and determined that once we were married all of our efforts would have been worthwhile. There were sleepovers and an occasional weekend getaway to Vermont or the Cape, but in public we acted like we were mere colleagues. This arrangement had been going on for well over a year. A reasonable question might be how was an attractive man in his late thirties still available? Answer: he'd been in several relationships, some serious. But with a high pressure job in the administration the modern feminist wasn't going to put up with long periods of inattention. That was until he met wonderful me.

"What's up sweetheart? How was your day?" He inquired.

"Fine, except Randy didn't show up for a meeting. Do you know where he is?"

"No." He responded, sounding distracted. I could always tell when he was doing paper work while speaking with me.

"Yeah, well, I called Randy's sister and she hasn't heard from him. Emily sounded concerned so I'm going to New York Friday to visit and find out what she knows."

He responded, "Let me know what she says. This is unlike him. I hope he's not sick or something." When does a man care about another man's health? We chatted for a while about how much we loved each other and how much we wanted to be together, and some gossip going around the administration before we said goodnight.

I thought Mary Jo should know I was leaving Friday morning. I went down the hall and saw the light on under her door. I knocked, "Mary Jo?"

"Come in," She was lying on her bed reading Time magazine.

"I'm going to New York Friday and then on to St. Louis. I may return Sunday evening, but most likely Monday."

"Have fun," was the empty response I received. So much for close roommates. Wasn't she interested in who I was going to see, or why I was going in the first place, or what I was going to wear? Our detached relationship continued.

I returned to my room and turned on the 10 o'clock news. There was a report of a body found in a burned out car in Fort Marcy Park. The body was burned beyond recognition and no identification was found. I got a sickening feeling.

Chapter 2

In the morning, before I boarded my plane for New York, I called an old friend. It was actually an old boyfriend and the breakup did not go smoothly, so there was some angst. Actually, more like panic, but I needed to find out what he knew about the burned out car in Fort Marcy Park. Eric Stutter was an FBI agent. He was the first person I dated when I moved to Washington, D.C. four years ago, right out of college.

A college friend, who lived in Alexandria, Virginia, took me to see a rugby game at George Washington University where the college friend's boyfriend played. After the match, as rugby games are called, there was a party where I joined in singing filthy songs and got roaring drunk. I needed a day to let go. That was where I met Eric. I had broken up with my college boyfriend, at least that was my recollection, and here was this really good looking guy all muddy and bloody. I don't seek muddy bloody men, but in my state of inebriation Eric looked pretty good.

We left the party early to go back to his place for him to take a shower and as they say, one thing led to another. After all, we had known each other for nearly eight hours. I'm not a one-night-stand type of gal, but I was lonely, and, alright, I wanted to be close to someone. It had been a while, okay? But Eric was a gentleman and called the next evening asking me out, rescuing me from living a life of shame.

I really liked Eric. He was maybe six feet and about 180 pounds, all muscle. He possessed that rugged look, beady eyes, thick brown hair that was perpetually mussed, and a cocky, self-assured demeanor.

The down side, and there's always a down side, Eric was ordinary. It's difficult to put into words without sounding snobbish, but Eric didn't pass the upper crust test. He wasn't top drawer if that makes any sense. He'd graduated from the University of Michigan and he was from Michigan. It's okay to vacation in Michigan, but not to be from there. He was always talking about Big Blue, whatever that meant. We had a great time together. I loved being with him and it was my fault we were no longer a couple. Just as I disparaged the other women in the office for seeking to improve their socioeconomic status by enticing other men, that's exactly what I did. When I met my current love I threw Eric over the side. Working for the FBI was alright, but it was never going to have the earning potential of a person working in the administration with the likelihood of becoming a high profile Washington lobbyist or government consultant. Looking back it was stupid, stupid, stupid.

At the time anybody with half a brain would have understood why Eric was history when I met my new, soon to be, fiancé. But it was time to call the old boyfriend, "Eric. Long time." I stammered.

"Susan, I don't believe it's you. To whom do I owe this honor?" the smart ass replied.

"Well, I wanted to stay in touch," I lied. "It must be over a year. What have you been up to?"

"Working hard trying to keep the nation safe from criminals and unscrupulous women," was Eric's cynical reply.

"You haven't called. I thought maybe you didn't like me anymore."

"When you said, 'Maybe we should see other people,' I took that as adios." He had a point.

"Silly boy, I just needed a breather." I had to give the little dear a glimmer of hope.

"Well, let's get together. How about tonight?"

I thought, 'that's not what I had in mind,' "Actually I'm flying to New York in about an hour, but maybe when I get back." I knew I shouldn't see him, but then again we did have fun.

"I'm curious, are you seeing someone?"

"Matter of fact I am seeing someone." Translated: I'm sleeping with someone. "You wouldn't know him."

"Who is it? I know a lot of people. I heard you were dating someone in the administration."

'How would he know that?' "That's ridiculous, it's not important."

"Why, is he married?"

"I'm not answering that. It's a delicate situation because of our jobs."

"You mean like fraternization?" Eric inquired.

That was enough, "I'm not discussing this anymore." I wasn't going to ask him if he was seeing someone. That could be construed as being interested. "What I called about, has the body found in the burned out car in Fort Marcy Park been identified?"

"How would I know?"

"I thought you guys would know about those things."

"One, no I don't know anything about it, two it's a police matter, not the FBI's, and three, I couldn't tell you if I did. Why are you asking?"

I wanted to be honest, "I'm worried about a friend of mine. He has been missing since Monday along with his roommate." I assumed his roommate was missing because I'd called every night and there was no answer.

"Is this the special someone?" Eric inquired.

"No, this is actually just a friend." Men think women screw every male they know. "If you hear anything would you please call me? It's important. I have this bad feeling something is terribly wrong. I'm flying to New York to speak with my friend's sister, Emily Berg. She also thinks something is amiss and didn't want to speak about it over the phone. His name is Randy Finkland. Please let me know."

"Okay, I'll keep my ears open. So when is our date?" Eric asked.

"I'll get back to you on that." I hung up. Old feelings came rushing back as well as some quilt.

13

Chapter 3

New York, what can I say? Love it, or hate it. There were world class shopping, hotels, restaurants, entertainment, and the financial capital of the world on the one hand. On the other hand there were world class assholes driving cabs, begging, con games, pickpockets, and moral degradation. Personally, three days was my limit.

After paying the cabbie a borough transfer fee for going from Queens to Manhattan and circling the Empire State Building three times I finally arrived at Goldman Sachs in lower Manhattan, three hours after my plane landed and 50 dollars lighter. I found Emily busy on the phone. Emily fit the stereotypical Wall Street hyper neurotic worker bee. She was dressed immaculately in a grey wool suit that was getting tight with the emergence of the baby. Maternity clothes were not going to be flattering in the male dominated financial sector of Wall Street. Her brunette hair was pulled back into a tight bun. The glasses gave her a scholarly look. Every time we were ready to leave for lunch another call came in, or somebody rushed into her office with something that couldn't wait. We finally got settled in one of those trendy restaurants with white table cloths, tuxedoed waiters (no waitresses), where the business men all looked GQ and the women were smartly dressed in Chanel suits, and exquisitely coiffed hair. Even though this was the Age of Aquarius and everyone wanted to be a hippie in one form or another, there were plenty of people chained to the establishment. These were the people making money.

Emily and I exchanged pleasantries and an update on the pregnancy. Emily's brother was the only link between us; hence we weren't close. I broke the ice, "So what do you think is going on? Randy has been missing for almost a week."

"I don't know where he is or what he's doing," Emily responded, "but something has been building up in Randy. He called last weekend and told me some disturbing things."

"Like what?" To me it seemed like a reasonable question.

14

"To be honest I'm reluctant to tell you because I don't know you that well, but on the other hand I know you and Randy are close. I feel I have to trust someone if I'm ever going to find my brother," Emily stated.

"I assure you; whatever you say will be held in strictest confidence."

"Okay, but I feel I'm taking an unnecessary risk. You can't repeat this to anyone," Emily glanced around to see if anybody was eavesdropping. "Randy told me that four Navy SEALs captured over a million dollars in Vietnam on a combat operation this past May. That's odd enough, but what Randy told me next really floored me. He said the money was headed for the President's re-election campaign. As it turns out the SEALs were killed and the money is missing. Randy said the campaign is trying to recover the money without drawing attention. He said he raised questions about the source of the money," Emily continued with her story, "and he asked me how money could be raised in Vietnam for the President. Randy suspected the money was being raised on the black market, but he couldn't be sure. He'd been having trouble legitimizing some of the donations coming into the campaign. Randy was responsible for making the campaign finances appear legal. He said people in the campaign told him to do his job and not worry about how the money was being raised, just make the donations legal. Randy told me he was considering going to the FBI or the government accounting office. He didn't want to be left holding the bag when this thing blew-up. The thing that really bothered him was the idea that the administration was getting its own servicemen killed in order to get the President re-elected. And now he's missing." I didn't think it was a good time to tell her about the burned out car with the unidentified body found in Fort Marcy Park.

I assured Emily, "I'll look into it. I'm sure everything will turn out all right."

We finished lunch and said we needed to get together more often. I assured her I would not rest until Randy's whereabouts were known. I speculated that he probably ran off with his friend for a few days of decompressing. Emily needed to rush back to her office for an important meeting or to do whatever people do that make gobs of money.

I had a bad feeling about Randy's whereabouts as I was sure Emily did. At LaGuardia that evening while waiting for the last flight to St. Louis I called my boyfriend. "I talked with Randy's sister. Randy told her that he thinks something funny is going on with donations to the campaign."

"Like what?" he responded.

I had told Emily I would hold everything in strictest confidence, but then again I said I would look into it. My boyfriend also worked for the administration and maybe he'd heard something. I felt comfortable speaking with him. We didn't kept secrets from each other. "Emily said over a million dollars headed for the campaign was captured in Vietnam by the military and now it's missing, and people in the campaign are looking for it."

I must have sounded alarmed because he responded, "Alright, calm down. Was anyone around you that could have heard your conversation with Emily?"

I answered, "No."

"Good, I have never heard anything about Vietnam in relation to the campaign, but I'll look into it for you." There was something odd about the inflection in his voice.

I asked, "How would the campaign raise money in Vietnam? And from what Emily said, the military captured it from the enemy. Are the Viet Cong raising money for the President's re-election? It would be a good idea for them to keep the President in office. He's been a great asset to them."

"Susan don't be preposterous," he retorted, "the campaign isn't raising money in Vietnam. And be careful what you say young lady. This is not a secure line. If your views were known it'd cost you your job."

I hated it when he talked down to me, "Okay, I'll be careful. But don't you think it's an awful coincidence that Randy disappears and then Emily tells me this story?"

"Yes, I believe it's a coincidence and that's all it is. Randy's suspicion that money is missing in Vietnam and that it is connected to the campaign is pure fantasy. I think his tale about missing money is a symptom of a deeper problem Randy was having. I know he was a friend of yours and I didn't want to talk badly about him in front of you, but Randy was a screwball."

'Randy was having problems, was a friend, was a screwball,' all in the past tense. That disturbed me. I knew I wasn't getting anywhere so I dropped the subject and lied that my flight was being called. I wondered if the enemy was raising money for the campaign to re-elect the President. That did seem farfetched, but then again why not? And if the Navy captured the money, Emily said the Navy Sea Lions or some group like that captured the money, then how could it be missing? Maybe somebody should have a talk with the Navy. I thought the Army was in Vietnam. Was the money on a sampan out in the South China Sea?

This was all too confusing. Maybe servicemen were raising money for the re-election campaign and the enemy stole it. Then the Navy re-captured it, but the men were killed in the process. So how did the President's re-election finance committee know the Navy re-captured the money if they were all killed? The simplest explanation would be that Randy was fabricating this story and nothing of the sort happened as my boyfriend mentioned. To be truthful, how would Randy have found out about anything going on in Vietnam in the first place? None of this was making sense. I'd be home in a few hours and be glad to drop the whole matter.

Chapter 4

I enjoyed going home to St. Louis. I was on familiar turf where I commanded and deserved respect. With being away at college and working in D.C. these past eight years I hadn't visited home for more than a few days at a time. My parents had kept my room as if I still lived there. I should have cleaned out some of my high school memorabilia long ago. The junior/senior prom corsage fixed to the corner of my dresser mirror was wilted, and the vibrant ribbon bow was now faded and drooping.

I remembered the anticipation and preparation for the prom. I spent days dreaming of the close dancing, the mirrored ball reflecting sparkles on the dance floor, and the quiet hushed conversations of couples in a tender embrace. The anticipation was more exciting than the actual event, sort of like New Year's Eve.

My escort to the prom my senior year was Chip McCully. It was one of those situations where I wasn't dating anyone, a common malady for senior high school women. For an underclass woman it was prestigious to date upperclassman and have his high school ring dangling from a chain around one's neck. However, when a girl became a senior and the old steady boyfriend was off to college, guess who sat at home on Saturday nights? That was my dilemma. My contemporary senior male friends, whom I'd snubbed when we were sophomores, now dated the young, perky, peppy, pretty sophomores and juniors, whom I must say, were all sluts. The way they dressed just flaunted it in the seniors' faces. I have to admit I repeated this scenario in college and now I was once again dating an older gentleman in D.C.

I have heard these events ran several more cycles in life. A man in his fifties may dump his wife for a younger, more attractive woman, and if he really made a lot of money he could stretch this into his seventies and even eighties. The more money the male made the greater the age difference between him and his trophy.

Some of my high school friends arranged the date with Chip. Chipper may have been my first gay date. That was my assessment and there was no factual evidence or rumors to support my belief. I considered myself attractive. Chip didn't try anything. He didn't try to kiss me goodnight, or hold my hand, or wrestle me into the back seat. Not that I would have let him, but he should have at least had the decency to try. After all I was a senior. He didn't even get falling down drunk. Now what does that tell you? What kind of senior did he call himself?

Late Friday evening my father picked me up at Lambert Airport. I was glad he came alone. I was sure my mother was exhausted from a day of doing nothing. It seemed I hardly ever got a chance to be alone with my father. "How's my little girl?"

"Fine, it's good to be home."

My father could sense I was withdrawn, "What's wrong? Something bothering you? Are you alright?"

"Nothing, I guess it's work, there's a lot going on," I answered.

"You want to talk about it? Not that I can help, but I can listen." My father was always considerate of my moodiness.

"A good friend of mine has been missing for a week. I'm worried there may have been foul play. You know Washington, D.C. All kinds of funny things happen." I didn't offer any details.

My father's advice was, "Stay out of it. Whatever it is, stay out of it. You are right, D.C. is a wicked place. Don't involve yourself. It can do you no good." We rode in silence the rest of the way home.

The next morning I went down for breakfast only to find my mother mulling over a cup of coffee and a cigarette, "Oh, Honey, it's so good to have you home. I'm sorry I didn't meet you at the airport. I was tired to the bone. You have no idea how much I worry about you. You look as if you're gaining weight?" My mother asked, "What are you eating? And your skin, are you using the lotion I sent? Are you taking your vitamins? How is that young man of yours? When are we going to meet him and his family? Where did you say he was from?"

Enough with the questions, "His family is from Connecticut. I've told you that a million times. He's very busy, but I'm sure you will meet him soon, maybe Christmas."

"Just being from Connecticut doesn't mean he is the sort of young man we would find acceptable."

"Mother, everyone from Connecticut is acceptable," I informed her.

"Susan, certainly they have help in Connecticut."

"The help comes from New York. In the morning the trains that deliver the executives to lower Manhattan return to Connecticut with the help. Then in the afternoon the trains return the help to the Bronx, Harlem, or wherever before taking the executives home." My mother contemplated that for a few moments.

St. Louis was peaceful and quieter compared to D.C., at least the part of D.C. where I lived and worked. Fall was my favorite time of year. Home was safe. I knew which restaurants, clubs, and boutiques I could go into and get whatever I wanted by merely signing my name. There was no reason to carry cash.

My mother looked the same; maybe her hair was a shade blonder. But my father looked older. My mother was going to be 50. Did people really live to 50? I was joking of course, but my parents were aging. The last time I saw my father was at Christmas. It concerned me how much he'd aged in 10 months.

When I came home from college it was either for the Veiled Prophet Ball, Thanksgiving, Christmas, or summer break. Spring break my family flew to our vacation home in Naples, Florida. Naples was a small fishing village on the Gulf coast, close to Ft. Meyers. We loved driving down Gordon Drive to the movie theater or to Beach Store to enjoy chocolate ice cream sodas while sitting at the counter. But the most fun was having bonfires on the beach.

We would throw coconuts into the fire and when they were glowing red we would scoop them out with brooms and play a sort of field hockey. Sparks would fly as we batted the coconuts up and down the pitch black beach.

During the summer I worked in St. Louis as a sales-associate at Saks Fifth Avenue on Maryland Avenue. My job was to call my friends and tell them about a new dress or a unique chapeau that had just arrived from

New York via Paris. If they hurried they would be the only one to have the latest couture from Paris. It's important for women to stand out.

I worked on commission and received a discount on clothes. It was embarrassing when two girls showed up at a garden party wearing the same huge chapeau that I said was, 'the only one.' By the end of the summer I had spent more at Saks than I made in commissions. I think that was part of their business model. Since college I rarely went home. My job in Washington, D.C. and living alone gave me a sense of independence. I cherished that feeling.

We lived in Ladue, a St. Louis County suburb. My parents owned a colonial house in Oakleigh Lane off Ladue Road. Across Ladue Road was the country club where my father spent most of his waking hours in the spring, summer, and fall. In the winter it was racquetball at the Missouri Athletic Club (MAC). Racquetball was a code word for a massage, a two martini lunch, and a nap either in a day room or a reading room in a huge, overstuffed leather wing backed chair with a fire, the lights turned low, and the St. Louis Post Dispatch for a blanket. It was one of the few practical purposes for that particular newspaper. 'Racquetball' left little time for work. I wanted my father's job but I'd been blessed with the wrong chromosomes.

My father's other obsession was flying. He owned a twin engine aero-commander. My mother wouldn't fly with him, believing small planes to be unsafe. This may have been his motivation to fly whenever he could. My younger brother David, my dad, and I would fly to Naples for our spring break. My mother would go commercial. Some of my fondest memories were flying with the men.

My mother interrupted my thoughts, "I've been up since the crack of dawn. I have a million and one things to do. Susan you and I have massages at ten then our hair and nails, and a pedicure. We will never be ready for tonight." My mother switched her attention to my father who was trying to enjoy his breakfast and read the morning paper. "Would it be asking too much for you to stop by Ladue Market and pick up the salmon, and go by the Women's Exchange for the napkins, and Ladue

Florist for the flowers?" I heard a grunt come from behind the Post. My mother took that as defiance. "I wouldn't dare want to interrupt your busy Saturday. What is it, golf, or are you flying around in your airplane?"

Mother gave me an exasperated look. "I guess that is just more I'll have to do today as if I didn't already have enough."

My father got up. "Well it's off to the coal mines. Actually I have to go by the office. I may run a little late. I'm playing racquetball with Jimmy Wider later." I knew why my father went to 'work' early and on weekends, and spent as much time as possible in the easy chair at the MAC. When he was home his time wasn't his own. My mother was always in a fluster about something and never hesitated to make demands on other people's time. I don't believe she ever worked for a wage in her life. Working the past four years gave me a perspective as to what was and what was not a priority.

"What's going on tonight? I thought your birthday party was tomorrow."

"It is, but we are having the Taylors over for cocktails and I thought we would have some nice hors d'oeuvres. I found this smoked salmon at Ladue Market. Whoever thought they would have decent fish? It is simply divine. You know, a little something before dinner," my mother chirped. "And then we are all going to the club for dinner. There's so much to do before tomorrow I didn't want to cook."

What was she talking about? "But Mother, you don't cook," I reminded her.

"I know, but you know what I mean, the kitchen being a mess and the help staying late cleaning up. I want to get a fresh start in the morning." My mother seemed defensive. I knew what she meant; she wanted to get blitzed at the club instead of at home so she wouldn't have a bunch of dirty glasses and ashtrays lying around in the morning. In all likelihood she would invite everyone back to our house for a nightcap and make a mess anyway.

Although it was good to be home I felt the tension. My mother and I got along fine when I was away at school, or away working. But when I was home my mother was critical of everything I did. My father was always the same. He never got excited. He just rolled with the punches. I don't think he worried about appetizers, napkins, or flowers. He could enjoy a cocktail without the frills. After a couple of stiff drinks the flowers were not important. And monogrammed napkins, who cared?

At dinner that evening I was the center of attention. I liked going to the club because the food was excellent and the service was superb. The service had better be superb or the waiter would be looking for a new job. Conversation at the club could be about politics, any religion but Presbyterian, other people's business (making deals was forbidden), sports (the ladies acted annoyed), talking behind other members' backs was always in vogue, travel, children, grandchildren (a very special topic), second homes, and anything that mocked the lesser people.

You noticed I did not mention vacations. My parent's friends did not go on vacation, they traveled. People who vacationed had jobs where they got two weeks off a year. My parents and their friends traveled when they wanted, to wherever they wanted, and for however long they wanted. Sex, perish the thought of that subject being broached unless it was about an affair or somebody's daughter having to go away to 'school' in Arizona for nine months.

What I didn't like about dinner at the club was the constant interruptions. It seemed everyone stopped by our table to say 'hi,' and since I worked in the administration everyone gave me their two cents worth of advice. I think my mother may have embellished my position a bit. "Will you tell the First Lady to tone down those print dresses? She looks like she's going to an afternoon tea with Eleanor Roosevelt." "What's the President going to do about these race riots? You have them right there in Washington, D.C. Of course he's always at his ranch so I doubt he even knows." "If he wants to be re-elected, he'd better show some leadership. This war of his in Vietnam is getting out of hand. If he expects to win he'd better kick some ass. A bunch of sloop heads pushing us around is unacceptable." "Great Society, my ass. Is he going to give welfare to every deadbeat in the country? I'll be damned if I'm going to work my ass off to support some low life drug addict." "I suppose there will be another tax hike this year." Those weren't exact quotes, but that was the general drift. My parents' friends were opinionated. Of course, I supported the President, but I wasn't going to get into arguments with my parents' misguided friends. My belief was why not help those less fortunate? Certainly the country had the means to do so. I was willing to help those in need as long as I got a tax break and it didn't interfere with the principle of my trust fund. I could be as charitable as the next person. The war was a different story. I was dead set against the war. I believed if a man was really a man he would refuse to fight in this immoral war in Vietnam. But that view had to be kept to myself if I wanted to work in the administration.

My standard response was, "I haven't had a chance to chat with the President about those issues. I'll bring it up at our next meeting." The alcohol probably stunted their ability to see through my sarcasm. Did these drunks really think I could just walk in and speak with the President?

The evening dialogue digressed to the women discussing what they were going to wear during the debutante season and what gifts to buy for the newly installed girls, and diets which, in my opinion, were not working. The men gravitated to sports, talking about the baseball Cardinals winning the World Series and worrying about off season trades. My friends from Boston didn't think the 1967 World Series went so well. The football Cardinals were hoping to improve with their second year quarterback Jim Hart, but nobody was holding their breath. If everything went according to rule, the football Cardinals would be booed coming onto the field, booed at halftime, and booed at the end of the game. Sports fans paid a lot of money to freeze their behinds off only to be disappointed. Why? I just didn't get it. I could spend just as much money at Saks and be very happy, and warm, and not disappointed. Well, happy until the styles changed or my father got the bill.

24

I knew one day I would have to grow up and act like an adult, and be pleasant towards people I didn't like. And I would act interested in boring subjects, but I didn't want it to be that day at the club. And maybe one of these days I would think like my parents' friends and would not be anxious to give money to people who, as they said, quit school, had illegitimate babies, resorted to violence, did drugs, and lay around on their fat asses while not working. But it wasn't that day.

Being home I wanted to see my friends and talk about important things like who was doing what to whom, and things along those lines. "If you'll excuse me, I promised some friends I would meet them for a drink. I so rarely get home." I got up to leave.

"But, Honey, you haven't had your dessert. Don't you want to sit and visit for a while? We never get to see you," my mother begged in a pleading tone. Then she snapped her fingers at a waiter, something that always irked me, and changed her tone to that of a domineering bitch, "James, James, we need to see the dessert menu." She referred to all waiters as James. She felt that dignified them. "We've been sitting here for ages. Can't someone clear these dishes for God's sake?" And then hollered, "And another bottle of chardonnay." Changing back to an authoritative tone while speaking to her guests, but loud enough for 'James' to hear, "I don't know what they are going to do about the help around here. It gets worse every day." Some people would think my mother a snob, but it really came down to perspective.

"We'll catch up tomorrow at the big five-o birthday party. It's going to be a blast. And besides, I've been eating too much as you can see." I hoped my mother got the message concerning her rude comment about my weight. I started walking away hoping not to be stopped.

25

Chapter 5

"Que pasa," I heard as I entered the men's bar at Busch's Grove. "What brings you home?" It was Scooter Prime speaking. I don't know what Scooter did for a living but it seemed he was always guarding the door in the men's bar at Busch's. It used to be a men's only bar but in the liberated sixties women were tolerated, and if a young lady showed an old codger enough leg she could drink for free. Scooter wore a tweed jacket, club tie, wool slacks, blue oxford button down shirt, and Bass Weejun loafers. In fact, all the men dressed the same, from 21 years of age to 71. Once in a while a rebel, who graduated from a public high school, would saunter in wearing blue jeans and a tweed jacket with no tie.

Busch's Grove was established in the eighteen nineties as a restaurant/bar on Clayton Road in Ladue. The men's barroom was paneled in dark wood with a long oak bar. The room was filled with heavy wooden tables and captain's chairs. It looked as if nothing changed since the restaurant opened nearly 100 years before. People believed the furniture was original as well as the employees. The bar was perpetually crowded and smoky, always smelling of cigars and bourbon, but nobody complained. It was a local's hangout. The bartenders and waiters were professional and absentminded. Order a hamburger and one was likely to get a steak sandwich. Who cared? It was good to be home.

"I'm in town for my mother's fiftieth. How are you doing?" I didn't want to hear the answer. "Have you seen Franci? She asked me to meet her."

"She's over there," Scooter pointed. He didn't want to answer about what he was doing because he was like so many recent college graduates; he was doing nothing worthwhile. The resume read private high school, Ivy League or some other prestigious eastern school, entry level, or uninspiring first job at dad's business. If a young college grad was pressed to explain their career path to fame and fortune, the line of bullshit was nauseating. There was a fair number of my friends going to medical or law school. They weren't putting on airs of self-importance, yet.

Franci was seated with her back to me at a table with some of my high school friends. I recognized her blonde hair. Maybe it was too blonde. She had a cute figure and dressed to emphasize the better aspects. Some people said she was flashy, but I had known Franci since kindergarten. Deep down she was insecure, and maybe she dressed and acted the way that she did to beg for acceptance. Psychologically I would categorize her as fragile, low self-esteem, and two pills shy of a nervous breakdown.

My high school friends were pretty tight. We didn't welcome strangers. Even in college on the East coast the St. Louis private school kids gathered on weekends and stayed close. It was lonely being away from home. I found myself dating Daisies (St. Louis Country Day School boys) with whom I wouldn't speak to in high school. Loneliness was a terrible thing.

So I was surprised when I came up to the table noticing a couple I didn't recognize. "Franci, can I squeeze in?" Franci's steady beau and soon to be fiancé Jeff, who was in his last year of law school at Washington University, stood and gave me a hug and peck on the cheek. They'd dated off and on starting in middle school. They'd fallen in and out of love a few times.

Jeff's break from Franci was well known. He dated a high society Boston girl while he was studying at Harvard and the Boston girl was attending Radcliff. I doubt anything happened.

I was one of the few people who knew of Franci's misadventure and she prays Jeff will never know. She dated, or should I say shacked up with a drummer from a rock-n-roll band in Philadelphia when she was matriculated at Temple University. If that wasn't bad enough the drummer wore a tattoo of a rose on his butt. I had to take Franci's word on that. The only reason I knew of the tryst was that Franci called in a panic one night because she was late. It turned out she wasn't pregnant, but it scared her enough to tell the drummer to get lost. I believed Franci engaged in the relationship to prove something to herself.

"Yeah, sure if you can stop making out with Jeff. Make some room for fatso here," Franci signaled for another glass of Chablis, as well as one for me while giving me a hug. Franci was my best friend. The reason we hung out at a local bar was the same reason anyone hangs out at a local watering hole. We were skeptical of people not like us and it gave us a sense of security.

Franci introduced me to the other couple, "I want you to meet Jim and Lisa. They went to Ladue High School. Jim is Jane Crotty's older brother."

Jane Crotty was a couple of years behind Franci and me at Mary Institute, an all-girls school where they taught young women to be ladies. Some would say snobs, but those people were jealous. The three of us played field hockey. I vaguely recalled Jane having an unruly older brother. I didn't remember where he went to school, but public school was where the underachievers went, or kids whose parents didn't feel like forking over exorbitant sums of money for a high school education. Then I recalled that he crashed my 16th birthday party. He was drunk at 16. My mother was throwing him out when he threw-up at the front door. Everybody had to leave by the patio door.

I must have been giving him a curious look because Jim said, "My sister tries to keep it quiet about having an older brother." He stood and reached for my hand. It was customary for men and women to shake hands now that we were equals in the new-age sixties. Even with equality ladies still expected men to stand when they approached, open doors, hold chairs, help with coats, fetch and carry, and put up with their incessant whining. Equality was fine as long as ladies were treated with the proper respect they deserved.

"Oh please sit down," I said while acknowledging Lisa with a, 'what's with this guy,' smile and flash of eyes. I tried to read something into him. He didn't look like the aloof, but insecure entry level job guy or the abused professional school student. The best way to describe him was his eyes burned like he was trying to say he disdained me and my social class.

I was about to ask, 'what's your problem?' When Franci said, "Jim's a Navy SEAL stationed in Coronado, California."

Navy SEAL, isn't that the people Emily said captured the money in Vietnam and then lost it? "Enlisted or officer?" was my first question to put Mr. Crotty in his place. I'd already formed an opinion.

"Enlisted," was his sharp answer. Just as I thought, an underachieving enlisted sailor. He probably spent his days chipping paint or mess cooking. In Washington, D.C., sailors marched in parades and stood guard. Not a very promising career.

I wanted to keyhole his social class, "So you hang around with Gidget on the beach?"

"No!"

I turned my head. I may have turned up my nose as I looked toward Lisa, "And what are you doing?" I'd asked rather aloofly.

"I'm working on my masters in psychology at Wash U," Lisa answered.

"Bravo for you," I smiled pleasantly, knowing it would take her ten or more years to work off the student loan.

Franci continued, "Jim was telling us about the time at the Lake of the Ozarks when a bunch of Missouri frat boys jumped off the Grand Glaize Bridge and almost swamped a Jon boat."

"Isn't that quaint, what loads of fun the state college boys have." I was still analyzing Jim. He seemed genuinely pissed with my 'enlisted' put down. I felt like rubbing more salt into his ego wounds. "Whatever made you join the Navy? College too much of a challenge?"

"I thought I was going to be drafted. I didn't want to go into the Army. The Navy seemed a safe bet." He said with a great deal of self-control. I wasn't getting to him, damn.

He was too chicken to go into the Army, "So you thought you were going to be drafted? I could have told you that people from this area don't get drafted. Didn't anyone tell you that?"

29

I braced myself for what was sure to be a smart ass answer, "I don't mind serving. Maybe you can answer a question for me. You look like a smart person. How come with all the equality in our society women aren't drafted?"

"Don't you dare patronize me," was all I said. What an asshole.

At that moment Lisa got up and headed for the powder room. I followed. I think she wanted to get out of range in case glasses started flying.

Once alone, I asked, "So what's the deal with your boyfriend? He seems like a class A jerk."

"He's not my boyfriend. We were friends in high school and bumped into each other at Papagallo's. Jim was with his sister and we decided to stop for a drink. Jane had a date and left just before you arrived. We were about to leave. Maybe catch a late movie. You care to join us?"

I thought the way she phrased her question was an affront. "Hardly, what's a Navy SEAL?"

"Jane said it's some sort of supercharged frogman. I don't know. He just got back from Vietnam a few months ago. He's pretty quiet. I don't think he's comfortable being home. I'm not pressing the issue. I thought maybe he'd like some company. My boyfriend is in Iowa visiting family so I asked myself, why sit home?" Lisa answered. "Jim and I never dated. We're just friends." We returned to the table.

We continued with small talk. Jim didn't enter into the conversation which I thought was either weird or rude. He kept staring with those steel blue eyes. That was beginning to bother me. Finally, I asked, "Lisa told me you were in Vietnam. You kill any babies?"

He gave me a look that actually frightened me. I was about to challenge him with a, 'fuck you,' but thought better of it and decided to drop the issue. Being a lady, I gave my most disconcerting look, turned my back to him, and continued talking to Franci. Jim gave Lisa the sign to leave. I didn't acknowledge their departure.

As soon as they left I asked Franci, "Isn't he the one who was always in trouble?"

"That's the one," Franci said. "Don't you remember he was one of the eight kicked out of Country Day for trashing St. Louis Country Club? All of them were sent to military academies, or boarding schools except Jim. His parents must have thought he wasn't worth the money, and sent him to Ladue High. He didn't change much. I heard he got busted for underage drinking and public disturbance his senior year of high school. I didn't know what happened to him until I ran into Jane today and she told me he was in the Navy."

"Okay, forget him. So what's going on?" I asked.

"Nothing much, I just need to get Jeff through one more year of law school," was Franci's answer. The conversation meandered around to what people were doing and such, but Randy's disappearance and what his sister Emily told me was heavy on my mind.

I got around to asking, "Jeff you're the big time lawyer. How do you find a missing person?"

"Well first, that is a law enforcement question. We don't get involved until an interested party presents us with a legal problem. But what's your real question; somebody missing?" Jeff asked.

"I don't know for sure. A good friend didn't come to work this past week and nobody has heard from him." I continued, "I talked to his sister and she also had not heard from him."

"I hate to ask the obvious, but did you call the police?" Jeff asked.

"You know, I don't know if anyone did," I must have sounded stupid. "I spoke with an old boyfriend who is with the FBI. He essentially brushed me off."

"As he should have. He wouldn't know anything unless it became a federal case, and then it would be a remote chance he would be assigned to the case judging by the size of the FBI." Jeff added.

"There are a couple of other things. On the news the evening my friend disappeared, there was a report of a burned out car with an unidentified body."

"Coincidence," replied Jeff. "Go on, you said a couple of things."

"Yes, I was concerned so, as I told you, I called my friend's sister. She didn't want to speak over the phone. I had lunch with her yesterday in New York. She told me this incredible tale that her brother learned a million dollars in campaign contributions to the President's re-election was missing in Vietnam. Does that make sense?" I asked Jeff.

"What have you been smoking?" Jeff eyed the rest of the tables.

"I'm serious," I reiterated. "What do you think I should do?"

"Nothing, let the police handle this. He'll show up," Jeff said. "And as far as the million dollars in Vietnam for the President's campaign, there must have been a misunderstanding."

"What about the unidentified body? What if it is my friend? They'll never know." I questioned.

"There are three ways to identify dead bodies. I think we learned this in criminal law and litigation, but for some reason I recall it being discussed in properties. The lecturer got side tracked. Anyway, one way is visual. A body is found in an alley. Somebody reports a missing person. The somebody goes to the morgue and identifies the body, simple enough. The second way is fingerprints. This is a little trickier because the dead person has to have fingerprints on file such as a criminal record or been in the military, or other government jobs requiring fingerprints like your FBI friend. And third are teeth. Unidentifiable victims that can't be identified visually and no longer have fingerprints can be identified by their dental records. That's if they have dental records, or teeth. Teeth aren't destroyed by fire. The trick here is to have a pretty good idea who the victim is, such as a plane crash where all the passengers are burned beyond recognition. Their names would be on a manifest which could be used to get the passenger's dental records. There's a fourth way under development. Scientists are working on identifying bodies by using their genetic code, their DNA, but that is years in the future." Jeff surmised.

"Genetic code, that's clever. There's one more thing," I said. "My friend's sister told me that the four Navy people who captured the money were killed."

"You need to read a good book, and get your mind off of missing persons, missing money, and whatever," Jeff stood, "As much fun as this is I need to edit a law review article this weekend and I want to get started, so if you ladies would please excuse me."

I turned to Franci, "Let's go to my house. We still have a lot to talk about."

Once settled at my house with a bottle of Chablis, I asked Franci, "So, what's the deal? When are you two getting hitched?"

"Don't tell anyone. This is top secret," Franci started, "You are the only one who knows. We are announcing our engagement during the holidays. My parents are going to have their usual big, boring Christmas party. Once everyone is there and fairly well plastered, Jeff is going to gather everyone around the Christmas tree to announce a special present. He's going to dig into the tree and pull out a little, bird's egg blue box."

"Tiffany?" I interrupted.

"Yes, let me tell you. I'm going to act confused, excited like, could this really be happening. I'll rip open the box and gaze adoringly at the ring. Tears will come to my eyes and Jeff will drop to one knee. My parents and his parents will come rushing. We'll all hug and kiss and cry, and act so happy, and pose for pictures. My dad is crying because he's already writing checks. We've rehearsed it a thousand times." Franci informed me matter of fact.

"So, when did you pick out the ring?"

"A month ago. We went to New York," Franci swooned. "It was so perfect. We stayed at the Plaza, shopped at Tiffany, and Bergdorf Goodman. We dined at the Russian Tea Room and Tavern on the Green. Of course we took a romantic horse drawn carriage ride through Central Park. We even got to see Cabaret, the Tony award winning Broadway musical that's impossible to get tickets for, but Jeff has a friend who does marketing for Broadway productions. We did the works. Anyway the ring is pear shaped with….. wait I want you to be surprised. I can't wait until you see it. You have to be there."

33

"Don't worry, I'll act surprised. You bet I'll be there. I wouldn't miss this for the world," I gushed. "Did you make love?"

"I know I said I would never make love with the man I was going to marry before we said 'I DO', but the day we picked out the ring is the same day we went to the play and then a late supper. It was too much. We went back to his room. There was a bottle of chilled Dom Perignon '62, and a dozen roses. He got me drunk." Franci rationalized.

I reminded her, "I remember you also saying you would never have premarital sex. But we know how that worked out."

"So I was a virgin twice. Is that so terrible? The first time with drummer boy I acted like a seasoned veteran. With my second partner Jeff, I acted like a virgin. What's the big deal? Do you want to hear this or not?" Franci asked.

"I definitely want to hear this," I demanded. "So you played the virgin card?"

"Of course I did. Jeff would drop me in a second if he ever found out. I cried and made him feel terrible. We talked about it and then did it again a half hour later. But the morning rituals have got to stop. I mean as soon as I stirred he was on me, morning breath and all, and I had to pee like a race horse. I must have looked a fright, but that didn't slow him down one bit. He was hell bent on one thing. There are going to be some rules about that." Franci demanded. "And one more thing, you ever refer to drummer boy, and you will die a slow, horrible death."

"Okay, no jokes about how drummers can pound for hours." I added.

"There'd better not be. I'm serious about this. I know I'm not the brightest girl in the world, but I have to make this work, and you know why." Franci was serious.

I figured what Franci meant was that she didn't want to work for a living and marrying Jeff was her chance to live the life she felt she deserved. Why she felt she deserved to live like a princess was the result of the culture in which we were raised. I'd always thought I'd work for a year or two after college and then go to law school or get an MBA. And then land Mr. Wonderful. The goal was to work if I wanted, but not to

34

have to work. And here I was, four years out of college and nothing. Well, there was hope with the current prospect.

"One more thing, would you consider being my maid of honor?" Franci asked off handedly.

"Would I consider? I would be honored." We hugged and maybe kissed each other's cheek. Tears came to our eyes, the way silly girls act. "I wouldn't miss this for the world. Go on."

"The wedding is going to be in June, the week after Jeff's law school graduation. The ceremony will be at Ladue Chapel and then to the club for the wedding reception with a string quartet in the foyer for the reception line, dinner orchestra, dance band. You know the usual rigmarole. We are going to Paris and probably hit a few other European capitals for two weeks, and then it's back to St. Louis. Jeff will be studying all summer for the bar exam. We'll have to sneak away to Nantucket for a long weekend just to stay sane. The Grays have offered their place in Madaket in August. They are going to be skiing in Chile. Jeff has tentatively accepted a position with Armstrong Teasdale but who knows?" Franci said.

"Is that all?" I asked.

"Well, we've made an offer on a house. Jeff will live there until I can legally move in." Franci added. "But I'm sure there will be a few conjugal visits."

"A HOUSE!" I was shocked. "How long have you been planning this?"

"You have to plan years in advance. Do you have any idea how far in advance you have to reserve Ladue Chapel for a June wedding? And the club, with all the debutante parties, and weddings we were lucky to get both on the same day. Anyway, the house is a small three bedroom, two bath ranch in Olivette, just a little starter home. It's not my idea of anything nice but it will have to do for a few years until Jeff gets established and we can move to Ladue. Our parents helped with the down payment. One bedroom will be Jeff's study and the other one in case a little visitor arrives."

35

"Wait, I have to catch my breath." I gasped. "The engagement and wedding were enough, but now you've bought a house and talking babies."

"It's time to move on. What about you? I thought you would have similar news." Franci said. "And when are we going to meet this mysterious man of yours?"

"Yes, that is a problem. You have no idea how hectic it is in D.C." I made excuses. "You'll meet him soon. I think we will be engaged within the year. We are having serious discussions." I lied.

Franci sighed. "You're four years out of college. You're not old but time waits for nobody. Tell him to get it up or take it someplace else."

"Franci, really! I know it's frustrating. When you work for the President your time is not your own. Our jobs are very demanding. There is a lot of pressure. Things will settle down once the President is re-elected," I said. I don't think I was fooling Franci. I needed to change the conversation from me. "You and Jeff really in love? I don't mean love like it's the proper thing to do because your parents approve. But love like you really feel he's the man for you."

"Jeff and I have our moments. I get fed up with his long hours at law school. His study group meets at all hours of the night. And people have told me it only gets worse when he starts practicing. But we have common goals of where and how we want to live," Franci said. I guessed in Franci's mind that's what passed for love, the proper address, the proper job, and the proper social standing. What else was there to life?

We covered the same ground several times talking about the meaning of relationships and how everybody was messed up except us. We gabbed until Sunday's break of dawn. It took more than a few bottles of wine to cover all the subjects. In a few hours the tent people and caterer would be arriving to prepare the house for my mother's birthday party. It was going to be a rough day.

Franci got up to leave, "Listen, I've got to get going. I'll see you this evening at your mother's party."

I interjected, "So now you are marching to the beat of a different drummer."

"Susan, I'm warning you. One crack like that around Jeff and I will make your life a living hell." Franci seemed vulnerable. She had a perplexed look on her face. "Do you think they know?"

"Know what?" I asked.

"Do you think Jeff knew I wasn't a virgin?" Franci asked.

"Would you like for me to ask him?" Franci was a mental lightweight, and it was fun to goad her.

"No, don't you dare. I think he would have said something. And drummer boy, I wonder if he knew I was a virgin."

"Was he high at the time?" I knew the answer.

"He was always stoned," Franci answered.

"Then I doubt he cared as long as he took care of his business." Franci worried about the most inane things.

The party was what I expected, a lot of people standing around making small talk. My parent's friends again asked me what I thought of the President's policies. Of course I defended the administration. I had no choice. It was amazing how an innocent comment could get back to Washington, D.C. and cost a person their job. I'd seen it happen.

The biggest topic of conversation was my mother becoming a grandmother in three months. This was yet another sore point between my mother and me. My younger brother, who worked in Chicago was about to become a father. And here I was not even engaged. My mother would have been mortified to learn I'd been involved with three men without so much as a proposal. She would have been horrified if she learned I'd been involved with even one man.

After the guests left, my father cornered me in his study. I could tell he'd had too much to drink. I couldn't blame him for being in a state of semi-consciousness. A bunch of half century old hags blabbering about who knows what could drive any sane person to drinking. "How is your job really working out?" my father asked.

"It's fine," which meant, 'things could be better.' "There's a lot of stress with the election, even though it's a year off. I think the President is losing popularity. The money for his re-election isn't coming in like it should."

"You'd better believe he's losing popularity," my dad roared. "This Great Society idea of being everything to everybody is a bunch of hooey. There will always be smart people and dumb people, people who can accumulate wealth and people who can't hold onto a dime."

"Yes, but don't you believe everyone should have an equal chance?" I asked.

"Everyone does have an equal chance. Some people just don't capitalize on it. It's a matter of making choices. The best and brightest will always succeed no matter what environment they came from. But the President's idea to spend exorbitant resources on a few bums who don't have the skill or desire to succeed is foolhardy. The government needs to spend money promoting those who will create jobs, create products, heal, teach, or serve others. A college education isn't for everyone, neither is a high school education for that matter. It's a cruel, competitive world. Some people are going to fall behind, but to spend time and resources out of guilt that everyone must succeed is pure folly. I'm sorry, I didn't mean to lecture. There's one fact in life that no government program can cure, life isn't fair. Be skeptical, especially in Washington, D.C. Politicians always have an ulterior motive to any program or policy, and it comes down to greed and power. Never hesitate to question authority."

"Some people believe they don't get an equal chance. They believe the deck is stacked against them," I argued. "You belong to a private country club and you're on the board of directors of corporations. People are shut out of such groups and never get a chance at wealth. There's a socioeconomic inequality. Those people don't feel they have the chance you espouse."

"I'll tell you a secret. You produce a product people need or want, price it right, manage it correctly, and I don't care who you are, you will be a success. It could be a chocolate chip cookie, fried chicken, or a portable phone you could carry in your pocket, it doesn't matter. It takes getting an education, hard work, believing in yourself, and patience. Try doing that in the Soviet Union or China. If you sit around believing you are a victim you are only going to get what the government hands out, and it will never be enough."

"Okay Daddy, I'll tell the President to screw the underachievers and promote the achievers," I said it with a straight face.

"Now you're catching on." My father could also be sarcastic. However, I still believed some people were held back by factors beyond their control.

I caught a late plane Sunday evening. I'd talked to and seen my friends, and accomplished all I wanted to in my short visit home. Something about living and working away from home made me anxious to return to Washington, D.C. I didn't live in St. Louis anymore. My life was in D.C.

Little did I know, but I was not going to be attending Franci's engagement party at Christmas, or be her maid of honor in her wedding in June. In fact by Christmas I wasn't even going to be in the country.

Chapter 6

Looking back this was where I made my biggest mistake in the past five months. Once I got settled in D.C. after my trip home, I gave my friend Eric a call at his FBI office. I should have dropped the whole matter of Randy's disappearance, but he was still missing, and I felt an obligation to Emily, and for selfish reasons I wanted to see Eric. "Eric, I bet you didn't expect to hear from me so soon. I was thinking maybe we should have that lunch."

"Just lunch?" he asked.

I knew what he meant. "Yes, just lunch and nothing more. How about today in a very public place?"

"Alright, I was kidding," he demurred, "how about the Capital Grille at noon?"

"Pretty fancy, I thought you would suggest an Irish pub where they sang filthy rugby songs and broke chairs over each other's heads."

"Actually now that you mention it that does sound inviting," he pondered. "But I have a seminar nearby and the Grille would be more convenient for both of us."

"Capital Grille at noon. You got it." I should have known better than to mention a pub.

I wore a Christian Dior suit I picked up at Bergdorf Goodman's while on my trip to New York when visiting Emily. Nothing fancy, an off white wool and silk waist coat with a high collar and three quarter sleeves, and a navy blue felted wool pencil skirt that barely came to my knees. Well not quite to my knees, but not tacky, suggestive, but not tacky. It fit really well. I mean really well. Something I wouldn't dare wear around my mother. And I wore three inch stiletto heels even though heels were now verboten according to feminists who believed heels represented male oppression of the female. Okay, I wasn't wearing my usual work uniform, but when having lunch with a dear old friend I thought it appropriate to look presentable. "You look great," Eric said as he gave me a kiss on the cheek, and held my chair.

"So do you." And he did. We got seated and ordered. Eric requested a hamburger and I a salad. I desired the hamburger, but I wanted to give him the impression that I was watching my weight. I don't know why. I wasn't trying to be alluring or anything. Or was I? We practically lived together for over two and a half years and he knew I ate everything. Why would I want to impress an ex-boyfriend? We caught up with what we'd been doing for the past year. Of course I played down my relationship with my boyfriend, saying we were just good friends. Eric would not commit to having a serious relationship.

I got to the point, "Have you found out anything about my missing friend Randy?"

"No." I could tell by the inflection in his voice he was lying. "To tell you the truth the FBI and the local police don't collaborate on such matters."

"Have you heard anything about the body found in the burned out car in Fort Marcy Park?" I asked.

"I told you the body was burned beyond recognition. They will never know who it was." Eric lied again.

"Teeth Eric, they can identify the body by the teeth." By the look on his face I knew I caught him in a lie.

"We can't compare the victim's teeth with every dental record in the world. There is no national or world organization capable of comparing dental records like there is for fingerprints."

"Check Randy Finkland's dental records and tell me what you find, why don't you?" I scolded. "Randy grew up in Vermont and went home for doctor's visits."

"I don't have the authority. I'm not getting involved with this," Eric answered. "Who besides me have you discussed this with?"

"Well, I told my boyfriend because he knew Randy, and my father, and some high school friends. One's a law student. He told me about the teeth. Don't you think you should have told me about the teeth?"

"I'm giving you some friendly advice. Don't discuss Randy's disappearance with anyone, and I mean anyone, especially your boyfriend." Eric was serious. "Never discuss Randy Finkland again."

"You're scaring me." I said sarcastically.

"You won't think you're so tough after I tell you a few things." I think Eric was pointing his finger at me. "Emily Berg, her husband, and unborn baby were killed this past weekend while you were shopping in New York.

"Emily and her baby?"

"Yes, they were sideswiped into a telephone pole on the Long Island Expressway. Emily was ejected through the front windshield and landed 50 feet from the car. Her husband took the telephone pole in the kisser. His mother couldn't recognize him. Since it was their car and his wallet was on the body they assumed it was Emily's husband. Randy Finkland's apartment was ransacked and his dentist's office in Vermont can't locate his dental records. There is evidence of the dental office being broken into. Another bit of news, a body was found in Maryland in a dumpster behind a grocery store with a bullet in the head, and a 0.30 caliber police special revolver in his hand. They've identified the body as Clay Ericison. Does the name ring a bell?"

I was wiping a tear from my eye, "Yes, he was Randy's partner. You know what I mean by 'partner?' They lived together,"

"I gathered as much by what was left of their apartment," Eric stumbled. "I mean some of the things in the medicine cabinet, furnishings and some of their clothes made it obvious."

"Wait, I thought you said you weren't involved?"

"Okay, I checked with a few friends from the local police departments," Eric admitted. "Except for the apartment and dental office everything I've told you is a matter of public record, if one knew where to look. You can draw your own conclusions." Eric seemed satisfied with himself, and he was right, I was worried. "There are a couple of other things that are not public record and I shouldn't be telling you."

I reached across the table placing my hand on top of his, "What is it? This is important to me Eric," I pleaded.

"Okay, but you have to promise you didn't hear this from me. It could turn out bad for both of us," Eric said. "The burned out car with the unidentified body was registered to Mr. Ericison. They got the engine block number and traced it to him. Also, there was a suicide note in Mr. Ericison's pocket. The note has not been released to the public. It said, 'I can't go on. Randy was seeing someone else. If I can't have him to myself then nobody will. I've destroyed the most precious person in the world.' The police are calling it a murder/suicide."

"Bullshit. Double bullshit!" I may have raised my voice. People were turning and looking at me. I lowered my voice, "No way. I'm not buying that for a second."

"I've already told you more than I should. I'm just saying, drop it. There's a lot more going on than you could possibly imagine."

"Like what?" I asked while caressing his hand.

"I said, I've already told you too much,"

"You have to know it was Randy in the burned out car. Why can't the authorities release his body to his parents so they can have a funeral?"

"There are people in power who don't want the body identified. It's not going to be identified. That should tell you something." Eric seemed to want to conclude our lunch. He removed his hand from mine then launched into a full explanation, "There was no blood splatter amongst the body in the dumpster."

"So?" I asked

"It means that Mr. Ericison committed suicide someplace other than the dumpster, understand?" Eric explained. "Suicide victims are usually found where they commit the act."

"Oh," I admitted.

"The gun was bought in Virginia a few days before the 'murder/suicide.' We traced the serial number. It was paid for in cash, no name or address. Someday we need a law where we know who buys these guns." Eric went on, "From what the police have pieced together from friends and witnesses they know Mr. Finkland and Mr. Ericison were drinking white wine spritzers, smoking grass and dancing at the Galaxy

Club the night they disappeared. The police surmise the abductors must have grabbed the victims in the parking lot, and disabled them, maybe using chloroform soaked gauze."

"The abductors knew the suicide victim would eventually be found and identified and the police would construct a timeline of the victim's final movements. And the abductors knew the police would cooperate with them on the murder/suicide scenario. The people who instigated this murder/suicide are immune to authority. You getting what I'm saying?"

"The abductors must have driven the victims to Fort Marcy Park. They put Mr. Finkland in the trunk, doused him with gasoline, and lit the car on fire. Before they did that they may have shot Mr. Ericison in front of Mr. Finkland to motivate him to give information. The abductors then drove Mr. Ericison's body to Maryland."

"What information?" I knew about the missing money in Vietnam, but I wanted to find out what Eric knew.

"That's it young lady. Our conversation is over. How about dinner tomorrow evening?" Eric calmly interjected.

I was distracted for a moment thinking of Emily and her baby. "Oh, I can't, I'm leaving for California in the morning, a Presidential site visit. I don't think it would be wise for us to be seen together." I hoped that clarified our relationship status.

"Alright, that's fine. If that's the way you want it. One more thing, here's my home number in case you don't have it anymore. If anything funny happens, I don't care what time of day or night, call me at home or the office," Eric said.

"Anything funny?" I asked.

"Threats, people following you, strange calls, or anything suspicious, I want you to call me anytime." Eric was serious.

I didn't like it, but I couldn't act scared, "Alright, I'll call if I see the bogeyman."

Eric paid and got up to leave, "You really do look good. I wish we could.....oh, never mind." And he walked away.

When talking to my boyfriend that evening I mentioned, "I heard at work that Randy's sister was killed in a car accident this past weekend. There seems to be too many coincidences." I didn't mention I had lunch with Eric, or any of the other things Eric told me. Why stir things up? My boyfriend knew I was involved with another man at the time we met.

"I don't know what to make of that. Susan, drop the whole matter of Randy's disappearance. Let the police handle this. It's only bringing you undue stress," he said. "He's going to show up."

I told my roommate Mary Jo that I was traveling to California on business. The trip had been scheduled for weeks. I'd never been to California and when a Presidential site visit popped up I shamelessly begged to be included. It was a fringe benefit. One of the perks of working in D.C. Mary Jo reacted with her usual lackluster response, "Have fun."

'Don't tell anyone, especially your boyfriend,' kept repeating itself over and over in my mind. What did Eric mean by that, what did he really know?

Chapter 7

The furthest west I'd traveled was with my family on ski trips to
Aspen, Colorado and Sun Valley, Idaho. My mother thought California was
too uninhibited for our family. One of my good friends in college was from
San Francisco and she was every bit the lady, so I thought California would
be safe.

The advance party checked into the Hotel Del Coronado, across the
bay from San Diego. This was the hotel where the President would stay. I
demanded my room be changed to one with an ocean view. My mother
taught me to never accept the first room offered. She said if you did the
hotel staff would not respect you. Once in my room with an ocean view
and a complimentary gift basket for being an obnoxious twit, I looked up
the number for SEAL Team.

Franci mentioned Jim Crotty was a SEAL and stationed in Coronado,
California so why not? There was a listing for SEAL Team One. I called
asking for Jim Crotty. The man who answered said Petty Officer Crotty was
on a jump or something. I tried to sound intimidating saying I was with the
White House. Whoever answered the phone didn't seem impressed. I told
him to have Petty Officer Crotty call Susan England at the Hotel Del
Coronado as soon as he returned.

He said, "Yes Sir, Petty Officer Crotty will receive your message." He
made 'Sir' sound like 'bitch.' I made a mental note of his name.

The person in charge of the White House detail gave us until lunch to
get settled. We got our day's assignments during a working lunch in a
conference room. After lunch we went about our assignments checking
out sites the President would likely visit. The secret service would have
final say on travel routes, entrances and exits, and time schedules, but we
scouted the locations the President was to visit for photo angles, lighting,
catering, bathrooms, rest areas, and all the other little things to make the
President's visit appear seamless. When I returned to the hotel a little
after five there was a message from Jim Crotty saying he would be at the

Trade Winds bar until six or seven. The concierge seemed mystified that I would want directions to the Trade Winds. He looked up the address, and was surprised to find it was across Orange Avenue from the hotel.

I rushed to the Trade Winds. As soon as I walked in I knew I wasn't in the men's bar at Busch's. No one was wearing tweed. It was like going to another world. Nowhere I'd traveled was a low life bar across the street from a first class resort. It was dark, smoky, with two pool tables and sparse furniture. The place was crowded and noisy. All the guys looked the same, sharp features, blonde, muscular, a few Fu Man Chu mustaches, and hard glares. Some had tattoos. When I said muscular I meant in comparison to the noodle arms that worked in the administration in D.C. There were a few body builder types. They grossed me.

I must have looked conspicuous because I felt everyone staring at me. I was about to leave when one of the blonde men with piercing blue eyes came up and inquired, "Ms. England is that you?"

"Yes, Jim?" I tried to sound familiar.

"I figured it must be you. Nobody would come in here dressed like that."

If he was trying to start off our evening on a good footing he was failing miserably. "What's wrong with the way I'm dressed?" I was wearing a charcoal gray Chanel suit and Ferragamo Philippa pumps. Certainly I was dressed appropriately. I looked around. The men wore shorts, flip-flops and tee shirts, the women wore blue jeans or those dreadful denim miniskirts with halter tops. Flab on the women was bulging out, without any effort to conceal the blubber. Some of the women displayed tattoos, ugh, make me barf. I didn't know how long I would last in that environment. I knew across the street was refuge in the Palm Room at the Hotel Del Coronado.

"Nothing, you look great. Can I get you something?" Jim asked. He actually had manners, which was a pleasant surprise.

"A Chablis would be nice, thank you." I could tell he was embarrassed to be with me.

"I think they only have beer and hard liquor. Hang-on, they may have a gallon of Thunderbird wine."

"Never mind, may I please have a club soda with a lime twist," I asked politely.

"Sure," he rolled his eyes. What was wrong with these people? The boys were playing pool and drinking beer, laughing and talking. The girls were lined up along the bar, some talked to the guys. One of the girls played pool, never taking the cigarette out of her mouth. I guess she was the tough one. Of course, she wore the shortest mini skirt of the entire herd. The guys got behind her for a glance when she bent over the table. One guy mimicked ramming his pool cue up you-know-where, how quaint. She knew what she was doing. The girls also drank beer. One dike was doing Tequila shots. Excuse me that was uncalled for. I should never refer to a member of the fairer sex in such derogatory terms. I noticed hair on her chest.

"Here you go," Jim handed me my drink sans the lime twist, "So, what's the deal? I didn't expect to see you again. Isn't this a little beneath your social class? The guy on duty said you were with the White House. Am I in trouble with the President?"

"In trouble with the President, are you in trouble?" I asked.

"Never mind," Jim responded. "So what can I do for you?"

"Actually I do work for the White House. I'm out here for a Presidential site visit."

"He's not coming to our area is he? We'll have to get haircuts and paint everything that doesn't move. Presidents are a pain in the ass."

"You should work for one. Since I'm out here can a St. Louis girl buy a St. Louis boy dinner? I'd had a little too much to drink the night we met, and I feel I was rude and owe you an apology."

"You don't have to take me to dinner, but I'm not too proud to pass up a free meal. Do you have someplace in mind?" Jim asked. "And as far as the apology goes, we enlisted pukes deserve to be treated like shit."

Okay, he was pissed. I deserved that. "I was thinking the Prince of Wales room over at the Hotel Del." I didn't want to talk in the bar. It was

48

too noisy. I would have to speak loud and I was afraid someone would overhear.

"You are full of surprises. That's not my usual hangout. I think its coat and tie. And it may be hard to get reservations this late."

"I have a White House ID. I can get reservations. Can you get a coat and tie?" There I go again, acting snobbish. It's part of my breeding.

"What time?" Jim asked.

"Is seven too early?"

"I'll be there. And yeah, I have a coat and tie." We finished our drinks in virtual silence. "If we are going to make seven o'clock I better get going. I'm pretty sure I know where I put that coat and tie." He turned his back, and disappeared into the crowd. I figured that was my cue to leave. I put down my glass and left.

Dinner was strained. We talked about his sister and a few mutual friends we had while growing up in Ladue. We figured out we attended some of the same high school dances. I remembered his crowd. They snuck in booze which led to fist fights and their cars were loud and fast. No way in the world would I have ever associated with that group, and here I was having dinner with one of them.

When we finished our chocolate soufflés we ordered after dinner drinks. I was dying for a cigarette. You'd think by now he would have offered me one. "Do you mind if I smoke?"

"No, go right ahead."

Okay, now was the time for Jim to pull out a pack of cigarettes, but no, he just sat there. I fumbled in my purse making a big fuss over the inconvenience. "Would you like one?"

"No thanks, I don't smoke," Jim answered.

Oh no, a health nut. He ordered prime rib so I don't think he was a practicing vegetarian. Certainly he must have a cigarette lighter or matches to light a lady's cigarette. I waited. When he made no effort to light my cigarette I again made a big show of lighting my own cigarette. I reared my head back and blew the first drag into the air, very elegant, very sophisticated. I should have blown it in his face.

Feeling more relaxed I asked, "Franci said you were a SEAL. What is that exactly?"

"It's the Navy version of the Army's Green Berets. The Navy commando's, counter insurgency, covert operations, unconventional warfare, operations like that," he answered.

"So I guess you don't chip paint or mess cook?" I asked.

"No, but there's enough bullshit that I'm getting out of the Navy as soon as I can."

"And your lady friend said you'd been to Vietnam?" I knew all this, but I wanted to get his reaction.

"Yeah," he answered. "Remember you asked me if I killed babies?"

"I'm sorry about that. Sometimes I don't think before I speak." I wasn't getting anywhere. Jim didn't seem like the talkative type. I had to take a chance, "Last May were four SEALs killed in Vietnam?" The look he gave me made me want to crawl under the table.

But he responded calmly, "Why do you ask?"

"I heard some people at the White House talking about it. Do you know what happened?" I couldn't trust telling him what I knew.

"I heard the platoon found an 82 millimeter ChiCom mortar on an operation and brought it back to their hut. They were disassembling it when it exploded," he answered. "I don't think that is top secret information. It was in the San Diego Union paper except for the part about the ChiCom 82 millimeter mortar."

"ChiCom?" I asked.

"Chinese Communist, they sell armament to the North Vietnamese," was Jim's reply.

"Have you ever considered that maybe they were killed intentionally?" This was a shot in the dark. My reasoning, having worked in D.C. for a number of years, was this; a large sum of money missing that was linked to the administration, people disappearing, people killed, equaled government involvement. And after what Eric had told me about the murder/suicide, the missing dental record, and Emily being killed, I was certain this wasn't a bunch of coincidences.

"You've caught me off guard. You presented yourself as a society snob with a do-nothing job in Washington, D.C. I was impressed when you mentioned Vietnam. I didn't think your type was aware there was a war."

"I understand your skepticism, but I have reason to believe they were killed by our government," Either Jim was going to walk out, or have me arrested, or kill me.

There was a long pause, "What did you say your job was again?"

"I told you. I work for the President. A good friend of mine and co-worker has disappeared. I believe his disappearance is related to the death of the four SEALs."

"I hope you are not some nut job," Jim stated. "You are sure acting like one."

"I can understand how you might think that. But my friend Randy may have found out something about the SEALs being targeted. I know this sounds crazy, but I need to know. I promised his family." Which was a little late for his sister Emily, but I had to say something, "Did the SEALs find anything that would have lead them to being killed?"

"You're scaring me, Lady. I don't know anything. I really should be going. It was great seeing you one last time," Jim started to get up.

I grabbed his arm. "I need your help," I pleaded. After what Eric told me I felt more compelled to get to the bottom of Randy's disappearance. It may have been my competitive nature. On the surface I knew it would be best to drop the whole matter, but deep down I was driven to find the truth.

He motioned, "Let's get out of here. You'd be surprised who could overhear us," as he reached for his wallet.

"No, I'll take care of this. I insist," I said. "Let the taxpayers grab this one. I have per diem." I signed the check along with a generous tip, and provided my room number.

We took our after dinner drinks to the pool deck, out of everyone's hearing range. It was chilly with the onshore breeze. Jim offered me his coat, which I didn't expect, but was nice of him none the less. I glanced at the label 'Brooks Brothers', maybe there was hope for him after all.

Jim asked, "What was that about something being found?"

"I was hoping you could tell me."

"I wouldn't know anything. I'm an enlisted puke. They don't tell me squat. I was leaving Vietnam when I heard about the explosion. I was in another part of the country. That's all I know." Then Jim surprised me with, "Why are you asking me? Is this some kind of trap to see if I'll disclose confidential information and get me in more trouble?"

"No, you have to believe me. I feel you are my only chance to find out what really happened. You're a SEAL. Don't you want to know?"

"Sure I'd like to know, but I can't go walking into the captain's office, and ask if the government killed four SEALs."

"I was hoping you could snoop around and find out. See if anybody knows what really happened."

"No promises, but if I hear anything I'll be in touch. Let me walk you back to your room."

At the elevator Jim's farewell was, "If I don't see you again, enjoy your visit."

As he turned to walk away I replied, "I'll be here for a few days. Please help." I felt I'd already said too much and that I could be in trouble. I should have forgotten what Randy's sister told me and gone back to my normal boring life. What I didn't know was there was no going back. The next thing I expected was the FBI to kick down my door and haul me off to prison.

Chapter 8

The next morning I woke up at four which was seven a.m. in D.C. It was still dark. I couldn't fall back to sleep so I read a little of <u>Death of a President</u> by William Manchester, appropriate for my line of work. When it was eight his time I called my boyfriend at his office. "How's it going big boy?"

"Fine, I didn't hear from you yesterday. I was worried," was his reply.

"We didn't finish until late. I didn't want to wake you." I skipped the part about asking another man to dinner. "But everything is going great. We really should come out here by ourselves. It's gorgeous and the weather is unbelievable. I have a room with an ocean view."

"As soon as the President is re-elected we are going to do all sorts of fun things. Four more years in the White House then we are set for life. We'll be married by then. When do you think you'll be back?" he asked.

I couldn't believe he mentioned marriage. "They allowed us a week, but I imagine we'll wrap this up in a few days. The President is only going to be here for one night. How many places can he visit? I can't wait to see you. Hey, have you heard anything from Randy?" Even though I was pretty sure I knew the answer.

"No, still no sign of him. Don't worry. He'll show up," he added. We bantered on for a while then he said he had to get to a meeting. I knew a brush off when I heard one.

After breakfast I went for a walk along the beach. I had the place to myself as there were very few people out that early. I was walking south when a group of men came running toward me. I stepped aside. All they were wearing were short khaki trunks. The first few who passed were fast. They were lean, muscular, and ran like gazelles. About mid pack I heard, "Hey, Susan." I recognized Jim as the guy with the big smile. The next 10 men or so must have heard Jim because they all offered good morning greetings. I heard comments like, "Whoa, Jim's getting lucky." And, "Hoo-Yah Susan," whatever that meant. The last few stragglers didn't look as fit. They were jogging along at a conversational pace.

For the next couple of days I got involved with my job, and almost forgot about Randy. I wished then that Jim would drop the matter and not call. I may have over reacted about Randy's disappearance. I should have left well enough alone and not gotten involved as everyone suggested. As time went by, I became less upset about the circumstances surrounding Randy's disappearance. I did make a habit of going for my early morning walks along the beach to watch the men run. Why? I don't know. Who wants to watch a bunch of muscular men wearing nothing but short shorts running along the beach with sweat glistening off their chests in the early morning sunlight? Certainly not a lady such as me.

Wednesday afternoon I was lying down for a well deserved nap when Jim called saying, "I have some news. I don't know if it will help."

I was about to tell him to forget the whole thing, but I'm the one who brought it up so I inquired, "When can we meet?" A light supper in town sounded nice.

"I'm in the lobby," Jim said.

"I'll be right down." Nothing like giving a girl a chance to get ready. I didn't feel comfortable having him in my room. I slapped on some makeup, checked my hair, and threw on a skirt and blouse.

Once in the lobby, he suggested we take a walk along the beach so as not to be overheard. "Tell me," I demanded. I wanted to get this over with.

"I work in the admin department. My job is to keep track of the message traffic. What I do is get the Team's messages from the message center on base. I organize them in order of importance from general messages such as weather and ship movement to classified which may deal with SEAL business to secret messages dealing with past or future operations. I give them to the executive officer or XO. He checks off who needs to read what. Then I take them around to the different departments to be read. It's a good job. I get to bullshit with everyone. I get to see what's going on in the armory, the dive locker, and the para-loft. It keeps me off clean-up details, and my time is my own. I have my own office and I can take a nap once in a while, just like an officer. I'm still an operator, so I have to train with my platoon, but the rest of the time I carry around the message board."

"The chiefs usually scribble their initials in the box by their department without reading the message. They know 99 percent of messages in the Navy are a waste of time. Ensigns read them twice. They're afraid the XO will quiz them. By the time they make lieutenant junior grade, they scan them once. But it is serious business. I'm responsible for the security of the messages. No unauthorized people can see them. The messages can't be left lying around. They have to be locked in a safe when not in my possession. They say you can go to prison for letting unauthorized people read them." Jim droned on.

Did he really think I was interested in any of this? Come on, get to the point fella, I'm missing my nap. "Enough already, what did you find out?"

"I looked at the post-ops for Charlie Platoon. That was the platoon of the four SEALs who were killed."

"And post-ops are?"

"Post operation reports, or after action reports that summarize the platoon's actions on an operation," he said as if I were some dense creature. "Anyway, a week or so before they were killed the platoon had a curious entry. On an ambush the platoon stated five KIA, three probable, government documents captured, and no weapons recovered."

"What does all that mean?" I asked.

"KIA is confirmed enemy Killed-In-Action, probable are likely kills, and 'no weapons recovered.' That is not good. Officers who make a living sitting behind a desk don't like the idea of enemy soldiers being killed without weapons. The report doesn't mean the enemy didn't have weapons, just that none were recovered. Sometimes we can't stick around to retrieve weapons. The desk warriors are afraid we might be out gunning down unarmed women and children."

"Does that ever happen?"

"I'll get you in a fire fight and you tell me if you care," Jim said.

Jim was starting to annoy me. Okay, I was getting into uncharted territory. Maybe there were some things people inside the Beltway didn't understand.

Jim continued, "These desk jockeys have never been in the bush. Their heads are so far up their asses that if a gook jumped in front of them, they would crap out their brains."

"I don't care for that sort of language Mr. Crotty, if you don't mind," I found his use of derogatory terms toward Asians distasteful.

"Very well, what I wanted to tell you is that something struck me as curious about the government documents that were captured. I tried to find follow-up messages dealing with the documents like Intel reports, but found nothing. Even in the top secret message traffic," Jim explained.

"Is that normal?"

"Well, it's not completely unheard of. Sometimes things get misplaced, but in the Teams we like to act on Intel from the field to set up future ops, and there was nothing."

"So what happened? What were these four SEALs doing?"

"From what I gathered they were a detachment from Charlie platoon and were ordered to the MAC-V compound at Rach Gia in the Kien Giang Province. Believe me; it is out in the boonies. There were reports of the Viet Cong building up supplies, and some high levels of VC cadre were in the area. The local Army commander wanted Intel on what and how much material was being moved into the area, and if possible a captured VC commander. The four SEALs were sent to do recon work and a body snatch if possible," Jim said.

"And MAC-V is?"

"Military Assistance Command-Vietnam, they run the all-expense paid tours to Vietnam for military personnel," Jim answered. "Vietnam is divided into four corps or combat theaters. I Corps borders North Vietnam, and is mainly the province of the Marines. And IV Corps is the southernmost area where Rach Gia is located. The Army's ninth infantry mans that part of Vietnam.

"Go on about what they were doing?" I asked.

"It sounds like what I said, reconning. They were gathering intelligence on enemy strength, equipment, and high ranking VC."

"What do you think the documents were?" I asked. I knew the documents must have been the money, around a million dollars. But I wanted to hear that from Jim.

"I have no idea," Jim answered.

"Could you find out?" I asked. Then I asked myself, 'why was I pursuing this? The best thing to do would be to drop the whole matter.' But there was a part of me that wanted to know if what Emily told me was true. Were these people so desperate as to murder a midlevel government worker like Randy, his lover, his sister, her unborn baby and husband, and four servicemen, all for what?

"There was a week or so between the operation when the documents were captured and the explosion that killed the four SEALs. By now, the boat crews that supported their operation and other people at the MAC-V compound, and the Naval Support Activity in Rach Gia have most likely left. They have either ended their tours in Vietnam, or been discharged from the service or moved to other bases, or been killed. I doubt you could find any of them. And if you did find somebody I don't think the SEALs would have told them about the documents. All Intel is supposed to be kept secret. If support personnel got a hold of some Intel and mumbled it to their prostitute girlfriend to impress her, and she passed it on to her VC cousin, it could cost people their lives so most people keep quiet."

"There's a slight chance that somebody my know something. One of the men lived for a week after the explosion which was either accidental, as the messages said, or intentional as you stated. The other three died at the scene. Nobody knows anything. The one who survived was in and out of consciousness until he died. From what I've learned he didn't speak at any length to the SEALs who visited him in the hospital in Saigon. Maybe a nurse or a doctor or a tech spoke with him. And even if they did I doubt he would have told them about the documents. But it's the only chance I can think of," Jim postulated.

I asked. "What was the name of the SEAL who survived for a week?"

"Lowell Meyer, he went by Wayne. He was in my training class," Jim said. "You really think our government killed him? I can't believe it? To think he was killed by his own government." Jim looked down while shaking his head.

"I didn't believe it either, but too many things are falling into place," I said. Jim and I walked along the beach in silence until we came to a fence with a 'Do Not Trespass, U.S. Government Property' sign. "What's this?"

"This is the boundary to the North Island Naval Air Station. Anyone can get around the fence. Over there, across the entrance to the bay is Point Loma," Jim was pointing. "We're a mile up the beach from the Hotel Del and two miles from the area."

"The area?" I asked.

"That's what we call the UDT/SEAL compound where we work. This is our four mile run, from the area to the North Island fence and back."

"I thought it was SEAL. What's UDT/SEAL?" I asked.

"Underwater Demolition/SEAL Teams, there's Underwater Demolition Team Eleven, and Twelve and SEAL Team One. We are all housed in the same buildings. From here back to the Del is called Center Beach. This is where we do most of our trolling."

"Trolling?" I inquired.

"Yeah, you know? Picking up girls," Jim said.

"You pick up girls?" Maybe that sounded demeaning but I thought picking up strange girls disgusting.

"Oh, I forgot to who I was speaking with. Out here, men don't wear white tie and tails, and the women don't wear long dresses with elbow length white gloves when introduced before they hop into the sack. We actually do things without chaperones."

"Don't you mean, 'to whom I was speaking with,'" I didn't like his tone one bit. "So you skip the formalities of actually being introduced and get right to it. I can see by the outfits these girls are wearing there isn't much to disrobe."

We continued walking back to the hotel in silence. I noticed he snuck a peek at a few skimpily dressed teeny boppers. Who would want to strike up a conversation with those? I doubt any of them read Chaucer or Christopher Marlow. Who could not have read Marlow, the epitome of the 16th century dramatic renaissance? There was more material in a scarf than what those girls were wearing. So they were skinny, so they had perky breasts, and long shapely legs, bronze skin, natural blonde hair, and perfect white teeth. And I don't even want to go to the buttock. Why would any man take one of those girls of easy virtue over one of my sophisticated, demanding, nothing is ever good enough, cold as a fish, bitchy friends? I couldn't imagine. Okay, I was making fun of some of my insufferable friends. But still, a gentleman would never give those beach babes a second look. I could've been wrong.

I wanted to make sure our line of communication stayed open, "Will you call me if you find out anything?"

"Huh?" Jim mumbled.

"I'm over here. Get your eyeballs off that jail bait," I demanded.

"Oh, yeah, sure" Jim said, "But I don't know what good it will do." He kept walking. I turned to go into the hotel. I'd never met anyone so uncouth. I assumed that was it. I had done my best to find out what happened. I didn't want to know anymore anyway since five people already died because of what they knew. I should've put this behind me long ago and gotten back to my own personal problems that, in my mind, were more pressing. And another thing, he didn't even ask me out to dinner, the putz, after I'd treated him.

I called my mother when I got back to my room. I could sense by her voice she was concerned about something. I'm sure nothing that amounted to a hill of beans. I told her I was working hard in California. She told me to stay out of the sun, it would ruin my skin. I told her if it made me look anything like those girls on the beach I would definitely stay out of the sun. She also warned me about people that would try to get me to take drugs. And it wasn't only men that would try to kiss me. I should be aware of girls who also wanted to kiss me and do other things. I assured her I would be careful, but that I was considering a tattoo. It took me a half hour to calm her down and convince her I was only kidding.

Next I called my boyfriend and told him that I still felt there was some funny business going on in relation to Randy's disappearance. He questioned me as to why I would think that. I only mentioned that I had spoken to some people and there were some unanswered questions. I wasn't going to tell him anything further. He warned me again to drop my conspiratorial notions. I agreed.

The next morning our group flew back to D.C. I felt satisfied with my efforts to find out what had happened to the SEALs and the captured money. I could close the book on the whole episode. In a few hours the book was going to be reopened for good.

Chapter 9

I thought the flight from California would never end. By the time I got my luggage, retrieved my car, and drove home, it was well after 10. When I entered my townhouse and flicked on the lights I felt something wasn't right, but I couldn't put my finger on it. The place was deserted. Maybe my roommate Mary Jo was spending the night with whomever. I was glad, I needed some quiet time. I collapsed on the couch.

Eventually, I got off my lazy butt and hauled my luggage upstairs. I put a few things away and gathered my dirty laundry. I slipped into a Lantz nightgown and terry cloth robe. Then I went downstairs and sorted through my mail which was piled on the kitchen table. There wasn't much, a few bills and some junk mail. I still had this uneasy feeling that someone was watching me.

Then there was a creak on the hardwood floor. I looked over my shoulder to see a man standing there. I sprung back toward the kitchen door, "What are you doing? I'm not dressed." A lean man, a little over six feet with close cropped hair, ruddy complexion and menacing eyes stepped out from the hallway. I could feel the hair on my arms bristle.

"There is no reason to be alarmed ma'am. I'm not going to harm you," he said. "My name is TJ and I work for the government."

I didn't care who he worked for, he shouldn't be in my townhouse. He wore a black trench coat over a dark blue suit. He looked like a secret service agent. But what struck me as strange was that he was wearing black leather gloves when gloves weren't necessary on a warm evening. "Let me see some identification. And I don't care if you do work for the government, this is breaking and entering."

"Calm down," TJ reached into his inside suit coat pocket and produced some sort of identification card encased in a leather bound holder. I didn't want to get close to him. From where I stood it could have been a junior lifesaving card.

"If you don't mind I'm calling the police." I went for the wall phone by the back door.

TJ cut me off, but he didn't physically touch me. "I told you to calm down. Now sit down. I have some questions."

At that point, a lady would offer a gentleman a drink, but I didn't. "If you're really from the government, as you say you are, you could have called or met me at my office." I had no idea what this creep's intentions were. I tried to act calm and collected, and started fumbling for my Salems.

"This has to be done face to face, in private, and now. You've been asking about missing campaign money. Why are you interested?" he asked.

I remained standing looking for a match, "I don't know what you're talking about. I would really rather you leave and make an appointment at my office."

"Don't play games. I'm not leaving until I get some answers. We know you have been asking around about money missing in Vietnam," TJ informed me.

The first thing I thought was Jim told TJ. I had to think fast. I didn't want to implicate anyone. Randy was missing and probably dead, and his sister was dead so no harm could come to them. I played the 'you're dumber than you look' game, "You have it wrong. A friend of mine is missing and he worked with campaign finances."

"Quit screwing around." TJ was becoming impatient.

"I'm not screwing around. What business is it of yours anyway?" I answered with self-assurance. "Now if you don't mind, please leave."

"Okay we're done here," TJ smirked, "You're coming with me."

"I'm not going anywhere. Get out! I'm going to find out who you are and report this. I've got an early start tomorrow." I was getting nervous.

"It's a national security issue. We need to go into D.C. and get a statement," TJ said.

"Can't it wait until tomorrow? I'm really tired. Good night," I said as I moved to show him the door.

TJ, or whatever his name was, cut me off again, "Let's get this over with," TJ ordered.

I had to get away from this guy. Where was Mary Jo when I needed her? "Well if you really insist I have to get dressed," I said as I headed for the stairs. TJ didn't try to stop me. He stood at the foot of the stairs. I imagined he'd cased the place and was confident there was no escaping from upstairs, or that I owned a gun. In my bedroom I picked up the phone. No dial tone. I was in trouble. I wanted to ask if we were going to Fort Marcy Park and if I was going to commit suicide by setting myself on fire or shoot myself in the head, and then crawl into a dumpster. I'd never been in a situation like this. I'd never been so frightened in my life. I put on a pair of grey wool slacks, a sweater, and a pair of tennis shoes so I could run if necessary. Did I really want to die dressed like this? Oh well.

There was a false panel to a crawl space, by a dormer window in the hallway, I used for storing luggage. The panel had one of those latches that opened when pressed and closed the same way. Nobody would know the panel was a door to a storage area unless it was pointed out to them. I went in the bathroom, opened the window, then went back into the hall and crammed myself into the luggage storage area, pulling the door shut. I waited. I felt this was my only chance. If he caught me hiding and killed me, I wouldn't be any deader than if I walked downstairs and left with him. After about five minutes, TJ called up to me. Not getting an answer he came running upstairs. I heard him rush from room to room, slamming doors. He yelled down, "She's gone." Somebody else was in the townhouse. My heart was beating so loud I was afraid TJ would hear it.

TJ ran downstairs. There was another male voice, "Where the hell could she go? Did you look in the closets?"

"Of course, I did. The bathroom window is open. There's a gutter drain pipe, but I doubt she could slide down that," TJ barked.

"Do you think she knows?" the other voice asked.

"Of course she knows, you dip shit. Why do you think she ran off? Don't worry, you'll read her obituary in the morning Post!" TJ yelled. "You wait here in case she comes back. I'll get her. She couldn't have gotten far. Does she know any of her neighbors?" I heard TJ ask.

"The couple directly across the alley," I heard the other voice call out. My God, the other person knew me. Who could that be? My mind was racing a million miles an hour. I couldn't concentrate. This was not how debutantes were supposed to live their lives. It felt like an hour, but was probably only 10 minutes when I heard TJ's voice again. I couldn't tell what the two were saying, but a few moments later I heard the front door slam. I didn't know if anybody was still in the townhouse. I didn't dare move. I sat in the dark. After what felt like hours I peeked out. My body ached from being curled up like a pretzel.

I had to use the bathroom, but I didn't chance flushing the toilet. Once I was confident the coast was clear I crawled into the hallway. The lights were on with the front drapes opened. I always kept the drapes closed. I didn't want to stand up in case they were watching from outside. Maybe they were hiding inside the townhouse ready to pounce on me when I materialized. What was I going to do?

I could have been overreacting, but with Randy's disappearance, Clay committing suicide then climbing into a dumpster, and Emily, her husband and her baby being killed in an auto accident, I felt my life was in danger. I needed to get to the police. On second thought, if the government was involved the police might be convinced I was wanted by the government for national security reasons. They would turn me over to TJ. If I could find out about the money the SEALs captured, maybe I could find out who these people were who were killing everyone. At that moment it seemed like an unattainable goal. Petty Officer Crotty said there was a slim chance Wayne Meyer, who survived the initial explosion, talked to someone. One thing for sure, I couldn't stay in Washington, D.C., and I imagined my home in St. Louis would be watched. I needed to go to California.

I climbed back into the storage space and tried to sleep. I had to go so bad. At around five in the morning I crawled to my bedroom. Staying below the window level I collected whatever money I could find, my purse, and documents I felt I might need, like my passport, check book, and bank account numbers. How was I going to get downstairs? The drapes were open with the stairs visible from the street. The front bay window faced east. When sunlight began to fill the living room I took a chance the glare off the bay window would give me enough cover to make my escape.

I grabbed a jacket and slinked downstairs. I didn't see anyone, but that didn't mean somebody wasn't hiding. I made my way to the kitchen on my hands and knees. Every sound, every creak of the hardwood floor was magnified. The next step was to open the kitchen door. I figured a gun would be in my face. With no gun in sight I skirted down the alley staying close to the buildings. I wanted to hide behind some garbage cans and relieve myself. It would be just my luck to get caught and arrested for public urination. I didn't want to take my car for fear of it being watched.

I took a cab to a coffee shop close to my bank. Notwithstanding my aversion to public rest rooms I made a bee line to the ladies' room. I called my boyfriend's apartment. There was no answer. Next I called his office on the chance he went into work early, again, no answer. Where could he be? I needed help.

I found Eric's FBI card in my purse with his home number. I was reluctant to call. I didn't want to give him the satisfaction that he was right. A sleepy female voice answered the phone. I hung up. How could I be so childish? My feelings were hurt because a former boyfriend was sleeping with another woman. For some adolescent and self-centered reason I figured once a man slept with me he wouldn't be able to look at another woman.

I spent the next three hours reading the Washington Post waiting for the bank to open, all the while keeping an eye out for TJ. I withdrew several thousand dollars in traveler's checks and a few hundred more in cash, from my trust fund. The bank teller gave me a suspicious look as I mumbled, "Last minute round the world trip. Doesn't that sound wonderful?" I thought he was going to push a button and TJ would appear. Then I headed for the Greyhound bus depot.

A couple of years ago, in a fit of independence and with my dad's help, I transferred the bulk of my trust fund to Washington, D.C. My mother would have never approved.

I was paranoid enough to think TJ and his goons would have the airports watched. So I took my first Greyhound bus ride to Baltimore and from there I flew to San Diego. Everything I'd heard about bus depots and buses was true. They were smelly, crowded, and occupied by unseemly characters. I sat next to a wino. Since I hadn't bathed in over 24 hours I don't know who offended whom. He was a gentleman and offered me a drink from his brown paper bag. I politely declined. He struck up a conversation explaining he was a Korean War veteran who'd worked in a coal mine in West Virginia the past 10 years, but was laid off. He was headed to New York to live with his sister and look for work. He'd better stop drinking and get cleaned up if he wanted a job.

On the trip to San Diego I had second thoughts about my plan. I again thought Jim Crotty may have gotten word to TJ. Or maybe Franci's soon to be fiancé and soon to be lawyer Jeff, felt compelled to uphold the law by telling the feds. My father snitching on me? I had to think about that. If he asked the wrong person about their opinion of what I told him about the missing money and the story got back to D.C., it could've gotten back to TJ. And then there was the unfaithful ex-boyfriend Mr. FBI Eric. Maybe he was a double agent. Nah, anyone who played rugby was too much of a free spirit to be caught up in political intrigue. And everyone else who knew about the money was either dead or going to die, along with a few innocent bystanders such as an unborn baby.

I know I was rude to the salesman sitting next to me on the plane. He started with the usual questions about where I was from and what I did for a living, and so forth. But when I told him I was going to California to see a specialist about some incurable sexually transmitted diseases he backed off. I was through being polite. I changed planes in Chicago and slept most the way to the coast. I hoped nobody was going to be waiting for me in San Diego.

Chapter 10

When I arrived in San Diego I placed a phone call to, "SEAL Team One, Petty Officer Gracio speaking, may I help you, Sir?"

"Jim Crotty, please," I requested.

"Hold one Sir," there was a long silence. "He's gone for the day. May I take a message Sir?"

Think, Susan think. I'd only been on the go for two days, "Would he be at the Trade Winds?"

"Is this an irate chick, Sir?" he asked. I couldn't tell if Petty Officer Gracio was trying to be funny or if that was a legitimate question. Regardless, I was offended by him referring to women as 'chicks.'

"No Admiral, just a friend," I responded.

"Yeah, the Trade Winds would be a good bet, Sir," Gracio answered. He knew he was speaking with a woman. I guess it had been ingrained in him to end every sentence with, 'Sir.'

I grabbed a cab in front of the terminal at Lindbergh Field. Fourteen hours earlier, I'd left my townhouse in D.C. by the back door, escaping death. On the cab ride to Coronado I formulated a clever strategy to find out if Jim was in cahoots with TJ. If I found out he was working for TJ, I didn't know what I was going to do. Maybe make a break for Mexico.

When I walked into the Trade Winds I saw him. He was wearing flip-flops, corduroy shorts and a t-shirt with, 'Peace through Fire Superiority, SEAL TEAM ONE,' printed on the front. I'd made a choice and this was the consequence.

He was leaning against the bar yakking it up with some flabby, gum chewing, tattooed, cigar smoking slut. As I said before I hated speaking of the superior sex that way, but really what was the value of hanging around with a woman like that? Just seeing him laughing and having a good time made me mad. I went up to him sneering, "TJ was waiting for me when I got home. I need for you to call and tell him I don't know anything. Thanks for almost getting me killed." I gave my best, 'I'm going to rip your eyes out,' look, clenched teeth, fixed lower jaw, and all. Come to think of it, maybe my strategy wasn't so clever. I was crabby after being awake for over 30 hours with only a few cat naps, airplane food, not bathing, no makeup nor brushing my teeth, my legs felt prickly, and I felt like I was about to begin my period. Yeah, I was on the verge of mass murder.

The slut vanished. "What are you talking about? Who's TJ?" Jim asked. "What do you mean, 'when you got home'? I didn't know you left."

I lit a cigarette to calm down and took a chance. I lowered my voice, "I flew back to Washington, D.C. yesterday. When I got home this guy TJ was waiting for me. I was lucky to escape. I had to get out of Washington. Remember I implicated the government in killing the SEALs and said a friend of mine, who is missing, may have known something? I think TJ is involved in his disappearance."

"I remember," Jim answered, but I think he really wanted to tell me, 'so what,' or 'get lost.'

"Well, I think they are trying to kill me. Doesn't that mean anything to you, you numbskull?"

"Okay, now you are starting to freak me out. I was hoping you weren't a typical narcissistic, neurotic, socially appalling, and insecure product of a private school education, but now you give me no reason to believe otherwise," Jim lectured. "The idea of our government killing four of my teammates, kidnapping your friend, and now being after you is ridiculous. I'll admit, there are a few inconsistencies in the message traffic regarding the operation, but that goes on all the time. You knowing about the operation is a mystery. But people being after you? Get serious. I thought the waiter at the Prince of Wales Room at the Hotel Del was going to kill you when you sent your salad back because the dressing wasn't on the side, but then again, he probably puts up with you snotty brats all the time. And who knows if you are talking about the right operation?"

This guy was a riot. I'm being chased by a killer and he's making jokes. There were a few things I would have liked to have told him about underachieving, socially unacceptable public school students, but I needed his help. I hated being in the position of needing someone's help. "You have to listen to me. If you don't believe me, I don't know what I'm going to do."

"And why is that my problem? Just out of curiosity, what are your plans for keeping the U.S. Government from killing you?" Jim asked.

"I thought you could help. You said there was a slim chance of finding out what the documents were. If I could find out maybe I could get the authorities involved. I don't think these people will rest until they kill everyone who may expose whatever they are doing," which was running a black market to finance the President's re-election. I must have sounded like I was about to panic.

"I may have said that to keep you quiet. But I haven't given it much thought." Jim turned to the bar.

I got in his face, bad breath and all, "Well, why don't you start thinking real hard before TJ shows up and blows me away? You have to help me!"

"Why do I have to help you? Listen, I'll get in touch. Where are you staying, the Hotel Del?" Jim asked while backing away.

"I don't want to stay in anyplace so public. They may check. They know I was just out here."

"Great, by hanging around you I'll probably get caught in the cross fire. So I guess you don't have a place to stay?" Jim looked like his next statement was painful for him to say. "You want to go to my place?"

"Would it be too much trouble until I figure out what to do?" I asked. "It would only be for a few hours until I collect my thoughts and get a room reservation. I've been up for nearly two days. Then you can get back to your fat girlfriend over there." Okay, that was mean.

"Girlfriend? Get serious. These are Team hogs. I would never walk out of here with one of them. I've never been that drunk. They work on base. I talk to them to keep up on rumor control. They know which captain is humping which commander's wife and which platoon is deploying where and when. These hogs know more about the war than the President. I didn't want to say it, but you look like hell. My place is not up to your standards, but if you're game I am. Where's your stuff?" Jim pushed away from the bar.

"I don't have any luggage if that is what you mean. I literally escaped from TJ and his goons with what's on my back." I needed to stop being a bitch. We walked out into the fading daylight. Jim drove a British racing green Chevy Corvair. The one Ralph Nader said was unsafe at any speed. It was powered by a rear, air cooled, four cylinder engine. A lot of my friends owned them in college. It was time for Jim to upgrade.

"Could we stop at a department store and drug store? I need to buy a toothbrush," and tampons which he didn't need to know. "And I don't have any clean clothes."

"I don't think there is a Saks Fifth Avenue in Coronado or Imperial Beach. I'm sure there's a Salvation Army. Let me think where that is." A smart ass, just what I needed at that time. "I'll tell you what. We'll go by the Base Exchange on North Island. Tell them you forgot your ID and you're my wife." I didn't like the sound of that. I was in no mood for hanky panky.

"When we walk in, you go get your stuff and I'll head to the sporting goods department to look at guns and check out the gals walking up and down the aisles. When you have everything, come find me. I may be over in the magazine section looking at pictures in Sports Illustrated or reading articles in Playboy. Act annoyed like a wife. I'm sure you are good at that."

"You better be reading an article in Sports Illustrated and not checking out centerfolds in Playboy." At one time I thought I wanted to be married, but I'm having second thoughts. Oh, what am I worried about? Whatever poor sap I marry I'll program him to attend to my every need.

The Exchange was like a department store with an appliance section, clothing section, electronics, housewares, the aforementioned sporting goods department, and so forth. The military uniform section was about the only thing not found in a civilian store. I bought my first pair of blue jeans, some tees, and sweatshirts, sandals, and other personal clothing items. I also bought a hideous bathing suit. Since I was in California I thought I might do some sunbathing.

With my skin condition, I didn't know if that was such a good idea. The lingerie department, if that's what it was supposed to be, left a lot to be desired. I didn't think I was finicky about bras until I saw their selection. And the panties, maybe they were okay for those girls at the Trade Winds, but not a lady. Their personal care section wasn't up to snuff. They didn't carry the lotions I needed for my skin. The make-up aisle was a little garish for my taste. I think the make-up came from the Bordello Line. I also bought a cheap suitcase.

We drove south from Coronado along the ocean. Jim's place was a duplex on the beach in the border town of Imperial Beach, California, about seven miles south of Coronado. His place was a dump. "What's that smell?" I asked.

"Smell? I don't smell anything." I knew I was in trouble. The furniture was something out of the fifties with the stuffing coming out of the couch. Nothing matched. The carpet was worn and I didn't even want to know what some of the stains were. The windows were filthy. The kitchen floor was linoleum. LINOLEUM, I wouldn't be caught dead living in a place with linoleum. The sink was full of dirty dishes. The trash can was overflowing and empty beer cans were everywhere.

I needed to use the bathroom. Jim pointed the way. I peeked in and sniffed. I turned on the light. It was gross. Hairs were everywhere, in the bathtub, and on the toilet. And of course the toilet seat was up. There were more hairs in the sink and on the floor. How could anyone live like this?

On my way back to the living room, I peeked into a bedroom. The mattress was bare as was the pillow. There was a blanket half on the bed and half on the floor. Dirty clothes were scattered helter skelter. I was shocked at the filth. Death was looking like a viable option. Where was TJ when I needed him?

"If I knew I was having company, I would have picked up a little," Jim apologized. "My roommates are slobs."

"No, no, this is fine, lovely. It must be nice living by the sea." I was a born liar.

"Yeah, I like it, a little more casual down here," Jim said.

'Casual,' is that the word for living in a cesspool? "I guess you want the whole story. I might as well tell you before I crash."

"You've got my undivided attention," Jim said. "You want a beer?"

"No thank you, not at the moment. I may pass out." I told him everything about my narrow escape from TJ, the assassin.

"Back to your problem, who besides me have you told about the SEALs being killed?" Jim asked.

"Nobody, I promise. Well I may have mentioned it to my father, and that night I met you at Busch's I asked Jeff, Franci's boyfriend, a question about it, and then there's my boyfriend."

"You have a boyfriend?" Jim acted surprised.

"Yes, is that so odd? Of course I told my boyfriend. I even told my ex-boyfriend."

"No, I guess you being in a relationship isn't that odd. You having had two boyfriends is. I suppose there's somebody for everybody. So what are you going to do?" Jim asked. "You have this blood thirsty guy TJ after you."

"I don't know. I can't go home or back to Washington," I said. "I'm going to be missed. I probably already am. I need to call my boss and call home. My mother will be frantic. Also, I have to call my roommate."

"How about the boyfriend or boyfriends?" Jim asked.

"Yes, of course. He'll be worried sick." Jim harrumphed. Maybe he didn't believe a lady of my class could be in an intimate relationship and he probably thought the guy was a total loser.

"I know this sounds insensitive, but I suggest you not call anyone. Your parents' house may be wiretapped and your boss may be under pressure to tell the authorities where you are. And the boyfriend, he may be the first one to call TJ," Jim said. "You are welcome to stay here until you know what you want to do. There're two bedrooms and the one bath. Dan and I sleep in one room and Joe has the other. Ski usually crashes on the couch. He's not officially a roommate but he seems to end up here most nights. I'll tell Joe he'll have to camp with Dan and me for a few nights until we figure out what to do."

I was close to telling him I couldn't possibly live under such conditions, but what choice did I have? I was so tired I felt I couldn't take another step. I didn't want to be alone in a motel. "Yes, thank you," I said. "I need to wash these new clothes and take a bath. I've been in what I'm wearing for the past two days."

"Let me take your clothes to the Laundromat. You can put on one of my sweat suits. I think I have a clean one. Do you want to get something to eat?" Jim asked.

"No, I'm fine, just really tired," I informed him. "I'll do my laundry in the morning. You've already done too much." Did he think he was going to handle my undergarments? Was he crazy?

"Okay, you take a nap. I'll put a note on the door that you are not to be disturbed. Do you need a towel or soap or anything?" Jim asked.

"A clean towel would be nice, but otherwise I think I have everything." I was ready to fall over. I wondered why he was being so nice all of a sudden. Jim escorted me to the bedroom and left. Being alone in a strange room was unnerving. I managed to take a shower and crawl into bed. I wore my socks and pulled the hood of the sweatshirt over my head. I felt somewhat protected from bed bugs.

The next thing I knew I was being shaken by Jim, "I think there is something you should see on the 10 o'clock news." I staggered into the living room. Jim's roommates were sitting around enjoying beer and pizza. All they were wearing were short khaki swim trunks, blue t-shirts, and flip-flops. "You just missed it. You have been reported missing. Foul play is suspected."

"Since you are here, let me introduce you to Dan Beck, Joe Stranton, and Frank Pulaski or Ski." The three sort of acknowledged with a nod of a slice of pizza, or a beer can. Dan didn't even look up. He was shorter than the rest of the men with blonde, thick, hair and a muscular build.

"What did they say on TV?" I asked.

"Not much, just that you'd been missing since yesterday. The police said from what they've found they suspect a kidnapping, but when questioned they wouldn't give any evidence. There was a picture of you. It looked like one that would be taken from your personnel file at work," Jim informed me. "Are you going to finger me as the kidnapper when they find you?"

"Of course not." Well, maybe I would to save my own ass. "What can I do?"

"You've been kidnapped?" Dan asked. "Jim told us he had a friend visiting from St. Louis. He didn't say he kidnapped you. I know Jim is desperate but this is ridiculous."

"I didn't kidnap her," Jim barked. "Susan had trouble at work and is hanging out here until things cool down. First thing Susan needs to do is change her appearance, like her hair, and identification cards, whatever. We don't want her to be found by the authorities until she has things under control," Jim said. "Also, we need a little help from Ski." Jim looked at Ski. That caught Ski by surprise. Ski was not the type of person one would go to for help.

Jim directed his comments to me, "Ski lives in San Fernando Valley, north of L.A., and was good friends with Wayne Meyer. You remember he was the one who survived for a week after the explosion. He fixed Wayne up with one of his friends named Linda. Linda and Wayne hit it off and were talking marriage before he deployed. When Wayne was killed, Ski went to console Linda. Now, I know this sounds terrible, but the consoling became........."

"Ski screwing her brains out." I couldn't believe I said that.

"Thank you, I wasn't going to put it quite that way, but yes, they were having sex twice a day, and three times on Sunday. Isn't that right, Ski? Am I leaving anything out?" Ski sat there perplexed. Jim added, "For her part it may have been some sort of grieving, psycho rebound. Ski is a habitual sport fucker. What can I say? He has no excuse. He's a sorry excuse for a human."

Ski defended himself, "What are friends for? Linda was hurting and besides she was always giving me the eye. It was only a matter of time. I knew she wanted me. Once Wayne bought the farm, Linda and I realized we were meant for each other and besides she's a great piece of ass."

'A great piece of ass,' is that how men speak of women these days? I could not imagine my boyfriend saying anything besides, 'Susan England is well mannered, polite, a pleasant conversationalist, always well dressed, and a delight to be around.' I needed to know, "Ski, did you have a girlfriend when you took up with Linda?"

"Sort of, but it was time to move on. She was becoming a nag. I'm sure the old hag is making somebody smile," Ski offered.

"Yeah, right," I sighed. "Was there any overlap with your old girlfriend and Linda?"

"Maybe a month or two at the most," Ski answered. "It was wearing me out."

Jim interrupted, "Anyway, I was thinking maybe Wayne communicated with Linda before he passed away."

Ski's teensy brain started to click, he asked, "Wait, you've lost me. How does talking to Linda in Van Nuys fit in with Susan being kidnapped in Washington, D.C.?"

"That's the problem. Wayne may have learned something in Vietnam related to Susan's work. She hopes Wayne wrote Linda about it. So that's why we need to speak with her." Jim looked at Ski. "We could go with you this weekend. Would that be alright?"

"Yeah, I guess so." I could sense the gears grinding in Ski's pea brain, but I knew he was not capable of putting it all together. Ski seemed worried that our presence would distract the 'great piece of ass' from her appointed duties.

Jim asked, "What do you think, Susan? You got a better idea?"

"No, I guess that would be alright. I can't think of anything," I said. "I'm tired, where are the clean sheets?"

"Sheets, I don't understand," Jim answered.

"Never mind," I said.

Jim walked me back to my room. Once out of ear shot of the other three he said quietly, "This TJ character sounds serious and if he's not already in California looking for you he soon will be. He'll check the airlines, buses, and trains. He'll figure it out. I don't want this place shot up. I can't afford to lose my damage deposit."

"I never thought of that. I would feel terrible if you lost your damage deposit. What is it, 25 dollars?" He may have been joking, but then again, he may have been more concerned about his damage deposit than my life. "What about the identification cards?"

Jim told me he would have Joe look into it. "Joe knows a guy in Tijuana who fixed a California driver's license for an underage girl."

"Underage, is that what you guys do out here, corrupt young girls?" I asked.

"Hey, Joe said she turned 17 shortly after they met. Believe me, he said she out performed most 20 year olds who already have three or four years of experience under their belts. She was grabbing his crank every 15 minutes until he cried for mercy."

"Thanks for that graphic description." I wanted to ask him what a 'crank' was, but I had a pretty good idea. Joe impressed me as the card sharp, lady's man type. He was just shy of six feet, probably around 170 pounds with receding jet black wavy hair that was brushed straight back.

At that moment I wanted all this to go away and everything to get back to normal. I was going to have to sleep in this place, and eat here, and live with these guys who corrupted underage girls, and spoke constantly of sex. Actually, what I'd heard about California girls, I don't know who was corrupting whom.

There was a world renowned resort right up the road. But I knew why I couldn't stay at the Hotel Del Coronado. I was scared. TJ was hunting for me and now being a 'kidnap victim' everyone in the world would be looking for me. And as soon as I was caught TJ would have me. In a short time I realized Jim's place was plush compared to the place we would be staying in the San Fernando Valley.

Chapter 11

I hardly slept. I imagined bed bugs crawling in my hair. At seven o'clock in the morning the four roommates got up and left. They didn't shower. There was some toilet flushing. They weren't shy about bodily noises in the bathroom. I had to wrap the filthy pillow around my ears to block out the sounds.

It was Friday morning and Jim said we would leave for Van Nuys as soon as he got off work. He said Fridays were usually half work days with administrative duties in the morning, along with a field day before the monster mash. Jim said when he first joined the Navy and heard the term 'field day,' he thought of summer camp and playing games. The Navy's version of a 'field day' was quite different. It was cleaning the area. The field day was followed by a monster mash. A monster mash was a race designed by the executive officer that included two or more athletic events such as running, swimming, obstacle course, rubber boat paddling, and other frogman type activities. Every Friday a different combination of events would be put together for the race.

Once finished with the monster mash the Team enjoyed a barbeque and beer with awards being given to the winners. The awards were usually dinner for two at the Chart House, a popular restaurant across Orange Avenue from the Hotel Del Coronado. Heck, everything in Coronado was close to the Hotel Del. The good runners and swimmers always won. They were skinny and probably didn't care about a big steak dinner at the Chart House, while the bigger guys who could eat their birth weight were dying for a free meal.

I wanted to be ready to go by noon. There was much to do. The first thing was to carefully ease into the bathroom. I needed to go badly, but I'd lost count of the toilet flushes. Were there three or four? I didn't want to find anything in there that would make me gag.

The next thing I did was call home. Jim told me not to, but I could not let my parents think I was kidnapped. I called the children's phone line.

Our maid, Lilly Mae, answered. "Lilly Mae is my father or mother available?"

"Miss Susan where are you? You have us worried sick. Hang on; I'll get your father. He's talking to the police on the other line." Lilly Mae was smart enough to get my father. My mother would demand to know if the kidnappers were keeping me out of the sun and allowing me to take my vitamins.

"Susan, is that you? Where are you? What's happening?" My father asked in staccato fashion.

"Calm down. I'm all right. I had to leave D.C. I don't want to tell you where I am because the phones may be tapped. I know this all sounds mysterious, but for the time being I think this is best."

My father asked, "Does this have anything to do with what we talked about?"

"Yes, everything. Listen, I have to go. I don't want this call traced. I love you and will call as soon as I can, but don't worry I'm all right." At least for now.

I heard my father say, "Don't hang up. I have to know what's........." I hung up.

Next I called my boss Bob Williams at his office. His secretary recognized my voice and put me through. "Bob, I want you to know I'm all right. I needed to get away for a while. I saw the news and I'm not kidnapped."

"Where are you? What's going on?" Bob demanded.

"I can't tell you. I'm sorry if this is causing you an inconvenience. Please believe me this is necessary. I'll keep you informed. I'll be back soon."

"It sounds like you are in some sort of trouble. If this is something so bad that you had to leave D.C. then you should go to the police. There is nothing that can't be straightened out, but you need to report this now," Bob ordered. "You can't be having the police and everybody looking for you if you aren't actually kidnapped."

I didn't want to get into a discussion, "I'm taking a leave of absence. I'll be in touch. I have to go."

Again I heard, "Don't go. You have to tell me........." I hung up.

I told my boyfriend the same thing.

I called Mary Jo, my roommate, at her work. As expected she was unmoved and said she would keep an eye on my things. She wanted to know when I would send the rent and phone money.

As upsetting as it was I put the phone calls out of my mind and put on my new unwashed jeans and a sweatshirt; if my mother could only see me now. I gathered my grey wool slacks and jacket along with my sweater and other new clothes for the cleaners.

The last time I ate was on the plane to San Diego. I walked from the duplex to the main drag of Imperial Beach finding a one hour cleaners. Next I spotted Lydia's restaurant. I entered to curious stares. Everyone looked Mexican. They spoke Spanish. The menu was in Spanish. The signs on the walls were in Spanish. Had I crossed the border and not realized it? I didn't see granola or a white egg omelet on the menu. Not being that fluent in Spanish I tried to order muesli, but only got, "No comprendi." People were giggling. I was seven miles from civilization. Right up the road was the Hotel Del Coronado where the staff kissed my ass. I pointed to numero cinco, huevos rancheros with tortillas, salsa verde and refried beans. I hoped the beans wouldn't cause a problem on the drive to Van Nuys.

Jim told me to change my appearance. I passed a tattoo parlor. I wasn't ready to go down that road just yet. I was desperate, but not that desperate. Then I came across a beauty parlor. I think it was a beauty parlor. There were photos of women with different hair styles in the window. When I walked in there wasn't an anorexic ding bat receptionist with big hair, a pound of eye liner, talking on the phone while chewing gum like in Ladue. But rather there was a plump senorita with huge hair, a pound of eye liner, chewing gum behind a cluttered counter talking on the phone in Spanish.

There was loud Mexican music. The place didn't look clean. I got my shoulder length auburn hair cut short and dyed darker. I thought it looked cute. Those girls were creative. I couldn't understand what they were saying, but I think I was the brunt of a few jokes. 'Americano puta,' I think I got the gist of that.

I picked up my clean clothes and went back to the duplex. After I found the cleaning supplies, I sucked up my pride and cleaned the bathroom. There's a first time for everything. There was an iron in the closet. Ironing my new clothes was another first for me. I was starting to feel better. I was still terrified, but I felt I was moving forward.

Jim and Joe got home a little after noon. "Whoa, look at you," Jim said.

I think I blushed, "You think I look different?"

"Yeah, you look different." Jim was leering. "You look great. I don't remember you wearing glasses." I could sense Joe was grabbing a gander.

"No, these are fake glasses. I thought they would make me look older or, at least, smarter."

I could tell they'd had a few beers. They told me Ski already left for Van Nuys and that Dan, and a few of the SEALs were staying at the area to make sure none of the beer went to waste.

"Here, we got you a present," Jim handed me sheets and pillow cases with NAB stenciled on them.

"Who's NAB? Is this somebody's bedding?" I asked.

"NAB is Naval Amphibious Base," Jim explained, "They supply bedding to sailors." Jim winked at Joe. "Just like they supply brooms, mops, trash cans, silverware, glasses, plates, soap, toilet paper, and just about everything else you see around here for housekeeping. In fact I think they provided Ski with a battery for his car."

"You mean you stole these sheets?" I asked.

"Cumshaw is a more correct term," Jim offered. "It's a Chinese term for gift or tip. I gave the supply clerk a genuine bolo knife taken off a gook I killed in a knife fight in Vietnam and he tipped me in sheets and some other things. We have a deal with the U.S. Navy. The Navy screws sailors every day and in return we steal from the Navy. Everyone is happy."

There he goes again with that gook term, "You killed someone with a knife?" I retreated a few steps.

"Hell no, but the better the story the better the tip. I found the knife in a bunker," Jim explained. "I have a dozen of them. Believe me, by the time that supply clerk gets back to Skunk Hollow, Tennessee the story will be greatly embellished. He'll be a war hero without doing anything more than handing out toilet paper while stationed at Naval Support Activity, DaNang."

Jim had spoken with Joe about the ID cards and Joe offered, "If you give me the ID you want altered I'll see what I can do. It will cost around 50 bucks."

I gave him my White House ID, District of Columbia driver's license, and 50 bucks. My impression of Joe was that it was going to cost him about 20 bucks, but I wasn't in a position to bargain. I kept my passport in case I wanted to return to being Susan England someday and for identification when signing traveler's checks. Also, I gave him a picture I took in one of those self-photo booths with my new hair style and glasses.

"Let's change the name to Susan Engler, that way not too many letters have to be altered. Change my hair to brunette, height from five foot seven to five foot six and weight from 115 to 110 pounds." I'll weigh 110 again someday.

Joe said he had to get going. He was rendezvousing with a friend. I bet it was the 16 year old, excuse me, 17 year old. He walked into the bathroom. "Whoa, what happened here?" Joe yelled.

Jim raced for the bathroom. "Good lord!"

I felt 10 feet tall. I walked up to the two stunned roommates, "I got down on my hands and knees and scrubbed the floor, something you should consider doing once in a while." I believed that was what females were supposed to say to make males feel guilty, 'I got on my hands and

82

knees.' I didn't even think about saying that, it just came instinctively like some primitive behavioral pattern.

"Thanks," they both said with sheepish smiles.

Jim said it in a way that sounded like he appreciated what I did. That what I did was unexpected. That was the first time someone thanked me for something I did, not for something I bought. When I bought presents people thanked me as if they expected more. And the more money I spent, the more they expected. Jim made me feel good about myself for simply doing something. Only my father could make me feel that way.

The drive to Van Nuys was interesting. Jim and I drove around San Diego's south bay and onto Interstate Five, heading north through downtown San Diego. Just north of San Diego was an off ramp for LaJolla. I'd heard the name. LaJolla was to San Diego what Ladue was to St. Louis. I recalled that being a correct answer on the SAT.

Further up the coast we drove through Camp Pendleton, the mammoth Marine Corps training facility. As we got close to Los Angeles, more lanes appeared on the interstate, the traffic got thicker and quicker, not faster, but quicker. Lane changes were made where there wasn't room. East coast traffic meshed together, out here it was quick. Rudeness prevailed on both coasts and it seemed the universal sign for being pissed-off was the display of an extended middle finger.

We got onto Interstate 405 and passed LAX, the Los Angeles International Airport. At the north end of Los Angeles, we started climbing the Sepulveda Pass. There were few structures along the pass. It was amazing how rugged the countryside looked having just left the country's third largest city. At the top of the pass, Jim said, "There it is, San Fernando Valley."

"Where? All I see is brown haze," I asked.

"That's smog. Don't worry," Jim said. "Humans live down there."

It didn't look healthy, "Are you sure it's safe?"

"The air is safe for millions. Guns and switch blade knives are another matter." Jim drove into the haze.

We got off the interstate and drove to Ski's house. I almost did an 'Oh My God,' but held my tongue. It was a beige stucco, one story house without a blade of grass on the postage stamp of a front yard. There was maybe four feet between houses. Every yard was fenced off, a style held over from the Conquistador days. A Studebaker was on blocks in the driveway and steel bars were on the windows and doors. The garage door was open, facing the street. I don't think a number two pencil could have been crammed into the garage; it was that full of junk.

I would take Jim's duplex over this, hairs on soap and all. "Why are there bars on the windows?"

"This is San Fernando Valley; it's a high crime area. Let's see if Ski's home. His car is here," Jim said as if nothing was wrong. A high crime area, could it get any worse?

There was a yellow Pontiac GTO in front of the house displaying a SEAL TEAM ONE sticker in the rear window. The sticker showed a seal standing, wrapped in a black cape wearing a black beret and holding a knife.

Jim banged on the door, "What the fuck you want? It's open," commanded the husky voice from inside.

We walked in. Ski was lying on the couch wearing only his short, short khaki swim trunks looking at a HOT ROD magazine. Something about those khaki swim trunks that brought one's eyes to them. Thank God no personal body parts were dangling loose. Maybe the reason men wore those shorts was the same reason women wore necklaces which was to draw one's attention to certain body parts. Actually, in Ski's case it was part of his SEAL Team uniform and I don't think these guys cared what they looked like. Ski was well over six feet tall and north of 200 pounds. He displayed a big cheeked, goofy smile that gave the impression he was harmless. His hair was light brown with tight curls. I would swear he had a perm. And he'd outgrown those swim trunks about 20 pounds ago.

Something caught the corner of my eye. I looked and almost jumped. In the corner of the room was a floor to ceiling statue of Jesus painted in bright, garish colors. I looked to Jim. He gave me a sign to not make a big deal about it. As I examined the room, there were several religious artifacts.

A woman burst in from the kitchen that I imagined was Ski's mother. She was in her late thirties to early forties, but with a heavily painted face it was difficult to say. The platinum blonde hair was a little much. Hefty and busty would describe her figure. She wore a pair of short shorts that were ready to split at the seams, a floral blouse tied off midriff, with a lot of cleavage showing, and clear plastic four inch heels. My first impression was she'd lived a hard life. In a hoarse, smoker's voice she said, "Hey Jim, give Momma a big hug and smooch," as she removed the unfiltered cigarette from her mouth while setting down her beer.

"Hello, Mrs. Pulaski." Jim hugged her. "I would like for you to meet Susan England. She's visiting."

"Hi Susan, Frank told me we were having visitors. We've got you in Brenda's room." I assumed Brenda was Ski's sister. "She's shacked up with that no good dope dealer in Northridge. She needs to get hooked up with somebody respectful like a sailor or a salesman. I wished you would have taken her out. I think you could have won her favors pretty fast. Lord knows every other deadbeat has." Mrs. Pulaski gave me a disdainful look. She slipped her arm into Jim's, pressing her big boob into his side. I winced.

"We appreciate the hospitality," Jim said.

I didn't have the nerve to say, 'I would rather sleep on the freeway.' I'd heard Bel Air was a nice part of town. Wasn't there a Bel Air Hotel?

After Jim got our luggage, which consisted of a parachute bag and my cheap suitcase, Mrs. Pulaski led us down the hall. "Here you go. As soon as you get settled come out and have a beer. No quickies now." No chance of that Mrs. Pulaski.

When I was sure she was out of ear shot, I whispered to Jim, "This looks like a little girl's room, all the dolls and stuff." There were a few posters of teen idols like Jimmie Hendrix and Joe Cocker.

"I think she is 17," Jim said.

"That's underage, what's her mother doing letting her live with some man? How old is the dope dealer?" I asked.

"Ski said he's 29 which mean he's probably 39. I know it's a little weird out here," Jim said. "I think he's only been to prison once which is respectable for the Valley."

"Let's go to a hotel. I'll pay," I begged.

"Ski expects us to stay. We are going to meet Linda tonight," Jim informed me.

"Can we go to a hotel after we talk to her? I really don't like this."

"It'll be alright. It's only for a couple of nights."

"Well, how are we going to work this? You didn't think......" I pointed to the bed.

"I'll sleep on the floor. You have nothing to worry about. Having grown up in Ladue I'm immune to your type."

That wasn't called for. "What, smart and sophisticated?" But I was glad he didn't expect me to sleep with him.

"No, playing dead in bed."

If only he knew. "Where's the bathroom?" I opened a door to a closet crammed full of junk.

"There's only one and it's down the hall," Jim explained.

"You're kidding?" I asked.

"Let's go have that beer. Try to be sociable."

"I have to go potty. I'll meet you in a minute." The all pink tiled bathroom was the size of a phone booth. The toilet lid was covered with fake lamb's wool. The grout was mildewed as was the shower curtain which was all black at the bottom. I wanted to scream.

I drank the first beer a little fast. In fact, I may have drunk the first three beers too fast. I was feeling okay when the five o'clock news came on. The lead story was about the girl kidnapped in Washington, D.C.

"She's dead," Ski's mom blurted. "The kidnappers will get the ransom and her parents will get the body. It's the way it always works. Mark my words."

"You think so. Maybe she ran away," I responded. Jim gave me a look like, 'don't screw around with this.'

"Ran away! They say she left her car and all her clothes. Nobody runs away and leaves their stuff," Ski's mom barked with a cough.

My picture flashed on the screen. It was me the night I walked in the Veiled Prophet Ball, St. Louis's presentation of debutantes. Only my mother would pick that picture. She wouldn't consider that if her daughter were kidnapped she may not be in a ball gown posing with her hair and makeup just so. "Do you think I could pass for her?" I asked Mrs. Pulaski.

"You! Look at you. You're a sweet little thing. You could never pass for a spoiled brat like that. Look at that bitch. She's one of those high society snots. You don't want to be like that. Stay just the way you are." My confidence soared. Jim was shaking his head.

Ski's idea of an evening out did not include going to the country club for cocktails and dinner. First we went to an In-And-Out hamburger joint to get something to eat. I'm not fond of fast food, but it was really good. There were no fast food restaurants or franchises of any sort in Ladue. Maybe the city council should consider an In-And-Out.

Next we went to a gentleman's club called the Hole-in-One, except there were no gentlemen. Scantily clad women danced in cages suspended from the ceiling. Other girls looked like they'd contracted a scathing yeast infection and were scratching themselves against poles. The lighting would make an epileptic go into seizure with strobes and flashing beams of multi colors. The music was ear shattering and awful. The men nursed their drinks with mesmerized eyes. I didn't get it. What was the attraction? Was this to stimulate the libido in some strange way? I could get more of a rise out of these deadbeats with a suggestively fitting skirt, sheer stockings, high heels and crossing my legs just so. I asked Jim, "So, this is your idea of fun?"

"No, Ski likes to come here. Guys come here to buy overpriced drinks and fantasize that virtuous, beautiful women will want them," Jim deadpanned. "In here, men can re-invent themselves. They can tell these

87

women they are professional athletes, race car drivers, or spies for the CIA. They can be anybody they want. They have their tough guy tattoos, facial hair, earrings and talk rough, then on Monday morning its back to pumping gas or flipping burgers. But this is their escape. This is where unattainable dreams are dreamt."

"What kind of women would work in a place like this?" I asked.

"The same kind, dreams unfulfilled, but the women are more practical. They need the money so they work under the illusion of a rich sugar daddy waltzing in, spotting her and taking her away from all this. It's happened, but rarely. Mostly when the sugar daddy and the pole princess get hooked up they shortly find out he is not an independently wealthy real estate tycoon, but rather an out of work wife beater, and the pole princess turns out to be a single mom with multiple kids by different men, and an expensive drug habit."

"This is a sad place," I observed.

"Yes, it is. This is capitalism at its best. If you can think it then you can fantasize it, and if you can fantasize it there will be somebody eager to take your money so you can pretend it."

We spent a few hours there drinking beer. It felt like an eternity. I went to the bathroom once. It was disgusting. I thought for sure I had contracted a lifelong sexually transmitted disease. Finally Ski had enough. I don't know what he had enough of, but he said, "Let's go."

While driving to Linda's apartment, Ski laid rubber at every stop light. He revved up the GTO and gave a challenging look to the driver in the car next to us. My neck was getting sore from being whiplashed. If one of his drag races turned into a fist fight I didn't know what I was going to do.

Ski knocked on Linda's door. A full figured brunette opened. She was wearing a uniform of sorts, probably from some fast food joint. I figured we killed time at the gentleman's club until Linda finished her shift, or maybe he was working up a fantasy. After three beers at the gentleman's club and the race car ride I had to go, BADLY! Linda noticed my distress. She pointed toward the bathroom.

Linda wasn't what I expected. She seemed normal in every way except her hair which was in a semi beehive and her makeup which was dark and heavy. The great-piece-of-ass was actually the humongous piece of ass. Her behind looked like two basketballs were stuffed in her trousers. I shouldn't say that because she was pleasant and polite, maybe two volleyballs would be kinder, but she had some major buns. After getting us a beer she said, "Ski said you wanted to talk about Wayne."

Jim looked at me. I said, "Yes, I'm very sorry for your loss." I was feeling dizzy and having trouble focusing. "I don't want to seem indelicate, but did you have any communication with Wayne after he was injured?"

"Not really. I got a letter from a nurse who treated him. If you want to read it, I'll get it for you," Linda said.

"Yes, very much." Linda retrieved the letter. I put it in my purse, "I'll read it tomorrow and give it back to Ski if that would be alright." I didn't want the evening to turn into a morbid affair and besides, I couldn't concentrate.

"Yes, of course. Can you tell me what this is about?" Linda asked.

"I work for the White House. Rumors have it that Wayne's platoon captured something. I'm trying to track it down." I lied. "He didn't do anything wrong. We are just trying to locate whatever it was they captured." I hoped that was enough. Linda didn't seem all that interested, and didn't ask any more questions. I didn't think she really cared.

Jim and I stayed another half hour or so. It was fun. We told lies about our embarrassing drunk adventures. I think I was the life of the party. I remember doing most of the talking. I ignored Ski waving his hands over his head for Jim to leave so he could get busy with the great-piece-of-ass. I thought Ski should rename her 'the humongous-piece-of-ass.' I was so mean. That was what drinking did to me.

Jim drove Ski's car back to the Pulaski house, without any drag racing, thank you very much. I don't remember much. I woke up in bed alone, thank God, but with a miserable hangover. Jim was passed out on the floor. Once he came to and we got organized, we went to breakfast at a greasy spoon. I pulled out the letter:

24 MAY 1967

Dear Linda,

I'm an Army nurse in Saigon and writing on behalf of Wayne Meyer. Wayne was injured four days ago and brought here. He is heavily sedated. When he is awake he speaks of you and wanted me to assure you he will recover and will be home soon. We are praying for him. He must love you very much by the way he talks.

He is facing his injuries bravely and remains in good humor. He wanted me to remind you to change the oil in his car. You are a very lucky woman and I hope Wayne can return to you soon.

Sincerely,

Teresa Volkman

"I need to speak with Teresa Volkman," I informed Mr. Jim Crotty. "How are we going to find her?"

Chapter 12

At breakfast I reiterated, "We have to find Teresa."

"We?" Jim asked.

"Aren't you going to help? You can't expect me to do all this by myself."

"I can't help anymore. I'm not supposed to leave the San Diego area. I shouldn't even be up here in Van Nuys this weekend. My platoon is deploying to Vietnam in early December without me. So I'll have the duplex to myself. You are welcome to stay with me until you figure out what you want to do, but I can't help. Besides, I don't know how you expect to find a nurse who served in Vietnam. You know, you are not going to beat these guys," Jim said. "They're going to find you. They have the whole country looking for you."

I contemplated what he said and he was right. But I was also sure somebody was going to kill me if I didn't do something to try and stop them. And the only way to do that was to have them arrested for doing something illegal which at that moment I thought was running a black market to finance the President's re-election campaign. The SEALs captured some of the black market money which was now missing. I needed to find out about that money.

Jim drove to Malibu's Zuma Beach. I brought along my hideous bathing suit. Jim told me to change in the car. "What if somebody sees me?"

"So what? They don't know you," was his answer. "I doubt you would ever see them again. It's not like people who hang out at Zuma Beach would show up at a St. Louis society ball. And I doubt anyone seeing you naked would gander a second glance." Well that was unkind.

Jim wanted to take a run on the beach. "A run? You mean run for no reason at all?"

"Don't you run or exercise?"

"They made us run around the hockey field at Mary Institute four times at the start of the season. It was the hardest thing I'd ever done.

You know how hot and humid it gets in St. Louis in late August? A lot of mothers, especially mine, complained that running would stunt our growth and cause big calf muscles which would make us undesirable to suitable gentlemen, and besides it was too hot to be outside doing anything. And college tennis was serious business. They worked our tails off. Since college I have retired from serious physical activity. I do play tennis occasionally." I thought that would set Jim straight.

"Did your mother consider your smoking may stunt your growth?" Jim asked.

Did he think he could get under my skin? "We didn't smoke in front of our parents until college. By then I was fully grown so it didn't matter."

"That's your reasoning, and you call yourself a college graduate?" Now he was insulting me. "Come on, I'll go slow. Your boyfriend won't mind big calf muscles if he really loves you. I'm sure he loves you for your mind, or at least your money."

Sometimes I just wanted to shout, 'FUCK YOU, you shit head,' but being the refined lady that I was I refrained from using such vulgar language. He wasn't going to intimidate me. So off we went running on the hard packed sand by the water's edge, Jim wearing his khaki team shorts. It seemed like we ran forever. Jim said it was 10 minutes, maybe a mile.

"Where can I shower? I'm perspiring," I asked.

"You're sweating. There's a difference. You can jump into the toasty warm ocean." I thought he was kidding, but Jim dove like a porpoise.

I walked into the ocean up to my knees where I got splashed by a breaking wave. The water was unbelievably cold. I'd seen those Beach Blanket Bingo and Gidget movies. Don't tell me prima donna actresses like Annette and Sandra Dee got in that water.

We ate lunch at Trancas Market by Broad Beach. I was starting to feel comfortable with Jim. He was funny in a sarcastic, cynical way. He was funny as long as the sarcasm wasn't directed toward me.

That evening, we went to Gladstone's By-the-Sea in Malibu. It was a place I would never have chosen in my pre-kidnapped days, but it was fun.

The restaurant was right on the water's edge where the foot of Sunset Boulevard met the Pacific Coast Highway. We drank beer, of course, and ate crab chowder and the biggest piece of chocolate cake I'd ever seen. The two of us couldn't finish one piece.

After dinner, we drove to Venice Beach and walked among the ocean side shops. We watched the ever evolving freak show. Kids smoking pot in public was legal, I guess. Nobody seemed to care and there was not a policeman to be found. Venice was a world of its own. I don't think the founding fathers of our country meant freedom to mean one could wander around in a drug induced stupor, whine about the war, civil rights, while being a freeloader at the taxpayer's expense. I think the founding fathers meant people were free to get off one's fat ass and make something of themselves. My God, I was starting to sound like my parent's friends, how frightening.

This was all new territory for me and I loved it. A man and woman walked by in evening attire. They looked out of place and uncomfortable. I realized that was me a few days ago. I was now a real person. I was no longer an out of touch elitist that couldn't relate, nor was I a freaked out weirdo who didn't have the capacity to relate. What it came down to was indifference at both ends of the societal spectrum. I saw kids smoking and realized I hadn't had a cigarette all day, and I didn't desire one. Maybe there was something to this exercising and being outdoors. We sat on a bench people watching. Something Jim said at breakfast bothered me, "Why aren't you supposed to leave San Diego?"

"Nothing that concerns you. Something happened on my last deployment which hasn't been cleared up yet," was his answer.

"Hey, I've told you plenty. Why I'm running, why I'm scared, you can tell me a little about yourself."

"Oh, it's nothing. I'm being investigated for murder," Jim said so casually that at first the statement didn't register.

"Murder!" I yelped. Should I yell for the police? Should I run? "Please go on."

"It's nothing. We were on a night ambush and I shot some people whom the government says I should not have shot." Jim shrugged his shoulders.

"Tell me about this," I demanded. My heart was beating a million times a minute.

"I don't know why you would be interested. It's all bogus bullshit." Jim started, "We were on a night ambush in the Rung Sat Special Zone. Intel had identified a VC official in our area of operation. VC stands for Viet Cong, the U.S. military's enemy, the hippie's hero. Anyway, the VC were to move this official down a river one night. We set up an ambush on the river bank where the river narrowed. In an ambush the officer in charge, better known as the OIC, sits in the middle with his men spread out on either side of him along the river bank. His job is to initiate the ambush when he thinks most of the enemy is in the kill zone.

He uses a starlight scope to watch for the enemy. It's a scope that sees in the dark. Sometimes the enemy will force civilians to travel ahead of them, hoping the Americans will kill the civilians. So it's the officer's responsibility to identify and kill as many of the enemy as possible."

'Kill zone, kill as many as possible,' I reflected. It was difficult to comprehend a boy from Ladue, my age, using terms like 'kill zone, and kill as many.'

"The Rung Sat Special Zone is a free-fire zone," Jim continued, "which means anything goes, so there should not have been a problem with killing anyone. And it was early morning, before the curfew was lifted. Even though we were in a free-fire zone and it was during curfew, we were still careful to avoid shooting civilians. Sometimes fishermen go out early, or as I said, the VC will force civilians to travel ahead of their patrols."

"About four o'clock in the morning, after sitting on ambush for five hours, and being eaten alive by mosquitoes, I heard engine noise on the river. The VC use small Briggs and Stratton engines on their sampans. I don't know if the American taxpayers are aware, but if it wasn't for the

94

U.S.'s financial and material support, the North Vietnamese would never be able to wage war against South Vietnam. It seems every VC sampan has an American engine. The engines were supposed to go to South Vietnamese fishermen. But most of the fisherman sell their engines to the VC, or have them stolen, or the fisherman is a VC in the first place."

"Anyway, I heard a sampan coming. The boat came closer and closer until it was right in front of me, less than five feet away. My night vision was such that I could make out the silhouette of an AK-47, that's the rifle the enemy uses, being swung around and pointing toward me. I couldn't wait for the OIC to get his trigger finger out of his ass. I blew the person away along with the other two people in the sampan. All hell broke loose. Everyone was firing. There was no return fire."

"When the smoke cleared I retrieved the AK-47 off the river bottom. The water was only about three feet deep, and luckily the weapon hadn't sunk into the mud. We found a few rice bowls and sets of black pajamas, but no documents or other weapons. We took the identification cards off the dead. There were five dead, an old man and four young females. They all carried South Vietnam identification cards."

I shuttered, but I wanted to know more, "Go on."

"Well, that's about it." Jim continued, "The OIC wrote up the post-op report stating five VC KIA, weapon and enemy material captured. He gave me a royal ass chewing about initiating the ambush. I explained what I saw and I had the AK-47 to prove it. Having South Vietnam identification cards doesn't mean anything because the VC are South Vietnamese who are rebelling against their government."

"So why are you in trouble?" I asked.

"Yeah, that's the curious part," Jim answered. "About two days later our OIC got a message to report to an Army major in Nha Be. The Army major stated that his ARVN, which stands for Army of the Republic of Viet Nam, counterpart reported eight civilians were massacred by Americans. I guess we didn't recover all the bodies. By going through the post-op reports in the Mekong Delta for that day he figured it was my SEAL platoon based on the location, date, and time of the ambush. Even though the incident took place in a free-fire zone during curfew, and a weapon captured, he wouldn't listen. The major wanted murder charges filed, probably to save face with his ARVN counterpart. My platoon was to return to CONUS, that's continental United States, in a couple of weeks, so the OIC sent me home early."

"My commanding officer has been understanding while trying to work things out with the Judge Advocate General, but I'm not to leave San Diego. No formal charges have been filed as of yet. I'm hoping the whole thing will die down and go away. In war shit happens, and as far as the victims being female, believe me a 10 year old girl can kill you just as dead as a 25 year old male soldier. Don't give me that crap about male or female or young or old. If they shoot you, you are dead. I've seen enough to know you shoot first, explain later. And the enemy knows that if they are to win this war they will win need the help of chicken shit protesters in the U.S. The ARVN officer reporting the incident was probably a VC and wanted to get the incident reported in the U.S. media to get the UC Berkeley student body worked into a state of hyper-conniption. Instead of supporting their own men our officers are gullible enough to go along with their ARVN counterparts."

Sunday morning, Jim and I drove back to San Diego. Jim taught me to drive his stick shift car. He was patient. He had to be. I murdered the gears. But this way, I could have the car during the day. Jim owned a Triumph Bonneville motorcycle that he could ride to work. He took me for motorcycle rides. It was so much fun. If my mother saw me it would have been coronary city for her.

I was in the kitchen when Jim got home Wednesday afternoon. I told him, "I know where Teresa Volkman lives."

And he told me, "I have something to tell you. But first, I know I'm going to regret this, how did you find her?"

"It took some nerve, but I went to the North Island Naval Air Station. First, I bought a new suit in LaJolla where they have some acceptable shops. I drove up to the gate and with the military sticker on your car, they waved me onto base. I asked the Marine sentry directions to the personnel office. At the office, I flashed my new White House identification card to the sailor behind the counter. That woke him up. He snapped to with a lot of, 'yes ma'am.' I told him I needed to speak with the officer in charge. Before I knew it, I was speaking with a commander. I told him I was out here doing some follow up work for the upcoming Presidential visit and the President wanted to give a medal to an Army nurse who served in Vietnam. I told him how politicians work, they trot out a representative from a group where they need votes and give the token person a citation or something. I said Teresa Volkman was recommended to the President as a heroic Army nurse who served in Vietnam."

"The commander flew into action. After a few phone calls, he gave me her date of commissioning, her date of birth, her date of discharge, where she enlisted, her last known address and phone number, and everything but her measurements, and I could've gotten those if I asked."

"He took me to lunch at the officers' club. I could tell he liked me because he held the door, and my chair, and fussed over me. He was cute and really nice. He made me laugh. I told him I would escort him to the President's reception. He gave me his card and wrote his home phone number. He lives right here in Coronado and drives a Corvette. He invited me for drinks at his place after work. I told him I would love to, but I had a previous engagement. I gave him your home phone number. I hope that was alright. I told him if he liked he could call me later and maybe we could get together for drinks. He was a fighter pilot in Vietnam. He dropped bombs on North Vietnam and made night carrier landings in storms. Doesn't that sound cool?" I waited for Jim's reaction.

"A commander, a fighter pilot, you're moving up in the world. So, when are you going out?" Jim inquired.

"I don't know." I goaded, "I'll have to think about it. A lady should never appear anxious and accept the first invitation from a strange gentleman."

"That probably explains all the times I've been turned down. Well, this sounds dandy. He can take over. We'll get your stuff and you can move in with the commander. I'm sure he expects you to. You two will make a cute couple. What about your boyfriend or is he just SOL? With the commander being funny, cute, a Corvette, and being a bad ass fighter pilot in Vietnam I don't see how any woman could resist. I guess for some women that's all it takes." Jim was pissed. That was beautiful.

"Yes well, as great as the commander sounds I think I can manipulate you easier. So you're stuck with me," I informed Jim.

Jim chewed on that for a moment then asked. "Where does Teresa live?"

"Salina, Kansas, you and I are visiting her the day after Thanksgiving," I ordered. "I've already called her and it's all set."

"I'm in the Navy. They take a dim view of people leaving without permission. I told you I can't leave San Diego. And it's November, nobody goes to Kansas in November. I'm living in Southern California, it's 75 degrees, the sun is shining, and girls are running around in bikinis. Why in God's name would I go to Kansas?" Jim argued. "See if the commander is free. He sounds eager. He can fly you there in his fighter jet."

"Don't you want to be with me?" I said with the sorrowful puppy look.

"Be with you? I don't even know you. You're dangerous. What if your assassin misses and hits me? I've got my own problems," Jim said. "I would have to take leave or be on orders, and I can't take leave. It can't be done."

"It's Thanksgiving break. Aren't you going home for turkey?" I asked.

"I told you I can't leave," Jim said. "The Navy doesn't care if I go home for turkey or not."

I ignored him. "We'll fly to St. Louis Wednesday evening. You do the turkey thing on Thursday, and Friday we'll take your mother's car and drive to Salina. We'll talk to Teresa and spend the night there or in Kansas

City, and be back Saturday afternoon. Sunday we'll fly back to San Diego. Any questions?" I asked.

"Let's say we go, which we aren't. Do we just walk into my house and I say, 'Hi Mom, hi Dad, this is Susan England. We're shacking up in my room and Friday night we're bedding down in Kansas City, but don't worry, we don't do the dirty deed. It's good to be home. Mom, you look ill,'" Jim explained.

"No, Silly, you say, 'It is my honor to present Ms. Susan Wellington England, Mary Institute, Smith College cum laude, Veiled Prophet maid of honor, White House associate and overall swell gal. We share the same bed, but we do not engage in any immoral sexual acts or behavior that would bring dishonor to our friends and families. At present, we are trying to solve a problem of national importance. If we do not succeed, we will be murdered.'"

"Oh now it's 'we will be murdered.' I liked it better when it was just you being murdered. Okay, where are you going to stay?" Jim asked.

"That's a problem. I was thinking of staying at the Kings Brothers' Motel. I would like to stay with Franci. You met her at Busch's the night we met. But I know she can't keep her big trap shut. She would blab everything to my parents. I would be captured and locked away."

"Doesn't Kings Brothers' only rent rooms by the hour?" Jim joked.

"I think you can get a room for a whole night." I should explain that the Kings Brothers' Motel was the closest motel to Ladue. As with franchise burger joints there were no hotels or motels in Ladue. Kings Brothers' was a dump where teenage couples went for their first experience of, 'going-all-the-way.' 'Going all the way,' in Ladue in the 1960s was the pinnacle event after years of going steady, proms, corsages, movies, dinners, dances, expensive Christmas presents, birthday presents, taking a truckload of crap from the female, and shameful begging from the male. Thousands of dollars of the male's dad's money was invested in the honor of, 'popping the cherry.' And after the grand event the male had to put up with a boat load of crap for stealing the girl's virginity. If those young men would have been smart they would have

99

ventured to the North County, picked up a nice girl at a Steak 'n Shake and gotten laid at a drive-in theater for the cost of a movie and a six-pack.

To keep the record straight, I did not succumb to the Kings Brothers' Motel. I fell for expensive champagne in college. And yes, I made him feel terrible for ruining my life. My mother told me people could tell if a girl had premarital sex by the way she walked. That was the sum total of my birds and bees talk.

Rumor had it that married couples also carried on at the Kings Brothers', but not with their respective spouses. Such was life in Ladue.

As we were talking the phone rang. I rushed to the living room and picked up. Jim yelled from the kitchen, "Tell the commander, 'hi'." I thought he would have the propriety to wait at least 24 hours. They must be horny at North Island.

I answered, "Hello, ...Yes, may I ask who is calling?" I turned my head with a roll of the eyes and gave my best, 'are you kidding me,' look, "It's for you lover boy, Emmy Lou. You said you had your own problems. This sounds like one of them. Is she of legal age?"

I retreated to the kitchen and acted like I was busy, but not so busy as to not listen. "Oh, she's out here doing something for the government...............no, I hardly know her.......... she's staying here for a few days so what.............yes, we stayed at Ski's.............I'm telling you nothing happened.........so I didn't call, it's not the end of the world................it's nothing like that...............hey, think whatever you want. I've got to go." Jim banged down the receiver. "Screw her!"

I came back into the living room, "I'm sorry if there is a problem on account of me being here." I lied.

"You did me a favor. Something I haven't had the guts to do," Jim stated.

He didn't seem upset. I asked, "Tell me what your news is."

"Oh yeah, I almost forgot." Jim started, "The CO, that's the commanding officer, called me into his office. That's never a good thing. There were two men in suits. That's really not a good thing. They wanted to know to whom I'd been talking to about SEAL operations. Of course, I told them nobody because all SEAL operations are classified secret, and we aren't supposed to mention them. They told me I'd been observed speaking to somebody, who works for the White House, about four SEALs killed in Vietnam. I told them a friend of mine from St. Louis who works in Washington, D.C. asked me about the operation last May. I told the CO that I didn't tell you anything that wasn't in the San Diego Union. One of the suits asked me why my friend was asking the questions. I told him that you thought the government killed the four SEALs, and the government was now gunning for you. I told them I thought you were paranoid. One of the suits asked me if I knew where you were. I told them sure; that you were shacking up with me, and if it wasn't too much trouble could they come and get you."

"You didn't? You did? Don't kid around about this." Was he joking?

"No, but I wanted to." I thought, 'what a shithead.' "The CO wanted to know if I'd heard any more about my murder case."

I made the 10 o'clock news again. The news report speculated that I may have known my kidnapper, and was traveling with a male. I wondered who would leak stuff like that to the press.

Jim snapped me out of my thought, "So, it's Kansas for Thanksgiving?"

Chapter 13

We were lucky to get a flight to St. Louis on the Wednesday before Thanksgiving. The food was terrible. I cannot eat with those tiny toy knives and forks and the pretend salt and pepper shakers. And the wrappers that cover the food, what are you supposed to do with those? Jim was anxious. If he got caught being away from San Diego his command would not support him, and murder charges would most likely be filed.

Jim checked me into the Kings Brothers' Motel on Lindbergh Boulevard. I worried that in the middle of the night I would be awakened by the rhythmic pounding of a headboard against the wall in the adjacent room. Jim came to see me a couple of times on Thursday and brought me leftovers from his Thanksgiving dinner. We ate pumpkin pie and finished a bottle of red wine. We sat on the bed and watched the nine o'clock news, and then Johnny Carson. My kidnapping was not a lead item on the news in my own hometown, how disappointing. The kidnapping came after the story on the proposed school bond issue, yawn.

There was a short interview with my best friend Franci in front of Mary Institute. They showed a picture of Franci and me skiing in Aspen. I was wearing a parka with the hood pulled over my face, however Franci looked radiant with the sun glinting off her teeth. I'm sure that was going to help someone find me. I got the feeling Franci was volunteering information to get her face on TV.

I told Jim he should spend the evening at home, that he didn't get to see his family that often. He said he would rather be with me. It was one of my more memorable Thanksgivings. Jim was alright even if he was rough around the edges. He was considerate even though he didn't want to give that impression. I wanted to go home so bad, but knew I would be picked up by TJ and his buddies. I was afraid they were watching my house.

Friday morning, Jim picked me up at five a.m. in his mother's Country Squire Ford station wagon. That was the de rigueur car for the suburban housewife. It was dark outside, cold, and windy. We were in for a long day. I'd never driven across Missouri and into Kansas. I resisted smoking out of consideration for Jim, but I needed a cigarette badly. Ordinarily I would have flown, but there were no connecting flights to Salina, Kansas, at least none that I knew of. I think the only airline that went there was Ozark Air, and the chances of arriving in one piece were slim. He'd packed some sweet rolls and orange juice. I drank a little orange juice, but passed on the fattening sweet rolls.

With stopping for gas, my frequent bathroom breaks, and food stops for Jim, it took us over six hours. Jim actually ate food bought in gas stations, stale donuts and candy bars. I didn't understand it. No way would I eat that junk. The bathrooms were disgusting. I had to put a half roll of toilet paper on the seat before I could think of sitting.

I called Teresa and asked if she wanted to meet for lunch. Salina wasn't much of a town. It was in the middle of Kansas on the main highway between Kansas City and Denver. Otherwise, I don't have anything to say about the place. I wouldn't live there.

We met at a truck stop diner just off the highway. It was dirty and the food was indescribable. I think everything was fried. After introducing ourselves we sat down to lunch. I ordered a salad and picked at it. Jim ate a hamburger and fries with a coke, and Teresa had a chicken salad sandwich with coffee. Teresa was thin, maybe too thin. Her hair was stringy and done up like most women in rural America. It was the chain smoking that bothered me. I smoked to be polite, but I couldn't keep up with her. Her hands were shaking when she asked, "You said you worked for the defense department and wanted to know about the quality of medical care in Vietnam?"

I could see Jim's surprised look from the corner of my eye. "I fibbed a little. I work for the White House. I need to ask you about a particular case in Vietnam."

"I could have saved you the trip, Deary. I handled hundreds of cases. I doubt I would remember any particular one," Teresa stated.

I explained, "This was last May. A Navy SEAL was injured in an explosion and died while in your hospital in Saigon." I was startled how

103

fast Teresa looked away, and took a long drag. She had trouble getting the cigarette to her lips. I could tell she knew what I was talking about. I needed to be careful. "We need to know what, if anything, you two talked about."

"There was a man in Vietnam asking the same question," Teresa said.

"Did he have a high and tight military haircut and a narrow face?" I asked.

"Yeah, we called him parrot beak. He was very demanding. I told him to fuck off," Teresa said. "Just like I'm telling you to fuck off."

"Did he go by the name TJ?"

"Yeah, how did you know? Is he a buddy of yours?"

"We've met. I assure you we're not friends," I said.

At that point Jim jumped in, "We're asking about Wayne Meyer. He was a classmate of mine in UDT/SEAL training and we were in SEAL Team One together."

"What class?" Teresa asked.

"Forty three," Jim answered.

"Your name again?" Teresa asked.

"Jim Crotty."

"Wait here," Teresa got up and went to a pay phone. She was gone about 10 minutes. It looked like she made several calls. Jim and I made comments about the patrons in the restaurant, mostly derogatory. I shouldn't say that. These were people who worked for a living, farmers, cross country truck drivers, mechanics, and many other jobs people like me took for granted.

"I thought you quit smoking?" Jim asked.

"I did. I'm just doing this to be sociable," I answered as I saw Teresa returning.

"You in Nam?" Teresa asked.

"Yes, ma'am," Jim answered.

"What platoon?"

"Kilo."

"Okay, now listen, that TJ friend of yours is bad news. I don't want noth'n to do with him, okay?"

I spoke, "He's not a friend. I think there's been some foul play."

"No shit Sherlock. Tell me something I don't know." Teresa blew smoke out the side of her mouth.

"We have to know what you and Wayne talked about. Lives may depend on it." I didn't mention that it was my life that depended on it.

"Okay, but you have to promise to never mention my name, or that we ever spoke," Teresa said. "If somebody comes around here I'm telling them I'd never seen ya."

"We promise," I said.

Teresa's hands were shaking worse. I thought she would cram that cigarette up her nose trying to get it to her mouth. "Wayne is the reason I left the Army. I loved the military, helping the wounded, serving in a combat zone. It was my life, but what that bastard did to Wayne made me get out." Teresa started to settle down. "Wayne was a fighter. I loved fighters. Some men gave up. Their wounds were bad and they thought they didn't have a chance so they died. Some men didn't know what end was up. They were scared and confused. But Wayne knew he was in trouble and he fought. He wasn't going to let his injuries kill him. He was going to beat it. He had a chance. He was almost stable enough to evac to Japan for further surgery. Then that parrot beaked, cocksucker TJ showed up."

"What happened next?" I asked.

"I knew something was wrong." Teresa said, "He demanded to see Wayne, not in a consoling way, or the way his SEAL buddies did. He wanted to interrogate him. I kept Wayne on a morphine drip, enough that he was out of it whenever the parrot beak was around. I don't know why, but I knew that cocksucker was up to no good. Call it my motherly instincts. I hovered around whenever the parrot beak was on the ward. I acted busy, like I wasn't paying attention. He kept asking Wayne where the money was, where was it hidden?"

"Then about 10 o'clock one night I got a call that a code blue was called on Meyer. I rushed over to the hospital."

"By the time I got there Wayne was in full cardiac arrest. The doctors did everything they could, but it was no use. When he was pronounced I saw the parrot beak duck out the back door. I don't think he saw me. Sally, another nurse, yelled, "Where's my potassium? It was right here." Now call me crazy, but I think the parrot beak killed Wayne by putting potassium into his IV line."

"The day before Wayne had told me he and his platoon hid the money under the pier where they found it. He said whatever you do don't let that bastard TJ know. Wayne told me that about a week after the platoon hid the money, they were returning to their hootch from an operation when someone spotted an 82 millimeter ChiCom mortar under a table. Wayne said he started to leave to get EOD as the other three platoon members walked toward the table. That's all he remembered. I don't know why Wayne told me, but he must have felt his life was in danger, and as it turned out, he was right."

"I ain't ever testifying in no court and you can forget you ever saw me." Teresa was looking down as a tear run down her face. She was trying to act tough. She fumbled to light another cigarette.

A gum chewing waitress sauntered up to the booth with one hand on her expansive hip. "You having pie, Hon?"

"I'll have to pass, thank you," Jim answered. "I think we should go." He took my arm and started to pull out his wallet.

"I'm paying," I said. I paid and left a nice tip. With a hand on her shoulder I told Teresa, "Thanks for your help."

Her face was still downcast, "How could they kill a serviceman wounded in combat? What has our country come to?"

Jim answered, "I don't know, but we are going to find out, and when we do people are going to pay." Teresa reached out and squeezed Jim's arm.

After we got in the car, I asked in a superior way, "So, do you believe me now?"

"I believe you but what's this about money?" Jim asked.

"I don't know," I lied, "I guess they found some money that TJ thought belonged to him. What pier do you think Teresa is talking about?"

"Hell if I know," Jim contemplated. "It has to be somewhere in Wayne's AO, or area of operation."

"What was that about Class 43?" I asked.

"If somebody says they are a SEAL, they're asked what Team they are with or what training class they went through, or platoon or something that pins them down. She probably knew some SEALs and called somebody to verify who I was. I think that's why she talked to us," Jim said. He seemed focused.

"And what's EOD?" I asked. All those military acronyms were Greek to me.

"Explosive Ordnance Disposal, they're the bomb squad. We work with them a lot. They defuse booby traps and other ordnance." That sounded like a marvelous job. Jim continued, "Wayne was probably leaving to get them when the mortar went off. From what Teresa said I think it was command detonated. In other words, TJ, or somebody who works for him, was waiting for the SEALs to go into their hootch, and then he cranked it off. But he screwed up. He didn't get the money first. He probably thought he knew where it was. Now he's in trouble."

I added, "Or he didn't destroy the evidence. He probably inspected the place after the explosion, and found no remains of the money. Okay, one more dumb question, what's a hootch?"

"A house or more accurately a thatched hut," Jim answered then asked, "What do you mean, 'destroyed the evidence?'"

I shouldn't have said that. "Oh, I was thinking out loud that the money may have been evidence in a crime." I didn't want to elaborate.

We drove back to Kansas City in relative silence, each digesting Teresa's statement in our own way. We stayed at a Hilton that night. I didn't demand a different room. I mean, am I going to ask for an ocean or mountain view room in Kansas City? Get serious. I didn't feel like being a bitch. I was humbled by what Teresa told us, how a person working for the President could kill one of our own servicemen. I had to stop TJ before he stopped me, and to be truthful I was worried about our government. Were we really killing our own servicemen so some jerk could be re-elected President? Jim seemed possessed. Teresa's statements must have affected him.

We ate steaks at a nice restaurant in the Plaza. I'll say this much for Kansas City, the steaks were great. It'd been over 24 hours since I last ate a real meal. Jim didn't say a word during dinner. He stared into space. His eyes narrowed. I didn't know who I was more scared of, Jim or TJ.

After driving a little over four hours we arrived in St. Louis before noon Saturday. "Can we go to Busch's for lunch?"

"Why Busch's, aren't you afraid of being recognized?"

"That's one of the reasons I want to go. And I want to find out what people think of Susan England being kidnapped."

We had to decide whether to eat in the main dining room where the ladies would dine, or the men's bar where the men would be having their two martini lunch while solving the world's problems. The cabanas out back were closed for the winter, and Jim said they would be of little use for overhearing other's conversations. Jim said the main dining room would be the best place for gossip, but the tables were spaced too far apart. The tables were bunched close together in the men's bar, but the cigar smoking men wouldn't be interested in talking about a kidnapping. We choose the men's bar.

Jim ordered a steak sandwich, and I a hamburger. I asked, "Do you recognize anyone? There's Mr. Scott, he's in insurance. Do you know him?"

Jim replied, "No, but I see Mr. Schock. He knows my dad. Do you know him?"

"No."

Jim caught Mr. Schock's eye. Mr. Schock came over to our table. "I thought that was you. What are you doing in town?"

Jim stood to shake hands, "I'm here for Thanksgiving. I go back tomorrow. I would like to introduce Susan Engler. She's a friend of mine visiting from California. She's a doctoral student in political science at UC San Diego writing her dissertation on, 'How Graded Socialism Leads to the Downfall of Democratic Governments'."

"Very interesting," Mr. Schock said to Susan, and then turned to Jim. "So, did I hear you were in Vietnam?"

"Yes Sir, I'm about to go over for my second tour."

"I see your dad once in a while. He told me you were a frogman or something in the Navy."

"Yes Sir, I'm with SEAL Team One out of Coronado, California."

"I knew some frogmen in World War II. They were always getting into some daring missions."

"It hasn't changed. I heard on the news that some St. Louis girl was kidnapped. I think I recognized her name. She may have been the same year I was in high school."

"Yes, Susan England, she went to Mary I. Horrible business, nobody knows what is going on."

"They don't say much on TV, at least in California."

"If anybody knows it would be Natalie Miller. There is nothing that goes on around here without her knowing about it. I saw her in the dining room. If you have a minute, let's go over and visit. I'm curious myself."

I gave Jim a nervous glance. Jim stood, "Sure let's go."

"Natalie, how are you?" Mrs. Miller was sitting at a table with three other ladies.

"Well, I'm just fine Taylor. How are you?"

"Very well, thank you. Let me introduce some friends of mine. I don't know if you remember Jim Crotty. He went to school here. He's in the Navy now. And this is his friend Susan from California. I'm sorry I've already forgotten your last name."

"Engler."

"It's a pleasure to meet you Dear. Taylor you remember Marie Nelson, Katherine Harris, and Caroline Boldt, don't you?"

"Of course, it's so good to see all of you young ladies enjoying lunch."

"Young ladies, listen to this Casanova trying to woo us. He must want something."

"Jim asked me about the England's girl's kidnapping. He said they haven't heard much in California."

Caroline Boldt jumped in, "What we've learned is she wasn't kidnapped at all."

'No shit, what makes you so fucking smart?' I didn't say that out loud, but instead asked, "I know this is none of my business, but what do they think happened?"

"Well, I know from a reliable source that she ran off with a man. I'm not at liberty to divulge my source, but that's what happened. She's living on a deserted Caribbean island with a native." I almost burst out laughing.

Katherine Harris couldn't hold back, "She's not living with a native. I happen to know from a really reliable source she is living in a commune in Vermont with a band of Gypsies or hippies or whatever they call themselves, doing drugs, and having premarital sex with multiple men." That drew a few gasps.

That was too much for Marie Nelson, "She happened to have run off with that older gentleman she was involved with in college who her family disapproved of. He's keeping her as a sex slave in Massachusetts. That's where all the sex slaves are." Now I was a sex slave. I loved that. I did date an older gentleman in college. He was a senior at Tufts when I was a freshman at Smith and he was the one with the expensive Champagne. He told me he was pre-med and had been accepted to Harvard medical school. I thought I was in love with him. I'll admit he was a smooth talker when it came to getting me to part with my better moral judgment and panties. My father saw him for what he was and made life difficult. Of course, my mother adored him. He came from a respectful Boston family. He was smart and wowed her. I'm glad my father intervened. It was a life experience that should have taught me something.

I heard later from friends he was never accepted to Harvard medical school or any medical school for that matter, but became a marketing consultant for a large biomedical tech firm in Boston. He was making more money than most physicians. Maybe I should have stuck around. No, he was a manipulative, controlling jerk. I heard he married. I'm sure his wife is living a comfortable life, but miserable. Do women ever learn?

I asked, "What makes you think she wasn't kidnapped?"

"No ransom note. Nobody has called demanding money." Mrs. Boldt added.

Damn, next time I do this I'm leaving a note. Should it be on personalized bonded stationery from the Service Bureau? I argued, "But the news said all her belongings were left behind."

"That was to make it look like a crime. No, she's living with some man," repeated Mrs. Nelson. "It's no wonder. That's what's become of our young ladies in today's free loving society with all these drugs and loud music. They run off and live with unsavory men. Not like our day when a young lady respected her family's position and was presented to suitable gentlemen."

Mrs. Harris contributed, "From what I hear from the other girls is that this is what they expected from England. She was always a bit of a free spirit." That stopped the conversation about me as the ladies drifted back to talking about recipes, clothes, and being too fat. 'Was,' was that what she said? I 'was' a free spirit, like I didn't exist anymore. Screw those ladies. They were all a bunch of asexual a-holes.

"Well, it was nice seeing you ladies. We best be going," stated Mr. Schock.

Once Jim and I were alone I wanted to know, "Where did you come up with that graduated school bit?"

"I don't know. I thought it sounded good."

"When do we fly back to San Diego?"

"Tomorrow morning early. If we get back in time we can go for a run on the beach," Jim informed me.

"I can't wait," which caught Jim by surprise.

Chapter 14

"How far do you think you will get before you're caught?" Jim asked me at 30,000 feet on our flight back to San Diego from St. Louis.

"I have to see this through. I have no way out. You know that, or I'm dead. I'm sure this TJ character killed my friend Randy, his lover, his sister, her husband, their unborn baby, and he killed the four SEALs. I know he wants to kill me because he thinks I know what Randy knew. He probably killed Wayne because he was afraid Wayne would tell somebody where the money was hidden. Teresa was smart not to let TJ know she talked with Wayne, or she would be dead."

Jim mumbled to himself, "So this prick TJ placed an 82 millimeter ChiCom mortar in their hootch and command detonated it when they returned from an op. He's a dead man." I didn't know if I should have taken Jim seriously. "How in the world do you expect to find the money?"

"I don't know. It's under some pier in Vietnam," I answered as I drifted off to a restless sleep.

Back at Jim's duplex in Imperial Beach, we sat around the kitchen table with Jim's roommates, Joe, Dan and the unofficial roommate Ski drinking Olympic beer while throwing out ideas. Jim told them the whole story. They didn't seem shocked. I imagined after a tour in Vietnam hearing the government killed four SEALs wouldn't be shocking. Jim and I needed their help. When Dan piped up, "You've got to go to Vietnam. That's all there is to it. You've got to find the money."

"And how do you propose I do that?" I asked.

Joe, the ID forger, offered, "Draw up fake orders for Jim to escort you on an advance site visit for an upcoming Presidential visit to Vietnam." He said it so nonchalantly it almost sounded feasible.

"Yeah, that sounds good," said Dan. Dan may have had too much to drink. All the guys were wearing their UDT short khaki swim trunks. The others kept their legs together and under the table, but Dan was spread eagle while leaning his chair back against the wall, displaying all his personals. I tried to avert my eyes, but it's like a woman wearing a low cut dress or a short skirt, eyes naturally gravitate there. The others knew what was happening, but said nothing. I didn't want to be to one to tell Dan to organize his junk.

"That would take some balls." Was that me talking or the beer, a Freudian slip. I'd been around these guys too long.

Jim rambled, "There are fake messages all the time. One time, we received a message saying a Marine Corps corporal was ordered to impregnate the President's daughter so she would deliver close to the time her Marine Corps husband returned from Vietnam. And every Annapolis graduate sends birthday greetings to every other Annapolis graduate like there is nothing better to do than route their personal messages. For a K-Bar knife I could get the message center to type a message on official paper with a date-time-group-order number requesting I escort you. I'll tell the radioman it's a joke. Radiomen know we SEALs are always screwing around. I'll route the message myself so the commanding officer is sure to read it."

"You think it will work?" I asked.

"Hell no, but I think it's your best shot," blurted Ski.

I liked the way these guys worked, no scruples, just whatever it took to get the job done. There was no talk of the consequences if I got caught. I think they liked the adventure, the risk taking, and the sticking it to the government. In Washington, D.C. there would be countless meetings on every decision to consider every possible angle to avoid blame. In D.C. the bureaucrats didn't care if the policy worked, they just wanted to avoid risk. And when the plan failed, as it invariably did, the finger pointing would start with, 'I told you so.' But what could happen to Jim and his friends? The government sends them to Vietnam.

Joe added, "And if Jim gets caught they'll add 50 years of hard labor to his sentence of death by firing squad for greasing those gooks. One more thing to consider, you better travel commercial. If you try to use

113

military transportation the orders are going to be scrutinized closely with a chance of being caught sooner. You're going to be caught. No doubt about it and you're going to jail, but going commercial will give you more of a chance."

Swell, that was just what I wanted to hear. I was going to jail for trying to save my life. "That's a comforting thought. Are the bathrooms clean in Vietnam?" I asked.

"Bathrooms?" Joe asked with a quizzical look.

I knew I was in trouble, but my life was at stake. Sometimes you just got to say 'what the fuck' and make your move.

Dan mentioned, "While you were gone a commander from North Island called about five times looking for Susan. You are to call him as soon as you get in town. He got real officious and huffy. I told him to screw himself. I didn't put it exactly in those terms, but I think he got my drift. I told him you were sleeping with the four of us and I didn't know if you wanted to take on a fifth, but I could be wrong. Did I say the right thing?"

I never knew when to believe these guys, "That's fine. I didn't want to speak with him anyway. Like all men, once they've served their purpose they're good for nothing." That got a smile from everybody except Ski.

The next morning I helped Jim word the message. I'd seen enough official government communications to make it sound real. A couple of days later Jim showed me the message. "I'll give it to the CO in the morning."

The following evening Jim told me the commanding officer called him into his office, and asked him if he knew a Susan Engler with the President's staff. Jim said he told the commanding officer he did, and that he and Ms. Engler grew up in the same town.

The next evening Jim came home with a problem. The commanding officer drafted a message suggesting Petty Officer Crotty be replaced by Lieutenant Hatelberg, an officer with staff experience. "I didn't turn the CO's message into the message center. I could be hung for this."

"Hung higher than you're already going to be? Don't turn the message in, I'll handle this," I said, "Give me the CO's phone number." I'd dealt with enough junior officers to know how to put the commanding officer in his place.

The next morning after eight o'clock Pacific Time, I called the commanding officer of SEAL Team One. I mentioned to the watch petty officer I was from the Secretary of the Navy's office. That cut through any delays and I was speaking with the commanding officer in a matter of seconds, "Good morning Sir, the Secretary of the Navy sends his regards. This is Elizabeth Hornsby, the Secretary of the Navy's chief of staff's senior administrative assistant." I imagined the commanding officer's anal sphincter slammed shut at that moment. "The Secretary received your message stating you intend to disobey his orders. This is off the record, but the Secretary usually doesn't have his orders countermanded by junior naval officers. I wish I had your nerve. Anyway, back to business, the Secretary orders you to be in his office at 1000 hours tomorrow to discuss your reason for not obeying his orders. I know it's a long trip from California to Washington, D.C., but he feels it's that important."

At that point the commanding officer interrupted, "He misunderstood my message. I didn't disagree with his orders in principle. I believe Lieutenant Hatelberg would better serve the President's envoy. And besides, Petty Officer Crotty is on administrative hold pending a judge advocate ruling. He's not to leave the San Diego area. I'm sure the Secretary will understand." I didn't say anything. I let his statement hang in the air. Finally he asked, "I'm curious, how did Petty Officer Crotty get chosen for this assignment in the first place?"

I answered, "Ms. Engler knows Petty Officer Crotty personally and requested him. The President's chief of staff felt a member of his administration would be more comfortable traveling with a person she knew. The President's chief of staff suggested Petty Officer Crotty's name to the Secretary of the Navy. The administration and the Navy Department were briefed on Petty Officer Crotty's potential legal problems and felt they wouldn't interfere with this assignment." Then I asked, "Petty Officer Crotty is qualified to escort a woman to Vietnam, isn't he?"

"Yes, I suppose so. It's not exactly what we train for," the commanding officer stated.

"And Lieutenant Hatelberg is trained as an escort?" I asked.

The commanding officer stammered, "As I said, it's not something we train for, but yes Lieutenant Hatelberg is more qualified. He's an officer."

"Very well then, 1000 hours tomorrow," I snapped.

"Well, wait a minute. I'll be happy to comply with the orders as written if he really thinks that's best," the commanding officer spit out.

"Of course he thinks it's best. That's why he ordered it. We'll see you at 1000 hours. The Secretary is meeting with the Chairman of the Joint Chief of Staff at 1030. He wants you here for three or four minutes to straighten this out. Please be prompt and be prepared with your reasons countermanding his orders. As you know the Secretary is a reasonable man if you present your argument convincingly. Dress blues with ribbons is the uniform of the day. Good day, have a nice trip," I said.

The commanding officer interrupted me again, "I'm flying across the country for a three or four minute meeting?"

"You have more pressing business than meeting with the Secretary of the Navy? I'll convey that to the Secretary. He'll be impressed. By the way, the Chief of Naval Operations may drop by. He was briefed on this matter and wants to hear your reasoning." I mentioned while repressing a giggle.

"No, no, you don't understand. I will comply with the original orders as written. Why don't we just forget my message?" the commanding officer asked. "I'll send a counter message."

"Don't send any more messages. You've already distinguished yourself in that area. The Secretary runs a tight ship. He doesn't like changing his schedule. When the President requests a meeting with the Secretary, he goes, no questions asked, no second guessing. He expects the same from subordinates. I'll see what I can do. I'll call you if I can cancel the meeting." I hung up. He could sweat all day as far as I was concerned. I would have loved to have seen his khaki soaked arm pits.

I called the commanding officer at four o'clock in the afternoon Pacific Time which would have been seven o'clock in the evening in Washington, D.C. "The Secretary was in meetings most of the day, but I caught him just as he left for dinner with the chairman of the House Armed Services Committee. He said he would cancel the meeting if the orders were followed as originally written."

The commanding officer sounded relieved, "They will be. Thank you for taking care of this and give the Secretary my regards."

"Yes Sir, I will," was all I said. What were the chances of this working? Something like when pigs can fly.

When Jim arrived home that evening, I asked him how it went. He said the commanding officer called him into his office after quarters and made him feel like he had done something wrong. The following evening Jim came home with orders to accompany me on the President's advance party to the Republic of Vietnam for an unspecified period of time, starting immediately. Jim was given priority travel authorization which meant he could bump anybody off a government plane. He could wear civilian clothes and carry firearms. It also mentioned he was authorized to parachute, use demolition, and scuba dive. I hoped he didn't expect me to do any of that. The orders were great, but we didn't want to travel on government planes with fake orders and my fake IDs, so we were traveling on my dime.

I worked out a tentative itinerary. First stop would be Hawaii, and then to Hong Kong, and on to Saigon. From there, Jim would have to get us to where the four SEALs captured and hid the money. What was I going to wear? Would I be able to eat the food? What were the bathrooms like? And the hotels, did they have clean sheets? I'd been to Europe and Canada, but never Asia. Did they have five-star restaurants? Could I get my nails done? What about my hair? A massage would be nice.

We planned to leave as soon as we could get airline tickets through to Hong Kong. While Jim was at work I called home, "I'm going to travel some."

My dad didn't like the idea, "I want you to come home."

"I think it would be best for me to get out of the country for a while until things settle down. I'll be in touch as soon as I return. Love you." I asked my dad to get in touch with Mary Jo and make sure my bills were paid. I wanted to get off the phone as soon as possible.

I called my boyfriend at work, "Susan, you can't be serious about leaving the country. Come back to D.C. Everything can be cleared up. The missing money, if in fact there is any money missing, isn't important. You getting back here safely, that's what's important."

"I don't believe I would be safe. Nine people have been killed. If TJ was in jail I would feel more comfortable. But as long as he is on the loose I have to keep moving. I don't trust anyone," I stated.

"You can stay with me. I know we agreed not to live together because of public perception, but we could keep it quiet for a few days until we get a handle on this TJ character," he said.

That was tempting to stay with him. Maybe that would move things along in the marriage arena.

"Well then, who are you traveling with? You aren't going by yourself, are you?" he asked.

"Yes, I'm a big girl and can take care of myself," I lied. I couldn't tell him I was traveling with another man even though I was sure nothing would happen.

"At least tell me where you are going."

"I'd rather not."

I was still paranoid about the phones being tapped, "Listen, I have to go, but I'm worried about my things at my townhouse and car."

"I've checked. Mary Jo seems to have everything under control. The important thing for you is to come home," he stated.

"Soon Darling, love you. I'll be in touch." I hung up.

Chapter 15

Jim and I flew to Hawaii and spent one night at the Royal Hawaiian before flying on to Hong Kong. We were booked into an ocean view room without requesting one. My reputation must have preceded me. I would have liked to have stayed longer. The air smelled like hibiscus and ilimas. The weather was beautiful. I questioned why I went to school in the East. I should have gone to the University of Hawaii. I'd never been in a place with such a different culture, even New York City. The Pacific Islander people were different. They were casual and relaxed compared to the on-edge U.S. East coasters. Their attire certainly was more casual. I didn't see one man wearing a tie. That evening, I watched the 10 o'clock news. They didn't mention the kidnapping of the girl from Washington, D.C. Nobody knew about me out here.

In the morning we went for a short run on the beach towards Diamond Head. A 20 minute run was now a short run. Then we ate breakfast on the terrace while watching the long board surfers off Waikiki Beach. With the swaying palm trees, it made for a romantic setting. Speaking of which, I was starting to wonder about Jim. We had now shared a room in Van Nuys, Kansas City and Honolulu. We shared a bathroom at his place in Imperial Beach and not once had he made a pass, or made any kind of sexual overture toward me. I wasn't that bad looking. And I didn't think he was a homosexual. Not that I was an expert on the subject, but I just didn't think so. His ex-girlfriend sounded like a young girl on the phone, a very young girl. I hope that wasn't the affliction. I could sense Jim's apprehension. Maybe he was nervous about what awaited us in Vietnam, or the illegal orders. I didn't want to start a relationship, at least not consciously, but then again I wished he'd shown some interest so I could gain the upper hand.

After breakfast we took a long board surfing lesson. Me surfing. If I'd been here with my parents my mother would have forbidden me to go in the ocean. She would have warned me about how dangerous surfing was, that there were man eating sharks and undertow, and all sorts of horrible things. Then my mother would go home and brag to everyone what fun we had going to a luau with hula dancers and half naked men dancing with flaming spears, and having a coconut split open right in front of our eyes.

The flight to Hong Kong took forever. I thought about my car, my townhouse, my job, and not calling my mother. I'd left a mess behind me. And my boyfriend, he was beside himself when I told him I was leaving the country. What was going to happen to me when this nightmare was over? At the time I felt I had no choice, but to proceed. On reflection, I wondered if I'd acted rationally. I was going to miss Franci's engagement party, oh well. On the flight I snuggled close to Jim to get some sleep. The plane was cold. He didn't seem to mind. He was going to be in deep trouble when the orders were found out to be phony. But he was going to be in trouble anyway for the fouled up ambush in Vietnam.

If the media got a hold of the ambush details he was going to be in prison or worse. And what if all my suspicions turned out to be coincidences as my boss suggested? Wouldn't I look like the fool? I would have spent all this money and caused all this trouble for nothing. No, Teresa suspecting TJ killing Wayne Meyer and the other three SEALs, Randy and his partner's death, Emily, her baby, and husband's death could not all have been coincidences. I had to push on. I mean, what was the alternative? I couldn't tell the pilot to turn around.

In Hong Kong we checked into the Peninsula Hotel. I heard it was up to my standards and it was. I felt so much in my element that I made them change our room for a harbor view, and at cocktail hour I sent back my drink and told them how to make a proper Manhattan. We had two days until the flight to Saigon. Jim tried to relax. Hong Kong was even more of a cultural shock than Hawaii. I thought the British had taken over the place. There were tons of Chinese.

The next day I went shopping. The concierge recommended several establishments where custom clothes could be made in a few days. In the shops a customer would pick items from the latest fashion magazines. I picked among several patterns for suits and skirts and then I selected the material. I picked a few sport jackets and shirts for Jim. He needed the help. We went for a fitting the next day. They said everything would be ready in a couple of days. I told them we would be gone for a week or so, and for them to deliver the clothes to the Peninsula Hotel to be held in our names until our return. Jim and I did the usual tourist attractions like visiting the New Territories, eating at Aberdeen on a floating restaurant, and going up the peak tram to Victoria Park.

A curious thing happened at Victoria Park. Jim said he caught a glimpse of a man that seemed to be eyeing us. The man fit my description of TJ. Jim said as soon as he caught his eye the man ducked behind a building. Maybe we were both getting skittish.

I asked Jim about what we could expect in Vietnam. "How long do you think we'll be there?"

"I have no idea. It could be a few days to a month. It depends on how long it takes to find the documents and what kind of cooperation we get," Jim answered. I figured I better take some personal hygiene items.

We spent Christmas in Hong Kong. It was a weird experience for me as this was my first Christmas away from home. The climate wasn't like the mid-west. It was chilly but comfortable. The British bars and restaurants were decorated for the holidays along with the Australian, British and U.S. warships in the harbor. I wanted to buy a warm jacket, but Jim convinced me I wouldn't need one where we were going.

Up to that point I wasn't homesick. Everything had been moving so fast, but Christmas was tough. Jim gave me a gold pendant. I knew he didn't earn much money. I felt bad I didn't get him something in return. Well, I did buy him a plane ticket from California to Hong Kong. We enjoyed a really nice dinner at the Peacock and Pheasant and then took a long walk. I thought of Franci's engagement in front of the Christmas tree which would take place in another 12 hours. That made me sad.

The next morning he broke the bad news, "You are going to have to carry all your belongings."

"Can't we hire a porter like in the safari movies?" I asked.

"We are working with a small group. Everyone carries their own equipment," Jim said.

As I was packing, he asked me, "What's all that junk?"

"Nothing, just my lotions, shampoo, conditioner, body rub, face cream, blush, hair dryer, brushes, face soap, a razor, body soap, curlers, deodorant, nail polish, emery board, nail clippers, vitamins, mascara, lipsticks. Do you like this shade? Just the bare essentials, I have to have these for my skin condition and hair," I stated. "I would die without them. This lotion is prescription. You can only get it in St. Louis. If Hollywood ever found out about this skin moisturizer there would be a riot."

"What's this fatal skin condition you have that you keep talking about?" Jim asked.

"I have xerosis." I thought that would intimidate him.

"That's dry skin. A billion people in the world have it. The only reason it's a big business in the U.S. and Europe is because naive women believe ridiculous marketing, then pay billions of dollars for worthless lotions believing it will save their lives," he blurted.

"What about my vitamins? You have to admit I would die without these." He was making fun of me.

"Vitamins only make you pee iridescent yellow. Leave that junk here, prescription or not. You'll die a lot faster from a bullet when you can't run because you are carrying all that stuff. You can pick it up when we return. Two pairs of jeans, two t-shirts, and sandals are all you'll need. We'll get you some jungle lug boots in-country. They make small sizes for the ARVN," Jim said. "You'll wash out one set of clothes while wearing the other."

"I'm not comfortable with this. What's this about bullets? I thought we were going down there and picking up the documents?" I asked.

"I doubt the SEALs left them in a friendly area. If they captured the documents from the enemy, the enemy is probably still close by looking for them," Jim said.

"You really think so?" I asked. "What about underwear? Can I at least take underwear?"

122

"You won't need it. You'll understand once we get there," Jim said. "Operating gear like canteens we'll get in-country."

"Is a toothbrush out of the question?" I asked.

"That's okay. You can use it to clean weapons," Jim said.

"I need a razor, and is taking deodorant asking too much?" I asked.

"You can use my razor, and yes, deodorant is asking too much" he explained.

Of course he was joking. I hoped he was joking. He couldn't be serious about underwear. No way was I going to wear jeans and a t-shirt without a bra and panties. Okay, I have a flat chest, but still, what kind of place was this?

Air Vietnam, subsidized by U.S. taxpayers, flew between Hong Kong and Saigon. This was the route civilian contractors took. Ordinary citizens couldn't fly to Vietnam. With my White House ID and Jim's orders he got us tickets. Tomorrow it was into the war.

Chapter 16

We flew into Saigon's Ton Son Nhut airport. The people on the flight looked like business men, or they may have been media people, or maybe government workers. I was the only female, and I got a lot of attention. Some government type asked me what I was doing so I flashed my White House credentials. He didn't ask any more questions. I didn't know what to expect. According to the five o'clock evening news there should have been bombs going off and I would be ducking bullets. The way things turned out, it was nothing like that.

Saigon was a beehive of activity. The weather was stifling hot, not like Hong Kong's more temperate climate. The airport was mass confusion. The terminal was filled with U.S. servicemen waiting for a flight home or new arrivals that didn't have a clue. It was easy to tell the difference. The men going home were deeply tanned with sunken eyes. They were all smoking. Their uniforms hung loosely on their shoulders. Their faces were gaunt and haunting. There was an angry look in their eyes and they appeared 10 years older than the new arrivals that were pale and fat. The new arrivals were joking, like this was all a big lark. I think their giddiness was masking their fear of the unknown. In 12 months something transformed these mommas' boys into men with a screw-the-world attitude. What that something was, I was about to find out.

There were long lines everywhere. I saw a soldier with a rifle. There was something frightening about that. I couldn't believe I was in Vietnam. People were shooting and killing each other and I was right in the middle. I wanted to go home. This was not suburbia where the biggest fear was being caught on radar by the Ladue Police.

I got in line to check in as a U.S. government employee and Jim got in line for servicemen. For one who does not stand in line this was demeaning. This was the first time Jim and I were apart. I felt every eye was on me. The men going home were the most frightening. I was afraid if one of them got me alone I wouldn't know what he would do. Maybe it would be for sexual pleasure to satisfy something fantasized over the past year. Or maybe I was symbolic of the American woman who, in their minds, had suffered little, and needed to learn what suffering was all about. I could handle the new arrivals with an emasculating insult.

I looked around. I didn't see another Caucasian woman. There were Vietnamese women wearing black pajama bottoms, white blouses, sandals and large conical hats. They were sweeping the floors, or making themselves appear busy.

Jim kept an eye on me. Once we finished checking in, he took me out front where it was even more chaotic. At least I got a breath of fresh air, even though it smelled like a sewer mixed with diesel exhaust. Motor bikes, rickshaws, military vehicles of all types jammed the streets. People were like ants meshing together. Jim spotted a soldier sitting in a jeep. "That guy is looking for something to do before somebody finds something for him to do. Go ask him for a ride to the Victoria Hotel."

I walked up to the jeep and before I could finish my request the jeep driver replied, "Well, I'm on a secret mission. Saboteurs have been hitting the airport. I'm with Special Forces setting an ambush. But, it's about my break time so I suppose I could slip away for a few minutes. Hop in."

"Great, I'll get my escort," I said.

"What escort? I'm not authorized to take more than one. You know in case there is any shooting or anything." The soldier hurried his words.

Jim showed up out of nowhere, "Hey dogface, watch our stuff while I go back inside." Jim threw our bags into the jeep.

"Who are you? This is a military vehicle. You don't give the orders around here," the soldier informed Jim. In the soldier's defense, he didn't know who we were. We were wearing civilian clothes. He was perceptive enough to notice I was a female which inspired his initial response of offering me a ride.

"Presidential staff, Ms. Engler show him your identification. Listen troop; you've got it pretty cushy here in Saigon driving around in your jeep. You give us any crap and I'm the guy who can have your chicken shit ass in the bush tonight on a listening post. Comprendi?" Jim said with authority. I got the impression the military in Vietnam was the same as the bureaucrats in Washington, D.C., it was all blustery threats.

A submissive, "Yes Sir," was the only response from the soldier. He probably outranked Jim and didn't know it.

Jim was gone for what seemed like an eternity. The jeep driver would not stop talking about how he alone was winning the war and about his life back in the world in Sioux City, Iowa. According to him he had the fastest car in the county and was dating Iowa's Miss Corn or Miss Pig or something. I supposed he thought I would be impressed. Other soldiers started gathering. I accepted a cigarette from one to be sociable. If what they told me was true the war should have been won months ago. These 'heroes,' according to them, had killed more VC, gooks, dinks, zipper heads, slopes, NVA and other not so polite terms for the enemy, to have wiped out the population of Southeast Asia. When they saw Jim returning, they quickly asked me to meet them at the Manhattan Club or New York Club or something. They all promised me a good time. I imagined their idea of a good time wasn't the same as mine.

Mine would have been enjoying a vodka martini in a chilled crystal glass on a veranda with palm plants softly swaying on an orchid scented breeze, then attend a play or opera, then a late supper at a five star restaurant, and then to bed ALONE. I imagined their idea of a good time involved beer, dope, and multiple sex acts that wouldn't be appropriate for a lady.

The streets were impossible. The driver honked and cursed. The traffic meshed together. Motor scooters zipped in and out, constantly beeping their horns. There was no sense of order. I was drenched with perspiration and felt faint. The jeep driver offered me a drink from his canteen. I couldn't believe I drank out of somebody else's canteen. The water was one degree from boiling. The sun was without mercy. Jim didn't seem in the least bit phased by the heat. It seemed at every corner there were sand bagged machine gun emplacements and armed Vietnamese soldiers. I didn't like it. I was scared. I continued to get looks from everyone, Vietnamese and Americans.

When we arrived at the hotel the driver helped me with the bags and reminded me, "Remember the Manhattan Club, eight o'clock. We'll toke up on some Thai Gold. It will knock your pants off." Wasn't that the idea?

The Victoria Hotel was the turning point of my life where I went from getting whatever I wanted, to where I was grateful for anything I got. Jim and I were lucky to get a room with a private bath and I wasn't about to complain about the alley view. The bathroom was large, but atrocious. It had a bidet which was embarrassing. After all, Vietnam was a French colony a short time ago. I didn't dare flush the toilet. I had no idea what would happen. I needed to use the toilet in the worst way. I didn't have the nerve to go at the airport. I wanted Jim to try it first. If I tried it and it didn't do what it was supposed to do, and the evidence was left on the ceiling and walls I would be mortified. I was funny about things like that.

The bedroom was large with maybe a 10 foot ceiling. A paddle fan creaked producing no detectable breeze. The plaster walls were cracked and water stained, probably mildewed. The furniture was old. I'm sure the room had not been refurbished since the French high tailed it out of Vietnam in the nineteen fifties. Jim went to the bathroom and everything seemed to function properly, so I followed.

I realized that bitching and moaning wasn't going to count for much around here. My status as a lady meant nothing. We went to the hotel's roof top restaurant for a beer. The view of the city was depressing. What was once the pearl of the Orient was now a refugee camp. Jim took it all in stride. He'd been here before so I guess nothing shocked him. Two Army officers immediately came over and sat down with us, elbowing Jim out of the way. I didn't think they came over to make friends with the two of us. They were blunt and to the point. They wanted me to go to the officer's club with them for drinks and dinner, and I could only imagine what they had in mind for dessert.

I realized this was going to be the de rigueur drill in Vietnam. I decided not to be the one to fulfill their fantasies. I showed them my

White House Credentials and said I needed their names and units for my report on my contacts while in Vietnam on the President's business. They vanished. I wasn't in the mood to laugh at their inane jokes, or act in awe of their self-proclaimed combat heroics. Everything was new and intimidating. I didn't feel confident. I never wanted Jim out of my sight. I always thought it would be wonderful to be the center of attention, to be a celebrity. Now I knew it wasn't for me.

"You're going to get hit on the whole time you are here. I should have warned you. These guys don't see round eyes unless they end up in a hospital where there are nurses, or they work in a hospital. There are some U.S. government secretaries at the embassy and other government facilities and some private contractors have female employees, but for the most part these guys are as horny as is humanly possible. Out in the boonies where we are going there will be even fewer round eyes."

"I get the picture," I said. "So what's the deal about the boonies?"

Jim informed me we were leaving Saigon the next day morning. "There's an Army slick going to Binh Thuy. I got us a ride using my priority orders," Jim said.

"And a slick is?" I asked.

"A helicopter, driven by a 19 year old Army warrant officer who 12 months ago was running moonshine in Kentucky."

"How do you know he was running moonshine?"

"That's a stereotype, but after you ride in an Army slick that's what you'll think," Jim said. My stomach started churning. We stayed on the rooftop restaurant for a dinner of noodles and fish-heads. It wasn't really fish-heads. It may have been cat's paws. What I was trying to say was that it wasn't Tony's in St. Louis. The food was way too spicy. I didn't eat much. I needed to acclimate to the food and the environment.

We drank a couple of warm beers for dessert. As it got darker, flares started popping up in the distance. Jim explained parachute flares were deployed around base perimeters to deter enemy infiltration. "You think the enemy would try to attack Saigon?"

"The enemy is in Saigon, probably your waiter tonight. The flares are around Army fire bases that surround Saigon," Jim said.

I heard a muffled thump, and then another. Jim didn't wait for me to ask, "That's H and I, harassment and interdiction fire. Fire bases shoot off 105 millimeter rounds toward suspected enemy locations."

"But they sound close."

"There are Indians everywhere. While riding in that jeep today a motor scooter could have pulled alongside and the scooter driver lob in a grenade. It happens." Wonderful, I was so happy to learn of the many ways to die a gruesome death.

Back in the room, Jim lit a coil that looked like an electric stove burner. "What's that?"

"It's a mosquito repellant. It gives off a unique smell. If you are in the bush and smell this, run. It means the VC are close, very close."

"If you are trying to scare me, you are doing a good job."

"I'm trying to tell you things that will keep you alive. TJ isn't your only worry," Jim said.

There was one double bed. I didn't know if I could fall asleep next to him. It would be cruel to ask him to sleep on the tile floor. The mattress sunk to the middle and smelled musty. Our sweaty bodies were touching. A window air conditioner that dripped rusty water on the tiled floor made more noise than it made cool air. But it wasn't loud enough to drown out the buzzing of the motor scooters and beeping horns from the street below.

I had never felt so vulnerable, so alone, so far from home, even with Jim next to me. I wanted my mommy. I wanted to go home and take the consequences of whatever this mess was. Nothing could be as bad as this. This all happened so fast. A few weeks ago I was sitting in my den drinking wine with Franci and look where I was now.

Soon I realized Jim was asleep. How could he sleep in this rat hole? Tomorrow we were going into the bush. Jim made it sound like it was going to be worse than this; impossible.

Chapter 17

Jim startled me. I looked at my watch. It was five o'clock in the morning and dark outside. I never realized I'd fallen asleep, but I guess I did. The bed was soaked with perspiration. Jim was dressed in a camouflaged uniform that looked intimidating. He handed me a bottle of water, "You need to stay hydrated. And we need to be at Tac Air by six. Do you want breakfast?"

"No, I'm fine." I went into the bathroom to dress and get ready. I was nervous. We were really going to do this. Going into the boonies where the war was, to recover some mystical documents to prove that people in the government were raising money illegally to re-elect the President. Hopefully, this would lead to TJ being arrested and sent to prison, so I could get back my life. Was I nuts?

Jim hitched a ride with Navy officers who were going to the airfield. Tactical Air Command was located in a hanger on the other side of the airfield from Ton Son Nhut's main terminal. There were a bunch of planes, green in color. Jim asked around and found our helicopter. I couldn't believe I was going to fly in one of those things. I'd never been in a helicopter. The airmen were busy working on their planes and didn't seem to notice that a woman was amongst them. A sergeant came over with a clipboard filling out the manifest. I showed him my identification. He wrote down my name as Susan Engler and my ID information.

I told Jim, "I don't think that helicopter looks safe. Are you sure you want to go?" He didn't answer, just gave me the look.

Three other men were flying with us to Binh Thuy, an Army officer and two enlisted. There were canvas seats slung along the back of the fuselage. I strapped myself in. Jim was sitting in the doorway with his feet dangling out the side. As the helicopter revved up I noticed the crew chief forgot to close the doors. First, I screamed over the engine noise at Jim, "Get in here you idiot!" Then I screamed at the crew chief, "The doors are open!"

Everyone gave me a curious look. The crew chief yelled back, "They are open so when we crash we can get out." We are going to crash, is that what he said? I pulled the seat belt tighter. I'm flying in a plane with the doors open, lovely. Jim ignored me of course.

The pilot took off slowly, rotating the helicopter 180 degrees. We flew low and slow over Saigon and then started to climb. The city gave way to outlying slums and then we were over rice paddies and tree lined canals. Occasionally, there was a village. The land was flat and didn't vary. It seemed like there were more canals than roads. We passed over a wide river which I assumed was the Bassac. We made a few steep turns and then dropped into Binh Thuy, which served as an Air Force Base and Naval Support Facility. The little I saw from the air, the base appeared to be a series of corrugated metal roofed buildings.

The crew chief threw off a couple of mail bags the enlisted men had brought. Jim grabbed our bags. We'd packed everything into two canvas bags that was designed to carry a parachute. I brought my bras and panties. I didn't care what Jim said. Jim called it a war bag. I noticed more men were carrying guns than in Saigon, and there were more sandbagged gun emplacements. A fence surrounded the perimeter with barbed wire at the top and guard towers were in the corners. I didn't like the looks of this place. We walked to a metal building that Jim said was the SEAL compound. When we walked in, I heard, "You're a little fucking late, aren't you? Your platoon has been here and gone."

"In case you haven't heard, I'm on special assignment, Numbnuts. Where's the CO?" Jim asked.

"Lieutenant Commander Pierce is over at the base CO's office straightening out a brawl that happened in town last night. Seems some Army pukes got a little rowdy and had to be calmed down," the yeoman said.

"And I suppose the SEALs calmed them down?" Jim asked.

"We're here to serve. We fight for truth, justice, and the American way no matter what uniform you wear. It's a thankless job. Commander Pierce should be back soon. Who's your swim buddy? Looks like the SEALs are getting cuter. All you other motherfuckers are so damn ugly," the yeoman stated.

"Susan, meet Yeoman Anderson. He's a puke assigned to the Teams. He's not an operator, which means he didn't go through training, so don't let him give you any shit. You could probably kick his ass."

"Hi, nice to meet you," I extended my hand.

"Nice to meet you, Ma'am. If you need anything let me know. I doubt this jerk would get it for you," the yeoman said.

At that moment, an officer burst through the door. "Get those three fuckups in here el pronto! They want 500 dollars to fix that damn bar. I could build them 10 bars for that amount. The base CO is threating to kick us off the base again."

"Sir, Petty Officer Crotty is waiting to see you," the yeoman said.

"Petty Officer Crotty? What's he doing here?" the officer asked while looking for something.

Jim walked over and handed Commander Pierce his orders, "Sir, I'm here on special assignment. I would like for you to meet Ms. Engler. She's with the White House." As Jim was speaking, I held out my White House identification.

"Weren't you just over here?" the commander asked Jim.

"Yes Sir, I was here with Kilo platoon six months ago," Jim said.

The lieutenant commander eyed Jim as he walked over and opened the door to his office. "I remember now, aren't you in some sort of deep shit back home?"

"Yes Sir, it's all a big misunderstanding," Jim answered.

"It's always a big misunderstanding with you guys. Crotty you wait here. Ma'am please step into my office and have a seat. Can I get you anything, coffee, water, a beer?"

"Water would be nice," I answered.

The commander walked over to a small refrigerator, got out a bottle of water and poured two glasses. "Tell me why you're here. And please don't tell me the President is coming to Binh Thuy to inspect the SEALs."

"No, nothing like that. In fact, Petty Officer Crotty has most of the details. Can he come in?" I asked.

"Sure. Crotty get your ass in here," the commander yelled. "Sorry ma'am. I'm not used to females being present."

"Quite alright, I understand," I said.

Jim opened the door, "Yes Sir."

"Come in here and close the door. Ms. Engler says you have details about this so called special assignment," the commander said.

"Yes Sir, this has to deal with the four SEALs killed last May in Rach Gia.".

The commander responded, "That wasn't a good time around here. As I recall, it was a Chi Com mortar round they brought back to their hootch and it went off. I thought that investigation was complete." The commander was perusing Jim's orders.

"Sir, there's evidence it may have been a booby trap set off by our own people. If I could have your yeoman pull some messages I think you will understand what I'm talking about. I have the date-time-groups," Jim offered.

"Our own people? You're shitting me? Excuse me, Ma'am. There I go again forgetting my manners," the commander said.

"No apologies necessary," I remarked.

Jim spoke, "Believe me Sir, I was skeptical at first but Ms. Engler proved to me that this may be the case."

The commander piped up, "I don't see anything in these orders stating that's why you are here. It says you are to escort Ms. Engler on a site visit for a possible Presidential visit."

"Yes Sir, that's the way they wanted to word the orders so as not to arouse suspicion as to why we are really here," Jim said.

"Ms. Engler are you some kind of secret agent?" the commander asked.

"No Sir, a sequence of events has put me in this position," I fumbled for words. "Believe me, I wish this could be handled a different way."

"This all sounds fishy to me, but I'll give you a chance to prove your point. Petty Officer Crotty you get the messages and we'll meet after lunch. I'm curious why the White House would send you two. This should be handled by some other agency like Naval Investigative Services," the commander wondered out loud.

"Sir, we think people in the administration may be involved," I said. "At the moment this is being handled externally."

"I respect your credentials Miss Engler, but I have to say at the moment I'm skeptical," the commander said. "Maybe I've been over here too long."

"Sir, let us show you what we have then you can decide," Jim said.

"Okay I'll take Miss Engler to the mess hall for lunch. Crotty you get the messages and get settled. We'll meet back here at 1300 hours," the commander said.

The yeoman knocked on the door, "Sir, the three SEALs are here."

The commander gestured toward the door, "Miss Engler please step outside for a moment. I'll be with you shortly." As we left, Jim made eye contact with his three roommates indicating they were in trouble. I also made eye contact with Dan, Joe and Ski in an effort to say hello. They scooted into the commander's office. If they had tails they would have been tucked between their legs.

I heard the commander's raised voice and the words 'shithead, dumbass, and worthless SOBs' a few times then the three SEALs hurriedly left the office with their heads bowed. The yeoman stayed busy at his desk. A short time later, the commander came out like nothing had happened and said, "Okay, let's get something to eat. Did you have breakfast?"

"No, we were in a hurry this morning. Is there a bathroom?" I asked.

"I'm sorry. I should have offered. It's on the way to the mess hall. I'm afraid we don't have a women's restroom unless we go over to the hospital or women's barracks. As I said we don't get many female visitors. I'll guard the door," the commander said.

The bathroom, or head as they called it, was Spartan to say the least. It smelled. I was going to have to get used to this. The mess hall wasn't much better. There were some decorations and fake flowers to make everything seem homey. The commander had head of the line privileges. I had never eaten off a tray. I took the fried rice. We drank 'bug juice' which was Kool Aid or some reasonable facsimile. I was getting the eye from all the men. It made me self-conscious. The hot, humid climate, the uneasiness of being in a war zone and constantly being gawked at, had left me with little appetite.

I told the commander about Randy's disappearance, about Randy's sister telling me the SEALs were killed by our people because they found the re-election money, and I told him about the subsequent death of Randy's sister. Also I told the commander about Jim retrieving the messages about the operation and Wayne Meyer's nurse telling us that the SEALs hid the money under a pier. And I told him the nurse thought Wayne was also murdered. "That's why we are here, to find the money. Hopefully, by finding the money the people responsible will be exposed and prosecuted." I felt I needed to tell the commander the truth. He would see through a lie.

"That still doesn't explain why you're here. I can't help but feel somebody else ought to be handling this," the commander said.

"I can see how you would think that." I had to tell him everything, "I think I'm also a target. When I returned home to Washington, D.C. after a trip to California, a man was waiting for me. I panicked, I thought I was going to end up like my friend Randy. I escaped and went to San Diego to get Jim's help. Jim and I are old high school friends. I knew he was in the Navy and thought maybe he could help." Okay, I fibbed a little. "So yes, I could have called other people, but I don't trust anyone except Jim, and I hope I can trust you. Whatever the SEALs found is still out there."

"I'm not even going to ask how Petty Officer Crotty and you got orders to be here," the commander said.

"Thanks for not asking. I believe my life is in danger and unless I prove what these people are doing is a crime, they will kill me."

"So, for the sake of argument, what do you expect me to do?" The commander asked.

"I want to go to where the SEALs operated and find whatever is hidden under the pier," I said.

"Okay, let me spell it out for you. If Petty Officer Crotty demonstrates to me there is money to be found then I will propose an operation to recover it. We are stretched pretty thin. We have more intelligence reports of suspected VC activity than we have men to operate. I admire your determination, but under no circumstances are you going any further than Binh Thuy. In fact, I don't like you being here. I will speak with Petty Officer Crotty as to why he brought you. You should go back to Saigon," the commander said. "In fact, you should go back to the States."

"I have to go. I didn't feel safe in Saigon," I replied.

"Safe, let me spell it out for you. I don't mean to be vulgar, but a couple of weeks ago an Army private was captured by the Viet Cong in the area you are proposing to go. They found him three days later. He died of suffocation. They cut off his testicles and jammed them down his throat. Before he bled out, he suffocated. I could go on and tell you atrocities that would make you sick. I can't be responsible for you going down there. If that's what they do to men, what do you think they would do to a Caucasian woman?" the commander asked.

I didn't want to think about it. Jim entered the mess hall and went through the line. "May I join you, Sir?" Jim requested.

"Sit down, Petty Officer," the commander said. "What are you doing bringing a lady down here?"

"Following orders, Sir," Jim answered.

"Don't give me that shit. I don't believe your orders specified taking a woman into a combat zone. I don't think you exercised good judgment, Petty Officer. Do you have the messages?" the commander asked.

"Yes Sir. Do you want to go over them here, or back in your office?" Jim asked.

"You eat then join me in my office. First, I have some business to attend to. Have you arranged housing for Ms. Engler?" the commander asked.

"No Sir, I was thinking of going to the hospital to see if the nurses could help."

"Good idea. You two come over as soon as you get Ms. Engler settled. If you'll excuse me," the commander got up and left.

"He doesn't think I should go any further. In fact, he thinks I should go home."

"I told you that from the beginning."

"You told me that from the beginning? Are you kidding? You and your sicko sidekicks were the ones all excited for me to go to Vietnam and recovering the documents, you jerk! Now you get me over here in this Hell hole and you're saying I should have stayed home, screw you." I got a little carried away.

"You're right. I apologize," Jim explained. "What I meant to say was you shouldn't go to Rach Gia. I want you to stay in Binh Thuy. I wanted you to come to Vietnam with me because I thought you would be safer here than in the States with TJ on your tail."

I calmed down. Jim finished eating. We went to the hospital. It seemed quiet and peaceful, but there was a sense of urgency. Jim asked the duty officer if he could speak with the head nurse. A lady in her mid-thirties came out and greeted us. Jim explained my situation. "We're pretty crowded as it is. They don't give us much space. I'll see what I can do. Come back at 1600," the nurse said.

As we left, Jim said, "She'll take care of you. Everyone wants to make you feel like they are doing you a big favor."

We met the commander. Jim explained the messages. They described the area of operation and that documents were found. But there was no follow up intelligence.

The commander kept a poker face. He didn't seem impressed or unimpressed. "I'll tell you what, I'll check out a few things. If we do decide to put together an operation I'll have to get assets such as, men, transportation, air support, clearance from Four Corps, a myriad of things. I have a good idea where I can get a couple of volunteers. Petty Officer Crotty, your platoon left this morning for Can Tho minus Pulaski, Stranton, and Beck. Those boys may want to volunteer to go with you instead of staying here on work details awaiting their punishment for tearing up that bar. Also, Chief Petty Officer Henderson is here on medical and may be available in a few days. He caught some shrapnel last week near Dong Tam."

Commander Pierce continued, "Ms. Engler, I strongly suggest you go back to Saigon, or as I suggested, the States. Petty Officer Crotty can stay here and help with the operation, if we decide to do one, or he can rejoin his platoon."

I felt my opportunity slipping away. For some odd reason I asked, "Was a man calling himself TJ here around the time of the SEALs deaths? He may have passed himself off as a CIA agent."

The commander said, "Go on."

"He has sharp facial features and acts like an arrogant asshole. He's the one who wants to kill me," I said.

"I shouldn't say this, but there was a man here fitting that description a few days after the operation when the documents were found. He didn't pass himself off as CIA, but rather as a special envoy to the President. Sort of the same bullshit you are passing off on me. Aren't you guys working for the same President?"

"Yes, but I think there are different factions in the administration. That's why I can't trust anyone," I explained.

"Be that as it may the man you described wanted transportation to Rach Gia. The day after the three SEALs were killed and one wounded, he passed through here again on his way back to Saigon. I'll be in touch, Ms. Engler. Consider going back to Saigon," the commander motioned to the door.

Jim took me to the hospital. God, it was hot. Maybe I'd already mentioned that, but it was worth repeating. It felt like the sun was 10 feet over my head. Jim said he would meet me at the hospital mess hall for dinner. The head nurse came out again, this time with a younger woman about my age. "This is First Lieutenant Smith. She'll help you," the head nurse said as she left.

"Hi, I'm Laurie. Let's get you settled," the nurse said.

"I'm Susan, thanks for helping. I'm sorry for barging in like this," I said as I followed Laurie down a hallway.

"No problem. A couple of girls are on R & R. We have plenty of room. It will be nice to have a new face. Tell me what the girls are wearing back in the world. Are the skirts really shorter?" Laurie asked.

Plenty of room wasn't the way I would describe it, but it was nice to be amongst women. The first night I heard machine gun fire. "What's that?" I asked Laurie.

"Oh that, the guards shoot their weapons once in a while to discourage Charlie from penetrating the perimeter. Reconn by fire they call it," Laurie said.

"Is that safe? What if somebody is out there?"

"There's a curfew. If anybody is out there it's the enemy, or somebody so stupid they deserve to be shot."

I looked out the window. There were parachute flares like I saw in Saigon, but they were a lot closer. I figured it was safe and went back to bed. I asked Laurie, "You really think the enemy is close?"

"Close, some of them work on base. Don't worry about it. Go to sleep."

"That's comforting," I remarked. 'Don't worry about it,' who does she think she is talking to?

Laurie added, "Wait till we get mortared. That'll make your sphincter pucker."

Oh goody, "I can't wait."

For the next few days, I hung around the hospital. The nurses were nice, and serious about their work. There was definitely a pecking order and personality conflicts. Cliques were evident. They joked and gossiped like any group of women, but when helicopters came with the wounded they immediately snapped into action. The sounds of helicopters were unnerving. There weren't only combat casualties in the hospital. There were many different medical urgencies including drug overdoses, venereal diseases, malaria, diseases of unknown origin, snake bites, insect bites, and meningitis.

I felt guilty sitting around so I started helping. The nurses issued me scrubs to wear so I would look official, like I knew what I was doing. The scrub tops were sleeveless with a low V neck. It was imperative to wear a bra. Most of the girls wore t-shirts and green fatigue pants with combat boots. I served meals and read letters to those who were blinded, or couldn't hold anything because their hands were bandaged or amputated. The more severely wounded were medi-vac'd to Saigon as soon as they were stable. The hard part was that these were kids, most of them younger than me.

The hospital was not without sexual tension. Doctors and nurses worked in close quarters day and night, ate together, and socialized together. It was easy to pick out who was with whom. Some had spouses back home in the USA but that didn't seem to matter. I was surprised that a lot of the nurses, who were commissioned officers, took up with the male enlisted techs and medics.

I was a red blooded American woman with all the hormonal driven emotions associated with being such, even though my mother tried to repress them. So when Dr. Arthur (Art) Morgan stepped into my life I was defenseless. He looked a couple of years older than me, and cute. He had dark, thick eyebrows. I was a push over for those. I noticed him the first day. I didn't make eye contact, but he must have noticed me. He came over and introduced himself, asking what I was doing. I gave him the song and dance about being on business for the White House and that I was going to be at the hospital for a few days.

From then on, when he wasn't treating patients, Art found an excuse to be with me. We ate together. The nurses avoided us. I could tell they were jealous. They became cold towards me, but I didn't care. Finally there was somebody to speak with on my own social level. The nurses wouldn't understand what that meant. We talked endlessly about politics, the war, religion, the people working in the hospital, and yes, we got around to talking about relationships.

I fudged a little on my current relationship status saying it wasn't serious. Of course it was, but I wanted him to believe he stood a chance. If a woman said she was in a serious relationship that meant hands off, but maybe she could be a friend. On the other hand if a woman said, as I did, she wasn't in a serious relationship, she meant to say she was sleeping with someone, but under the right circumstances she would entertain a change of venue. 'Fuck off,' meant she didn't even want to speak with you.

His side of the story was he'd been so busy the last few years with medical school, internship, and being drafted into the Air Force Medical Corps and shipped to Vietnam, that he hadn't had time for a relationship. I believed him whole heartedly. We talked about the future such as settling down, having a family, and where we wanted to live. It was amazing how many ideals and goals we shared. I was surprised how close I felt to Art after knowing him for only a short time. Jim and I never broached the subject of life long goals.

One day, he asked me, "I'm going to Thailand for R&R next week. You want to go with me?" It sounded heavenly, a nice hotel, good food, shopping, touring, being with a nice man, why not?

I had not seen Jim in days. I don't know if he was avoiding me on purpose or busy putting together an operation to recover the documents. As far as I knew he may have already left. I didn't care. I welcomed the change. I was starting to feel comfortable with the idea of going to Thailand while Jim traipsed off to retrieve the documents. Art was a distraction from the war zone of sleeping in an un-air-conditioned barracks, sharing a barbaric bathroom with 20 other women, taking lukewarm showers, drinking bug juice, and eating fried rice off a metal tray. This would be quite a story, me meeting my future doctor-husband in Vietnam. From what he said, I gathered he was from a blue blood Philadelphia family. My mother would be so excited.

The day was New Year's Eve. I was able to borrow a lipstick from Laurie. That's about all there was for a girl to make herself look presentable. Art and I planned to go to the staff party as a date. I felt everyone was watching us. The other women left us alone. We mostly talked to the doctors. The party was in the hospital mess hall. Small groups gathered at tables. Liquor was bring-your-own. There was a stereo playing, but it was drowned out by the loud chatter. A few couples danced. When we danced Art held me tight. There was no doubt he was aroused, and to be truthful, so was I.

The mess hall staff made hors d'oeuvres out of spam and other mess hall food scraps. There were a few streamers hanging from the ceiling to give the appearance of a gay New Year's Eve party. After a couple of drinks I was feeling pretty good. I don't know what Art was mixing, but it was doing the trick. At midnight he kissed me long and tenderly. His hand slipped to my buttocks. He pulled me to him and pressed. Through those thin scrubs I could tell he was big and ready. I have no idea why, but I grabbed his buttocks and pressed back. That was all the encouragement he needed.

We snuck out when nobody was looking. People were pretty smashed. Art shared a room with another doctor. He said he made arrangements for his roommate to find another place to crash. Once in his room he wasted no time. Art removed my scrub top before I could catch my breath. I helped him remove his. I heard loud voices in the passageway.

"Who's that?" I asked.

"Nobody," Art got back to the task at hand of removing my bra, and then untying and pushing down my scrub bottoms.

I was untying his scrub bottoms when I heard a male voice, "Is this the room?"

"Yes." The door flew open and slammed against the wall. Silhouetted by the passageway light was Jim in his cammies. He walked up to Dr.

Morgan, whose scrub bottoms were down to his knees and his erection was in the full upright and locked position, and kicked him in the nuts. While poor Art was bent over clutching his family jewels Jim upper cut him in the nose. I heard a sickening crack. Blood flew everywhere as Art went sprawling across the bed.

"Get your clothes on, we're leaving." I looked at poor Art who was rolling over holding his nose and groin. I turned my back to Jim while I pulled up and retied my scrub bottoms. I grabbed my bra and scrub top and finished dressing. When I turned around there was a crowd of nurses at the door with scornful looks. I didn't say anything as Jim hurried me down the passageway like a scolded child. I tried to act annoyed and pissed off. I kept pulling my arm from his grasp. He practically had to drag me down the passageway.

Chapter 18

"My God what hit me?" I moaned to Jim who was standing over me.

It was five o'clock in the morning New Year's Day, 1968. I was lying flat on my back on the helo pad. It was dark so no one noticed me. Laurie Smith, the nurse who helped me get settled, was standing next to him. "I think she'll live. I'll be back in a minute." With that Laurie turned and walked away.

"What's going on? Where am I?" My head was pounding.

"From what I gather you were the life of the party," Jim said.

"Tell me what happened. I don't remember a thing." I was getting concerned.

"When I walked in you and the good doctor were attempting to consummate your relationship."

That scared me. "No, that can't be true." I tried to sit up, but felt I would be sick if I did. "This is serious. Don't kid about this."

"I'm not kidding. You two were wrestling with each other's clothes," Jim said. "You were practically naked."

"So we weren't, you know, in bed." I was sobering up with the realization that I may have been caught in the act.

"Not from what I saw, but it was only a matter of moments."

"Oh my God," I started to weep out of frustration. "You saw me naked?"

"It didn't turn me on if that's what's you mean." That comment didn't deserve a reply. Crap, how could I be so stupid? How could this happen? It wasn't my intention to sleep with him, at least not yet. I was holding out for Thailand. Jim continued, "Right now we have a bigger problem than you luring men into bedrooms. We're taking off in 15 minutes and I don't know what to do with you, send you back to Saigon, let you bed down with the doctor here, or take you with us. I feel somewhat responsible."

"You don't have to worry about me. I can take care of myself," I responded.

"Yeah, I saw how you can take care of yourself along with anybody else who wants to jump into the sack," Jim commented. "Are you going to write your boyfriend, or do you want me to?"

That made me mad. Did he really think I slept around? Well Eric the FBI Rugby player was rather quick, but that was different. At least that's what I kept telling myself. "Hey, fuck you. Listen, I don't know what happened, but something is not right. I'm not like that. And just to let you know my boyfriend is a gentleman and he would be understanding, and be supportive." There, I told him even though I didn't believe it myself. With that Jim left.

Laurie reappeared out of the darkness. "Here are your personal items. I put them in your bag in case you want to leave. What are you going to do?"

"First, tell me what happened?" Laurie must have known.

Laurie explained. I thought she was judgmental, "Dr. Morgan is notorious for hitting on new girls. He wows them with being a doctor and all that crap. He tells them what they want to hear, good values, home, family, and all that other bullshit that goes along with it. He usually invites them on a trip. Once he gains their confidence he serves them his special concoction of, what we believe is, benzodiazepines and amphetamines. The girl submits without resistance and they don't remember much the next day. Once he makes his conquest he moves on to the next victim. He has no intention of maintaining a relationship. Besides he's married and has a little girl back home. You can check his personnel record if you don't believe me."

"No, I don't believe it. That can't be true," I stated. "Nobody would treat me like that."

"You, who are you? Everyman's dream. Okay, don't believe me." Laurie got up to leave.

"No wait, I'm sorry. It's just a little hard to comprehend at the moment." I was confused and about to vomit.

"I can give you the names of several girls if you want to speak with them," Laurie said.

"No, I guess I believe you, but a doctor?" I asked.

"Yeah a doctor, who'd ever think? They can be jerks too you know; big surprise."

Jim returned, "What's it going to be?"

I didn't want to stay in Binh Thuy and face Dr. Morgan. I certainly didn't want to go to Saigon by myself. Going deeper into Vietnam didn't sound appealing, but I felt I'd run out of options. "Do you mind if I tag along?"

"You're not going to like it, but let's go." Jim hoisted our bags over his shoulder and started heading to the helicopter.

In my bag was a pair of jungle lugged boots, scrubs, and fatigue pants I got issued while at the hospital. That's about all I owned except for the blue jeans, underwear, and t-shirts I brought from Hong Kong, and my toothbrush.

Laurie was kind. Before I left she said, "I'm sorry about what happened."

"I made a fool of myself, didn't I?" I pondered.

"You're not the first." Laurie and I walked behind Jim to the helicopter, "At first you acted like you knew what you were doing. You looked like you were having fun. So we left you alone. You probably thought we were envious, you stealing away the handsome doctor and all. But, believe me we weren't. We should have warned you. None of the girls can stand him because he has hurt so many of us."

"I hate men," I said.

"Welcome to the club."

"How did Jim know?" I was curious.

"You started acting funny at the party," Laurie stated. "All of a sudden you were all over him. We knew he'd probably spiked your drink so we sent the hospital orderly to fetch Petty Officer Crotty. By the time he showed up you'd left. We figured the doctor had taken you to his room. I must say those SEALs don't hesitate. Not like he politely knocked on the door to ask if you were alright or if you needed anything. He kicked in the door and went straight for Dr. Morgan."

146

At the helo pad I caught up with Jim and followed him onto the helicopter. He carried a rifle.

The crew chief grabbed me. "Who the hell are you?"

"I'm with the White House. I'm going," I said, showing him my ID.

"Not on my plane, you ain't. You're not on the manifest," the crew chief stated.

I was in no mood for his nonsense, "Well then get me on the manifest. Call the President. Here I'll give you his number." I started fumbling in my pockets. I didn't know how long I could fake looking for a nonexistent number.

Jim heard the commotion and turned around, "She's with us, Chief."

The crew chief hesitated like he didn't know if we were telling him the truth. I sat down. The crew chief looked at Jim. Jim shrugged his shoulders like, 'what can I say, she's a pain in the ass.' The crew chief waved a ground crewman over. He took my ID and wrote something on a clipboard. The crew chief threw my ID back at me. Then he talked into his headset. I couldn't hear what he was saying, but the engines started to whine. Pungent exhaust fumes filled the passenger compartment. I felt nauseous. The engines revved. The helicopter vibrated. We lifted off, tilted forward, and started to climb.

The helicopter flew lower and faster than the ride from Saigon to Binh Thuy. Out the left door, or port side as they called it, the sun was rising. It was beautiful with the jungle below, but I knew there was danger down there. Jim, Joe, Dan, and Ski sat with their legs out the side. It made me nervous.

Riding on the helicopter in addition to the four SEALs were the two pilots, two door gunners and the crew chief. There was another SEAL I didn't recognize. He looked older. They all had guns and wore harnesses with canteens, knives, pouches for magazines, flares, and hand grenades. The guns weren't fancy shotguns like my father used for duck hunting with wood stocks and fancy engravings on the side. Their guns were black and looked menacing.

All of a sudden the Gulf of Thailand came into view. We circled the village of Rach Gia. There was a barbed wire encampment with lookout towers at each corner. It didn't look as luxurious as Binh Thuy, and Binh Thuy was the pits. There were a bunch of long one story plywood huts with corrugated tin roofs. Once on the ground the first thing I noticed was the men were scragglier than in Saigon or Binh Thuy. They were unshaven with longer hair and deep tans. They wore paisley headbands, John Lennon style tiny round lens sunglasses, and love beads around their necks, and of course, no shirts. Again it was the eyes, the sunken eyes with the far off stare that scared me the most. They looked like a bunch of hippies in fatigue pants with guns. And then there was the way they looked at me, everywhere I went I got the look. Hadn't these guys ever seen a woman?

We checked in with the OIC at the Naval Support Activity shack. He got right to the point, "We don't have females stationed on this side. Are you a nurse?" I was still wearing my scrubs from the New Year's Eve party. "What I'm saying is we don't have accommodations for you here. I think you would be more comfortable with the nurses over at the Army's medical facility."

I looked to Jim. I didn't want to stay in a hospital again, "I'm not a nurse. I was helping out at the hospital in Binh Thuy. Can I stay with these guys?"

The officer explained, "I'll tell you what, I'll bunk with some of the officers from the mobile riverine force, and you can have my room. That way you will be closer to your men. You'll only be here a few days, right?"

"I hope not that long," I said.

"We'll have to make some arrangements about the head. Right now there is no privacy. Also, our perimeter is being probed every night. Something is in the works. The natives are restless." I was starting to get a sickening feeling.

The lieutenant's room was the back part of the office. It was a trash heap. He packed some personal items. I saw him quickly grab a girlie

148

magazine that was by the bed. I acted as if I didn't notice. "Where's the bathroom?"

"The head is over there." The lieutenant pointed to a shed across the path.

"It looks kind of small to have a shower," I stated.

"There are no indoor showers, Ma'am. There is no running water, no sewer system. We have diesel generated electricity for lights, communications, and refrigeration. We have butane gas for cooking. There's no air-conditioning, no TV, no radio, no hairdryers, no nothing. This is the edge of civilization, and we have it 10 times better than the Vietnamese who live in the village," the lieutenant said.

"Clean towel and sheets?" I was hesitant to ask.

"Sheets?" the lieutenant smirked. I didn't ask any more questions. I knew I wouldn't like the answers. The lieutenant left. I sat on the bunk despondent, depressed with a terrible headache. If there was another word for hopeless I would have used it.

Jim entered and sat next to me, "Happy now?"

"You hate me don't you?" I asked.

"I don't hate you. I don't know what to think. I can't believe I'm sitting next to a St. Louis debutante in the middle of the jungle in a war. I can see the society section of the Post, 'Susan England, daughter of Mr. and Mrs. Dennis England of Ladue, spent the winter abroad exploring the many fascinating sites of Southeast Asia including Vietnam. While she was there she delighted in tasting the unique cuisine better known as mystery meat on a stick. Susan's travels included a firsthand look at the war. She was thrilled while being shot at. Upon Susan's return she reverted back to being a snob and general nuisance.' Girl, you have no idea how deep you're in it. We're meeting in the office in a few minutes. The chief is going to give the warning order. If you want to sit in at least you'll know what our plans are," Jim said as he got up to leave.

"Do you think I'll be shot at?" I was scared out of my mind.

"The VC probably took pot shots at us on the helicopter ride down here," Jim said.

"Could you take me to the bathroom? Helicopter rides always make me have to go," I asked.

We walked across to the head, "You're not going to like this," Jim said.

I can't even begin to describe the smell. I don't know what else to say. It was dark, suffocating hot, but the smell. The flies buzzed in a flurry when I opened the door. I looked for toilet paper to put on the seat. I stuck my head out the door, "Hey, there's no toilet paper."

"I have some in my bag. I'll be right back." He returned with the toilet paper and I completed my business. What had my life become? Was I really expected to walk around in public with a roll of toilet paper in my hand? What kind of madness was this?

We walked back to the office. People were gathering and mulling about. Jim said, "Everyone, this is Susan Engler. She's the reason we're here. Susan, you know Petty Officer Beck, Stranton, and Pulaski. After they got in trouble in Binh Thuy they 'volunteered' for this operation.

Besides, this operation is partly their idea." That comment created curious looks from the others. "Over here is Chief Petty Officer Henderson. He'll be the OIC for the SEAL detachment. And this is Trung, a Chieu Hoi who has been helping us. He knows the area where the documents are supposed to be. The chief is going to brief us."

Trung looked like he would be just as happy to slit my throat as to shake my hand.

"Alright people listen up," Henderson started, "At zero one we'll meet at the boat. We have a PBR that Operation Sealords cut away for us to use for insertions and extractions. Trung will navigate us to our insertion point. We've studied aerial photos and can't find a pier, but with triple canopy jungle that ain't no surprise. Trung doesn't know of a pier, but translating pier into Vietnamese may be the problem. Anyway, from their post-op reports we have an idea where the four SEALs were operating the night the documents were captured."

"We'll patrol to the location and try to recover the documents and capture any VC or other Intel in the area. We'll patrol to our extraction point here." Henderson was pointing to a map on the wall. The insertion point and extraction point were different. He went on about forward air control, safety, weapons, ammunition load out, medi-vacs, radio calls signs, moon state, tides, reported enemy strength in the area, and a bevy of things I didn't understand. When he got done he told everyone to get their personal gear in order and get some rest.

Everyone left except Jim who stuck around studying the map. I asked him, "What's a Chieu Hoi?"

"That's a VC defector. Chieu Hoi means, 'open arms.' Psych ops, or psychological operation's people put out brochures inviting the Viet Cong to surrender, and we will welcome them with open arms. We promise they'll be treated well, and that we'll give them money and food. We have to be careful though. Some VC defectors are still working for the enemy. Never turn your back on one, especially if he has a weapon," Jim informed me.

"Okay, then tell me why one place to insert and another to extract?"

"You really want to know?"

"I'm dying to know." Why was I being sarcastic at a time like this?

"In case we are detected going in we don't want to walk into an ambush on the way out," Jim answered while still looking at the map.

"That seems kind of silly. What's the chance of that? Wouldn't it be easier to park the boat in one place? Then you would know where it is," I asked. "It seems kind of stupid to be moving the boat all over the place in the dead of night. You may not be able to find it."

Jim turned to me, "You want to bet your life on that?"

It dawned on me, this was life or death. These guys weren't playing games but as a woman it was my responsibility to point out everything that seemed stupid. "Okay, I assume a PBR is a boat. What does PBR stand for?"

"Patrol Boat River is a 32 foot fiberglass boat with twin Jacuzzi pumps, twin 0.50 caliber machine guns forward, M-60 machine guns amidships, or Honeywell grenade launchers, and a 0.50 caliber machine gun aft," Jim answered.

I didn't know what any of that meant, but I figured I'd already asked too many questions. "You mind if I hang out with you? Can I help?"

"Sure, let's get something to eat." We went to the mess hall which was a plywood shack with folding tables and chairs. No white table cloths or starched white jacketed waiters. We got a tray and I stuck with the fried rice and bug juice. I figured it was safe. I was beginning to realize that people actually lived like this all the time.

I wanted a steak; I mean a real steak, a Kansas City steak. When they had steak night at Binh Thuy everyone got excited. What passed for steak there I wouldn't have thrown to my dog. And an orange, I wanted an orange I could peel and feel the juice run down my chin. And cold, fresh milk, not the warm powered stuff they served in Vietnam. And a fresh egg, I won't go into what they passed off as eggs. I wanted a warm bath and air conditioning. I wanted to go home.

I would find and tell TJ I didn't know anything and I won't tell anybody anything. I would tell him I'm sorry about Randy and the SEALs being killed, but I can't take it anymore. I was tired. I was still hung over and hadn't had any rest for over 24 hours. I came within moments of having carnal knowledge with an unscrupulous married man. I was soon to find out that things were going to get worse, a lot worse.

Chapter 19

After lunch we headed to the shack where Jim and his detachment were staying. I asked Jim, "What are those things around Trung's neck, they looked like prunes?"

"Those are his ears," Jim answered.

"Excuse me, his ears?"

"Yeah, when he kills someone he cuts off their right ear and puts it on his necklace. Who knows, some may be American. Remember, once he was a VC," Jim answered. "It's bad form to cut off the left ear." I stared at Jim. I couldn't believe what he was saying. He said it so convincingly I felt he was telling me the truth, not making a joke. Was I still on planet Earth?

The guys were getting their equipment together and discussing the operation. Some were lying on their bunks grabbing a nap. Jim pointed out his bunk. I lay down and must have dozed off. Before I knew it, Jim was shaking me and asked if I wanted to go to my room.

While I slept, someone had covered me with a camouflaged poncho liner. I felt rested. I should have. I'd slept for over 11 hours. When I focused on the men, I was startled. Their faces were painted green and black. They wore vests bulging with ammunition for their weapons, hand grenades, flares, a big knife and things I didn't recognize. Ski carried a big gun which he said was an M-60 machine gun. Belts of ammunition crisscrossed his chest like a Mexican bandit. It was real. It was right in front of me. This was no movie or play. These guys were going into combat because of something I suspected, causing me to feel responsible. Jim said they were about to leave. It was half past midnight. Jim walked me to the office with a quick stop at the latrine, or head, or outhouse. Everybody had a different name for the shitter. My God, I was sounding like them.

Jim left me off at the office, "You can lock the door, but I don't think anyone will bother you. Oh, and by the way, you snore." That was not what a lady wanted to hear. About 10 minutes later I heard automatic

153

gun fire then the boat engines started. A few moments later the sound faded away.

I couldn't sleep, I had nothing to read. There was the occasional machine gun burst. I was getting used to that, the harassment and interdiction fire used to discourage the VC from entering the camp. I heard men talking in the office. I went out, "I forgot to take my malaria pill. Does anyone have water?" In Binh Thuy the nurses gave me quinine pills to prevent malaria. I was supposed to take one every day while in-country.

"Sure help yourself," one of the men pointed to a metal water jug. There was one coffee cup tied by a lanyard to the jug. I guess everyone shared the cup, so I shared.

"Do you mind if I sit and listen?" I asked.

The officer, whose room I was using, said, "No, it's pretty boring. We monitor the FAC radio. That's the forward air controller. It's a twin engine Cessna that flies in the vicinity of the SEALs to relay messages back to us. We did a comm check when they left. The boat will move around like it's patrolling so as not to give away the SEAL's position. The SEALs contact the boat and FAC, and the FAC contacts us."

"You think there will be trouble?" I asked. They didn't answer but the looks they gave me were alarming. What was I thinking? This was war.

Every once in a while there would be a 'click,' on the speaker. At that moment whoever was at the radio would key the mike in return. One of the men explained, "That's the FAC checking in. They key their mike to let us know everything is okay. The platoon clicks the FAC. The FAC clicks us. We click back to let them know we received their message. Nobody speaks because the SEALs might be close to the VC, and besides the VC monitor our radios."

"The VC can listen to our radios? Is that fair?" I asked. Everyone looked at me like I was a total idiot. Okay, I lived in Washington, D.C. where reality was a far flung concept. I didn't like this one bit. They were out there. So close to the enemy they couldn't speak. Hours went by. I was getting more and more anxious. The men acted calm with nervous talk and laughter while playing cards, drinking coffee, and reading but I could feel the tension. They wanted the operation to be over as much as I did. I'm sure all of the men in the office didn't have to be there. They could have gone to bed, but they waited, and waited.

Finally, "Base, Rat One, they're 10, over."

"Rat One, Base, 10, out," the petty officer said into the microphone. "They're 10 minutes out. Let's get to the pier." I stepped outside the office. This was the first place I'd been in the world where it was hotter at night than during the day. Walking to the pier I was marauded by mosquitoes. I couldn't get away from them. Somebody handed me a bottle of insect repellant. The smell would keep anything away, but the mosquitoes fought through.

I didn't see the boat until it glided up to the dock in complete darkness. A couple of men from the mobile riverine force handled the lines. The men unloaded. They were caked in mud and looked exhausted. Dawn was about to break. I found Jim. "How'd it go? Did you find the documents?"

"No, this isn't going to be easy" he said. The men dragged themselves back to their hut. The first thing they did was strip down to their khaki shorts and started cleaning their weapons. I asked Jim if I could help.

"Sure," Jim said as he disassembled his weapon. "This is the bolt action assembly with the firing pin. Here, I'll take it apart. Soak each piece in this pan of solvent then scrub them with the wire brush to get the carbon off then dry them and apply a light coat of oil. I'll show you how to put it back together. Don't lose anything."

While I worked, Henderson came in with the Naval Support Activity's OIC to debrief the operation. "Continue what you are doing, men. Alright, we don't have any fresh Intel for this area so it was pretty much of a crap shoot last night. We inserted here." He pointed to the insertion point on a map hanging from the wall. "Coming up empty, not even a hootch or a barking dog. Not even a shot fired from a lookout to warn the VC we were coming. That's how lost we were. We know last May the SEALs were in this area. From the Intel they were using we should have been close. Back then they had fresh Intel of a high level VC cadre meeting in this area. That was their op, a body snatch. There were supposed to be four hootches, three on one side of a canal and one on the other. Trung says he doesn't know of hootches in this area. I'm going to talk to MAC-V in Binh Thuy to see if I can get better Intel on exactly where the SEALs were operating. Get cleaned up, get some chow, and then get some rest. Depending on what I find out we'll try again in a day or two."

I felt disheartened, "You mean you don't know what you're doing?"

Jim replied, "It's not that. There are hundreds of canals off the river. That's how these people get around. They don't travel by road. They travel by sampan. Some of these canals are natural and some are man-made, centuries old. The SEALs who found the documents may have been lost themselves. The four hootches may have been destroyed along with the pier. Usually on operations we burn the hootches. There may be nothing there. If they hid the documents under a pier, the tides may have washed them out to sea. Who knows, we could have patrolled right over the documents last night. Who said this was going to be easy?"

"So this may be all a waste of time?" I asked.

"It may be, but Commander Pierce thought it important enough to send us down here," Jim said. "I'm convinced the four SEALs were killed by your buddy TJ. We're going to keep trying. A lot of SEAL operations come up empty. On some operations we insert in the wrong place or the enemy finds out we are coming and sets an ambush, or the Intel is bogus or communications break down, any number of things. Be patient, we're going to keep trying."

I'll admit, I didn't understand combat or how the SEALs operated. After I finished with Jim's weapon, Ski called me over and asked if I would help clean the M-60. He was flirty, but it gave me something to do and made me feel worthwhile so I said, "Sure." I knew Ski was a 'sport fucker,' as Jim described him so I was cautious not to give him the slightest encouragement. After cleaning the weapons and gear we went to eat. On

156

returning from eating, the guys got into their bunks for a nap. There was an empty bunk above Jim's. I didn't ask. I climbed up there.

I was starting to know the guys. Dan and Ski were protective of me. Jim didn't hover over me, but I could feel his presence. Joe gave me the impression that he thought I should be pursuing him. I felt they accepted me, probably for no other reason than to speak with a girl. I listened to Dan's and Ski's war stories and training stories and how good they had it back in the world. Their girlfriends were the best looking gals in the county, they drove the fastest cars, and they were going to make a million bucks once they got home. It was always about fast cars, fast women, and making money, in that order. First came the car which would attract the women and the money would come easy. I'd been in Ski's car. It was fast, but not the fastest. I'd seen Ski's girlfriend, Linda. I doubt she was the best looking girl in her apartment building. I looked at the pictures of Dan's girlfriend, Kelly. She was cute, but I doubt anybody mistook her for Miss Corn Cob. A picture of Dan's car looked like it was one step from the junk heap.

I got the impression Dan and Ski barely had high school educations. Armed robbery was the only way I could see them making a million. But I loved them. They were so alive, so into life. They had goals and aspirations. Chief Henderson was a different story; he was a lifer, or a person making a career of the Navy.

Henderson looked at me as if I was a big inconvenience. He didn't appreciate a woman being amongst his men. I know he didn't like me or my type. These were his men, and he didn't want a woman distracting them. He may have been only a few years older than his men, but in life experiences he was many years older. His hair was shaved high and tight. He had a ruddy complexion, and looked mean with yellowing, crooked teeth. There were tattoos on his big hairy forearms that were faded, indicating they were of poor quality and old. He probably got them in Taiwan during his steaming days when he was 16 years old after lying about his age to enlist in the Navy. He was simply a big stocky man, all muscle. His gear looked worn. The chief didn't bunk with the men, but rather stayed with the senior enlisted on the base. He would joke with the men, but never befriended them. There was a definite line of authority.

The chief's story was that he was on his a second wife who lived in Chula Vista, California, with the kids from his first marriage, and he had a Filipino wife who lived in Olongapo, Philippines. I doubted the chief belonged to a religious order that encouraged polygamy. It was a matter of convenience.

For a weapon the chief carried a Stoner. It was an automatic assault rifle developed for the Army Special Forces, but used exclusively by the SEALs. I believed the chief slept with his Stoner. Nobody touched his weapon.

The men counted the days until they could return home and make something of their lives. It seemed the closer they were to death, the more they wanted to live. Jim didn't confide in me about those things which I found strange, but I knew he thought the same way as the others. It seemed Jim purposely avoided conversations with me that would draw us closer.

The next day we were sitting around playing Hearts. I asked Dan, "What do you plan on doing when you get out?"

"I'm talking to a guy back in Michigan about going in on an 18 wheeler. You can make a bundle of cash as an independent trucker. My father wants me to take over the farm, but I busted my ass on that farm since I could walk," Dan said. "And I think Kelly, my girlfriend, wants to move to the city."

"You ever think about college?" I asked.

"Naw, that's for rich kids," was Dan's response.

"What about you Ski, what do you want to do?" I was afraid to ask.

"A friend of mine has part interest in the Hole in One Club. You remember the place we went that night. He said I could get on as a bouncer. It should be easy to score with the ladies who work there. They always have problems and need comforting," Ski rambled.

Could that be a meaningful goal in life; comforting troubled ladies? I could see his resume under occupation: sport fucker at a gentleman's club. I didn't ask Jim for his goals in life for a couple of reasons. I didn't want him to think I was interested, and I was afraid he would say something like, 'I want to be a beach bum,' or something ridiculous like that.

The next couple of days were boring. The hot sun, playing cards, napping, reading whatever books the boys had lying around from smutty novels to Michener's Hawaii. The pages with sex scenes were dogged eared for those who didn't want to be bothered reading the whole book. It was always around page 100. Oops, I guess I slipped up there. Okay, I checked a few passages just to get a sense of the writing style. It was disgusting, nothing a lady should read. I got used to the parachute flares and machine gun fire at night. I slept in the SEALs' hut on the bunk above Jim. Was it ever hot up there? They didn't seem to mind. I felt safe with them.

I cut my blue jeans into shorts. It was so hot. I may have cut them too short. I think walking around barefoot, with skimpy blue jean shorts and a t-shirt with no bra was getting to the boys. Short shorts and beer was a lethal combination around a bunch of horny men. I was careful not to show favoritism to anyone. I didn't want a firefight to break out between the SEALs and the mobile riverine force. I knew girls who loved to have men fight over them. It justified their existence. But if I got things stirred up I was afraid Chief Henderson would ship me to Saigon. So I played it cool, and was friends with everyone, but I let it be known that I was with the SEALs.

The mobile riverine force sailors were an enterprising lot. They wore black berets and called themselves the Brown Water Navy. There were different ribbons attached to their berets indicating combat experiences or something. They were constantly making deals with any boat or helicopter that came our way.

Every night we watched a movie they wrangled from other commands. I shouldn't have worried about the food. Somehow there was always a refrigerator full of cold beer. And the food; steaks, lobster, fresh milk, eggs, ice cream, and of course, fried rice. They hired a woman from the village to cook and a few women to do laundry and clean the barracks.

The pay was food. Money wasn't of much value in the village, everything was barter, or cumshaw as the men called it. That way, the men weren't breaking any laws like hiring a foreign national without a security clearance to work on a U.S. military base. No, they were giving some locals a gift or tip for cleaning and cooking. The help was probably VC, but the black berets didn't mind. So there I was at the edge of civilization and living better than I did in Saigon or Binh Thuy. Those black berets could wheel and deal a sno-cone machine to Eskimos.

On days the men didn't operate, the routine would be to get up, PT or physical training, go to breakfast, shoot their weapons, clean their weapons, work on their equipment, nap, eat lunch, then hang out with the black berets working on the boats or fishing. Fishing was tossing a concussion grenade into the water. The SEALs would then retrieve the knocked out fish. We had some great seafood. They let me shoot their weapons. The first time I shot an M-16 it was louder and kicked more than I expected.

We started playing volleyball and drinking beer around four o'clock or as soon as the hottest part of the day had past. I participated in all of the activities.

I never realized volleyball was a full contact sport. Occasionally they played the Vietnamese who worked on base. I shouldn't spill the beans, but the black berets also hired day laborers from the village to help with their projects, in other words to do all the back breaking work. There was always something to be built or fixed. The laborers were paid with building supplies. Every day the laborers hauled off plywood, two by fours, nails, paint, tools, and anything else they needed to build a better place for themselves in their village.

In the volleyball games, the Americans would try to spike the ball every chance they got, usually hitting it out of bounds or into the net. The Vietnamese perfectly placed the ball just out of the reach of a diving American. The Vietnamese won more than their fair share of games.

Several of the American losses could be attributed to too much beer. I was getting annoyed with the Vietnamese big toothy grins and mocking laughs every time they made an American dive hopelessly for a ball while spilling his beer. I got into a few games. I never mastered the one handed set while holding a beer. I more enjoyed sunbathing and watching. There's something about sweaty men in khaki shorts.

The stereo would blare Creedence, Moody Blues, Doors, Cream, Steppenwolf, Hendrix or something uplifting. Those who didn't engage in the volleyball games would play cards, read or write home. The Vietnamese cook would fire up the barbeque. Steaks, chicken, pork and mystery meat, as the men called it, was grilled, and of course fried rice. Then we got ready for the movie as darkness descended. It was outdoor seating with a sheet for a movie screen, and mosquito repellant for perfume. I was gratified to learn the Navy's actual use for bedsheets.

After the movie some of the boys slipped off to the guard towers to smoke pot. The odor was unmistakable. One of the cleaning ladies brought party packs every morning, which were 10 rolled marijuana cigarettes that cost 10 dollars MPC or Military Payment Certificate, the American scrip used in Vietnam. I shouldn't admit this, but I befriended some of the black berets and joined them at the guard tower a few times. Man, was that stuff potent. If I could have gotten that stuff back to Boston I could have retired a millionaire in a year. Afterwards I helped raid the mess hall to satisfy our major munchies.

The evenings I didn't go to the guard tower the SEALs and I would go to the mobile riverine force's bar. The bar was a refurbished Quonset hut. The walls were covered with Playboy centerfolds. It must have been every centerfold ever shot. Did I ever get the look? A bunch of drunken men, and me, the only girl, wearing short shorts and a t-shirt, what could go wrong? I was nowhere near centerfold material, but I was breathing, and at the moment that was all that mattered.

I got to know some of the black berets. Beyond the unshaven, un-bathed, ratty look, most of the boys were nice. There were a few weirdos, but that was to be expected with any group. Some were loners, some talked too much, some were too flirty and some just stared. I would hate to know the fantasies of the ones who stared. For the most part they were lonely. Like everyone else, they wanted to go home.

I asked one of the black berets, "Where was the hut that blew up killing the four SEALs?" He stated he wasn't there at the time, but he thought it was where the new armory was.

Mail call was a big deal. The black berets got all the mail. The SEALs mail hadn't caught up with them. I noticed Dan, Ski and Joe wrote letters. Jim did not. I could only imagine Ski's letters to Linda written in crayon; 'How the fuck are you? Remember the time with the whipped cream and cherries? Can't wait to tie you up again, Ski.'

As the OIC mentioned, there was no indoor shower. The shower was a 55 gallon drum sitting on a platform about eight feet off the ground. The drum was filled by pumping water from a water buffalo, which was a tank on a two wheeled trailer. A hose was attached to the bottom of the drum. The procedure was to unstop the hose, wet down, plug the hose, soap up, and unplug the hose to rinse off, presto, a shower. Only problem was there was no privacy. The first time I went to take a shower a nude man was standing there in the open. I asked some of my new black beret friends if they could help. They structured an enclosure out of ponchos. It was only neck high. I noticed a lot of men were in the guard towers whenever I took a shower. I think they were trying out their new telephoto lens; war, what fun.

The OIC would let me change in the office bedroom. I'd wash one set of clothes and hang them out to dry, just as Jim said, and I no longer wore underwear. What was the point?

It was probably a couple of days after the first operation when Chief Henderson stormed into the barracks. "Listen up, you shitheads. Crotty is under arrest for striking an officer. They want him shipped back to Binh Thuy on the next chopper." I about panicked. I couldn't be left alone in Rach Gia. "The OIC and I have convinced them to let him stay until we complete our mission." Thank God. "Also Dan, Joe and Ski are being docked their pay until the bar they dismantled is paid for. I'm the first one to admit all officers deserve a swift kick in the balls, but don't do it in front of witnesses. We'll deal with this stuff later. You people better start shaping up."

One evening Trung invited the men, which now included me, to dinner at a friend's place in the village. As we walked into the village, a Vietnamese woman squatted down in front of us, pulled up one leg of her baggy black pajama pants and relieved herself on the side of the road. I looked at Jim. He shrugged his shoulders, "It's a third world country. Did you forget?"

As we passed hootches I looked inside. There were dirt floors, no electricity, and I assumed no gas, running water, television, air conditioning, telephone, or sewer system. I knew people lived like that. I'd seen it in National Geographic, but it was different seeing it firsthand.

The Vietnamese looked at me as if I was from outer space. What would these people think of the way women dressed in the U.S., not to mention our supermarkets, big cars, paved roads, restaurants, air-conditioning, country clubs, and everything else we took for granted? And then hear us bitch when the coffee wasn't warm enough, the service wasn't fast enough, the check-out clerk wasn't polite enough, the filling station attendant wasn't respectful.

Trung's friend's place was like the other hootches. Three kids climbed all over me. They would touch me, giggle and run away. Then they would sneak up, and repeat the whole thing. They probably had never seen a Caucasian woman. There were probably 10 Vietnamese in the hut along with the five of us. We brought the beer, Black Label. Jim told me to drink up, that it was insulting not to eat what the host served. He told me I would want to be well fortified. He was right. The main dish was salamander on a leaf. There was some sort of sauce they called nuoc nam which I was told was fermented fish sauce. I looked for another dish, possibly some hors d'oeuvres like egg rolls or chestnuts wrapped in bacon or small crab cakes. My father's club in St. Louis made the best crab cakes. Surely, I thought, there must be some bruschetta or cheese puffs or maybe those little basil pesto bread pieces. No such luck. It was salamander or my Vietnamese host would lose face. Henderson got staggering drunk, or totally shit faced as the men said. I thought he was cruel by the way he insulted the mamma and papa san by mimicking their speech and the way they squatted on their haunches.

We were back in our hut by 10. Around midnight I woke up with chills and a cold sweat. I had horrible stomach cramps until about four in the morning when I started throwing-up. The diarrhea came next. In the morning, the black beret corpsman gave me a shot of something and some pills. He told me if the vomiting and diarrhea didn't slow down he was going to start an IV and medi-vac me to Binh Thuy. I didn't want to leave. I certainly didn't want to be treated by Dr. Morgan. I didn't think I could travel, but on the other hand I didn't want to be a burden to the boys. I wanted to die. I don't think I'd ever been so ill in my life. I told Jim I was moving back to the officer's room. He insisted I stay in his bed. He didn't want me in the bunk above him for good reason.

The other men helped. They brought me water and soup, but I couldn't keep anything down. I felt weak standing, so I just lay in bed. Dan spent most of the time with me, telling me about his farm and girlfriend. They put a bucket next to the bed. Jim was the one who washed it out every time I used it, which was often. And he washed my clothes often. There was no way I could keep myself clean. I seemed to have an accident every five minutes. Any sense of self-dignity was long gone.

The boys enclosed my bed using poncho liners. That gave me some privacy to change my clothes and use the bucket. Jim washed me. It was understood he was the only one to be with me when the ponchos were up. The noises and smells were horrific. I think any sexual thoughts the boys may have had toward me no longer existed. It may have even discouraged Ski. After 24 hours, I was a little better, but not strong enough to be out of bed for more than a few minutes at a time. I lay in bed playing cards and listening to Dan's stories.

Forty eight hours later I was almost back to normal when Henderson barged in, "Listen up, there's no new Intel for this area so we are going to get some of our own. We're going out at zero one, briefing at 1600. Trung's been in town, and thinks he has the location of a suspected VC tax collector."

That afternoon, they loaded bullets into magazines, taped down the spoons on grenades, stripped and cleaned their weapons. No one seemed excited. They went about their business like it was an everyday occurrence. Dan was loading bullets. I went over, "Can I help?"

"Sure, first you load a regular round then two of these red tipped ones into a 20 round magazine. They're tracers so when you see two red streaks you know it's time to lock in a fresh magazine. The regular round in the chamber leaves the weapon loaded." I didn't understand any of this. "Next, you put on the speed loader and push in 10 rounds. Then push in another seven. I'll carry 10 of these 20 round magazines. I'll have a 30 round banana magazine in the weapon to start," he said. I went to work loading magazines. I felt I had to do something to help. By then I could field strip an M-16, an M-60 machine gun, and now I could load magazines. I was ready to sign up for SEAL training as soon as I got back to the world.

Jim told me, not in a demeaning way, "It's a weapon, not a gun and it's a round, not a bullet." I was starting to get the lingo.

I felt strong enough to go to the mess hall with the guys for some fried rice. Coming back from dinner we heard a commotion behind the mess hall. We ran back to find a rat, the size of a small dog, in a trap trying to free itself. I screeched. The boys looked at me as if I was a debutante. I didn't want to be a debutante. I wanted to be one of the guys. The Vietnamese cook came out and clubbed the rat over the head. She took it from the trap and carried it back into the mess hall. "What's she going to do with that?" I asked.

"I wouldn't eat the fried rice tomorrow," Dan suggested. I almost lost it.

Chapter 20

Again, it was another long night sitting by the radio in the MAC-V office. Before the guys shoved off they test fired their weapons. For the first time I went to the boat dock with the platoon. Jim let me shoot his M-16. The tracers streaking over the water were awesome. Chief Henderson carried the Stoner. Nobody asked to shoot the chief's weapon. The Stoner fired at a much faster rate than the M-16 or M-60. Every fifth round was a tracer. When the chief buzzed the water it looked like a laser beam. The Stoner fired the M-16 round and was high maintenance.

Some of the black berets also came down to shoot. Ski had his M-60 machine gun. It was a heavy weapon, but Ski was built like a pack mule with the corresponding brains. Ski let me shoot the M-60. The SEALs cut off the bipod and front site to lighten the weapon so it could be handled by one man. Of course Ski had to stand behind me and wrap his arms around me to help support the weapon. I felt a few pushes on my butt. I think Ski's motives for teaching me to shoot the M-60 were less than honorable.

Joe was sort of the weapon's guru of the detachment. When he first saw me firing Jim's weapon he came over and gave me a few pointers. "When you shoot hold the weapon tight against your shoulder, and step into it, especially if you are firing automatic. The weapon will rise. Here, put it on automatic." Joe flipped the selector switch to full auto.

I pulled the trigger, "Holy crap!" A burst of rounds went down range. The tracers zipped across the river. The last tracer cleared the river bank. Okay, I didn't step in aggressively enough to keep the barrel from rising. I wanted to try it again. I ripped off another burst. It was way too cool.

Joe was smirking. Jim stood back and didn't interfere, but I think out of kindness he was suppressing a laugh. Joe said, "Well if anybody was standing on the opposite river bank they're either dead, or running for their life. See that log out there? Try to shoot just short of it. That way when the barrel raises you'll walk the rounds through the target, and if you don't hit the target the rounds kicking up dirt in front of the enemy will scare the shit out of them."

The second time I was more aggressive. After a few tracers went out I could put the rounds right on the log. "Yeah, that's it, thanks." They reloaded their weapons, got on the boat, and departed.

In the office some of the men were smoking. I hadn't smoked for weeks, but it was tempting. I weakened and bummed a cigarette. When the radio came to life I jumped and ran to the pier. It wasn't only the men who got off the boat. There were three blindfolded Vietnamese with their hands bound behind their backs. One was older and the other two were probably in their mid-twenties. They looked mean like Trung. The older one looked scared. The younger ones looked like they'd had the crap beaten out of them. All they wore were baggy cotton black shorts, no shirts, no shoes. They were skinny, and looked undernourished, probably from eating too many salamanders.

Camp personnel took the prisoners to a different building. We went back to our hut and started cleaning weapons. The guys talked about the operation. Evidently they snuck up on two hootches and set a perimeter. Henderson and Trung stormed into one of the hootches. A VC ran out the back and was gunned down by Dan. Two VC ran out of the other hootch and were greased by Ski. That's the word they used, greased. I understood what they meant. Ski said one of the VC ran straight at him. In the dark he probably didn't realize a SEAL was waiting. Ski said he cut him in two with the M-60. Jim heard a struggle in the hootch that Henderson entered. He ran in to find Henderson and Trung wrestling with three Vietnamese. Jim helped secure the VC. Once the VC were subdued and their hands were tied behind their backs, the men started moving them to the extraction site. Nearby VC responded to the shooting, and started firing in the direction of the SEALs.

They said it was a running gun battle in a swampy canal. The VC prisoners weren't cooperating and had to be dragged, and carried. And I imagined clubbed over the head and given a boot in the pants. For some reason I wasn't shocked or offended. I was sitting amongst men who in the past few hours killed three men and captured three, and I wasn't shocked. That was the part that bothered me; I was alright with this.

We went to eat. I had soup and avoided the fried rice. We returned to the hut to get some sleep. I kept my bed enclosed which I liked and I kept the lower bunk. Jim could roast in the upper bunk.

The sound of a helicopter woke us. The whole platoon went outside. It wasn't a green helicopter like I'd seen in Vietnam. It was silver colored and a different shape with Air America stenciled on the side in small letters. Two Americans and a Vietnamese man stepped out and went directly to the building where the prisoners were held. They wore khaki safari type uniforms, not the greens American soldiers wore.

It wasn't long before they emerged with the three bound, blindfolded prisoners. The prisoners appeared frightened. Their knees were wobbling as they were dragged to the helicopter. The older Vietnamese put his hands together in prayer formation and kept bowing and pleading with his handler. The man pushing him along wasn't impressed.

The helicopter started to wind up its rotors. One of the safari clad Americans and the Vietnamese man along with two of the prisoners got on the helicopter. The third prisoner squatted on the helo pad.

Jim grabbed me, "Let's go inside."

"Why? I want to watch the helicopter take off." I wanted to stay outside. Maybe I was having an adrenaline rush with the excitement of the men coming back safely and seeing the enemy up close.

Jim dragged me, "No you don't. Let's go."

"Who do you think you are pushing me around? You have some nerve. Why can't I watch?" I asked.

He shoved me through the door. "We can go outside in a minute. Just wait with me."

I heard the helicopter's engines whir to a high pitch and then the WHOMP, WHOMP, WHOMP as it lifted into the air. The sound faded, but the sound didn't disappear altogether which was odd. It seemed the helicopter was hovering high above the camp. Jim seemed to be anticipating something. The helicopter sound lingered for a few moments

then I heard a blood curdling cry and a sickening thud. The hut shook.
"Okay, it's over. You may want to wait here a while," Jim said.

"What's over? What was that?" I asked.

"That was a prisoner being prepared for interrogation," Jim said.

"Don't bullshit me."

"Alright, I'll tell you. It's a prisoner interrogation method that works
100% of the time. They take two prisoners up 1000 feet. Toss one out, the
other talks. It never fails," Jim said matter of fact. "In this case with three
prisoners they left one on the helo pad. He watched his buddy try to defy
gravity. He'll talk. The interrogators will compare the stories of the
prisoner on the ground with the one in the helicopter. I'll bet they're the
same."

"You can't be serious. The U.S. would never indulge in torture."

"It's not the U.S. It was the Vietnamese doing the tossing," Jim
explained.

"Even so it was a U.S. helicopter and U.S. personnel were complicit in
this act," I said. "I didn't see anyone trying to stop it, including you."

"The helicopter isn't registered in the U.S. And as far as U.S.
personnel being complicit, I don't know. That would have to be hashed
out in a court of law. Are you filing charges?" Jim asked.

"I may."

"The information they give may save your life. Is your life worth it?"
Jim asked.

"Oh no, you are not putting this on my conscience. We can't be doing
this," I said. "It's wrong."

"If those prisoners captured you, what do you think they would do?
This isn't the country club out here, Babe," Jim sneered. "You people from
Washington make me sick. You are so out of touch with reality, so holier
than thou. There are bad people in the world that need to be dealt with in
terms they understand. You self-righteous jerks need a wake-up call. You
know, people who sit in air-conditioned offices in D.C. should not be
making policies for people getting their asses shot at in the bush."

"This is not who we are as a country. These aren't our values."

"You better check your history Ms. England. How do you think we remain a country; not by succumbing to Britain, France, Spain, Mexico Germany, Japan, or now Communism? Somebody is always out to steal your lunch money. These teetotaler, limp dick, chickenshit politicians want to give it all away, and for what? Their warped sense of values!"

"You don't have to demean me. I just never thought we did things like that," I said.

"Good, then I'll spare you the really gruesome methods of persuading prisoners to talk. It's always acceptable for the enemy to use torture, but never us." Jim said as he stormed out of the hut.

Left alone I couldn't sleep, I couldn't read, I couldn't do anything. It was as if my brain was paralyzed. I felt sick. A couple of hours later I heard the helicopter, 'Are they doing it again?' I asked myself.

A moment later Henderson burst in with the rest of the guys. There was a big smile on Henderson's face, "We got good Intel. We really lucked out. Trung did us right. The old man was a VC Commissar. He happened to be visiting the tax collector. The tax collector was the one to bolt from the hootch that Dan cut down. The gook who did the full gainer in the pike position with a half twist and 10 foot bounce off the helo pad was the tax collector's son. I think we know where the documents are. We were within a klick of them the first op." A klick was a kilometer or just over half a mile. When Henderson briefed, he always said they were going to patrol so many klicks. "And something else is brewing, something so big we have to work fast. We're going out tonight. Be at the pier at zero one."

The guys went to work as if nothing happened, joking about the operation. This was how things were done. I should have been euphoric about the Intel, but I couldn't believe the emptiness I felt for the human price it cost. Maybe they could find the documents and I could redeem my life, but at what cost? Men were losing their lives and nothing had been accomplished. War was too horrible to comprehend.

Chapter 21

At half past midnight we were at the boat dock. Dan insisted I fire his weapon. I'd cleaned his weapon and loaded his magazines so maybe this was my thanks. I did much better keeping the tracers going down range and not zipping through the village across the river. The men loaded the boat and in a matter of moments they were out of sight. The engine noise faded.

I waited in the office, and waited, and waited. The night dragged into early morning. I couldn't bear it. There was the occasional radio check 'click.' Then there were none. It was past daybreak. They'd never been out so long. I knew something was wrong. I must have been dozing when I heard, "Medi-vac, medi-vac!" The office cleared except for the radio operator. He started contacting Binh Thuy. Everyone, including the black berets, were at the pier by the time I got there. Word must have traveled fast around camp. It was a few moments before we could hear the PBR. The boat came roaring around the bend. I'd never seen a boat move so fast. The engines were screaming. The boat was still going full blast when it got to the end of the pier. I moved back anticipating the boat crashing onto shore. The coxswain flipped the Jacuzzi jets into reverse, revved the engines, and stopped the boat in a matter of feet. Waves from the boat's wake rushed onto shore.

First I noticed holes in the bow. Then I saw the blood. The deck was awash in blood. One of the SEALs was lying on the deck with an IV in his arm. With their face paint, they all looked alike and I couldn't tell who it was. The black berets helped get him off and rushed him toward medical. The black beret corpsman rode on the PBR when the SEALs operated. He held the IV bottle as they ran the SEAL to medical. I ran as fast as I could and couldn't keep up with them. By the time I got into the hut they had his equipment and shirt stripped. An IV was hanging. The corpsman ordered more plasma expander. A pressure bandage was on the left side of his chest at about the diaphragm level. It was soaked with blood. It was then that I noticed the trickle of blood coming from the corner of his mouth. I felt Jim's hand on my shoulder. He said, "It's Dan. He was covering our extraction and got hit boarding the boat."

The corpsman yelled, "Someone get that Army doc." Two of the black berets ran out of the dispensary.

I didn't ask if the mission was a success. Nothing was worth this. The corpsman kept checking to see if Dan was breathing and feeling for a pulse. He asked about the medi-vac. "How long God dammit!?" I looked around the room. Everyone stood frozen, unable to move or speak. It was morbid.

The radio operator ran in, "It's 35 minutes for the bird. They had a fuck-up in Binh Thuy."

The corpsman yelled, "He doesn't have 35. I can't stop the bleeding. Where's that fucking doctor?"

I took Dan's hand. He wasn't conscious, or at least he wasn't opening his eyes. Suddenly the corpsman became concerned. It seemed as though Dan's body deflated. I can't describe it in any other way. The corpsman started chest compressions. He ordered me to give Dan two breaths. I didn't know how to do CPR. He yelled at me to pinch Dan's nose, tilt his head back, cover his mouth with mine, and breathe twice, and do it every time he ordered, 'breathe.' Without thinking I did. We kept this up for what seemed a long time.

The door opened, and in walked who I assumed was the Army's ninth infantry's doctor wearing bloody scrubs, holding a cup of coffee. He looked like he'd been up all night. He calmly walked over to Dan, took one look and shook his head. He spoke with the corpsman in hushed tones. I imagined he wanted to know the corpsman's assessment. After trying to take a pulse and listening for a heartbeat he sighed, asked the corpsman to help roll Dan onto his right side. The doctor stuck his bare finger into the entry point of the wound. "I'm pretty sure he nicked his descending aorta." The doctor spoke as he maneuvered his finger inside Dan. I almost fainted. "By the blood around his mouth I would guess the round passed through the inferior aspect of the left lobe of the lung. It must have passed just below the left ventricle of the heart. He could have been shot on the operating table and it would have been touch and go. Sorry, I'll pronounce. Get me the form."

I didn't know what to do, should I continue CPR or what? I just stood there and stared at Dan. He was asleep, so peaceful. I took his hand again as if that would do any good. It was clammy. There was no life. After a while the corpsman got a black rubber bag off a shelf. Henderson, the corpsman, Ski, Joe, and Jim maneuvered Dan's body into the bag. Nobody spoke. There were no tears, no outbursts, no hysterics, just numbness.

The medi-vac arrived. The black berets carried Dan to the helicopter. Jim came out with a war bag. I went to hug him. I needed to be held. He wasn't warm to me, "You're leaving. I'll catch up with you in Binh Thuy, but you can't stay here. The camp is going to be hit tonight. That was the other Intel we got from the VC prisoner; no arguments, no discussion. There is something very important you need to do. Go to graves registration with Dan. They'll put him in an aluminum transfer case. Do not let them ship him to Saigon for transit home until I get there. Use your White House ID, or whatever it takes, understand? Dan is not to leave Binh Thuy until I get there." He took me by the arm and helped me onto the helo and gave me my belongings. As I got on, Jim's grip on my arm slipped to my hand. He squeezed and gave me a reassuring look. I squeezed back. I felt something connect between us.

I watched the camp fade away. The men watching from the helo pad got smaller as the helicopter gained altitude. Dan's body bag was on my feet. That was the longest helicopter ride imaginable.

At Binh Thuy, the Air Force medics met the helicopter to get Dan's body. I followed them to graves registration. I told the person in charge the body was not to leave Binh Thuy until Petty Officer Crotty arrived.

"Ma'am, we have standing orders to get the deceased to Saigon as soon as possible. I don't care what Petty Officer Crotty wants," the officer said.

"Well then, let me put it to you this way. I work for the White House and I want the body to stay here until Petty Officer Crotty arrives," I ordered.

"Yes, we know all about you working for the White House. We've been briefed. You are to report to Lieutenant Commander Pierce upon your arrival."

I got a bad feeling the way he said that. He didn't show me respect. In fact he was defiant. I walked over to the SEAL building. "Step into my office Ms. Engler or England or whatever your name is." LCDR Pierce said. "I hate to be the one to break it to you, but you are no longer employed by the White House. I did a little checking when you left. They want you back in Washington, D.C. yesterday. It appears you have no authority to be over here."

My body went numb. I sat there with my head down, "I know. You have to believe me about them killing the four SEALs, my co-worker, and wanting to kill me."

"Make that five SEALs. I have to write a letter to Petty Officer Beck's mother and father. What do you want me to say? Your son was killed while participating in an unauthorized operation concocted by a delusional woman."

I had not cried since Dan's death, but I found myself making a fool of myself in the commander's office. I couldn't stop crying. My world was crashing around me. He wasn't sympathetic. "You're confined to the women's barracks at the hospital. I'm arranging secure transportation for you to Saigon and from there they are flying you straight to D.C. with a State Department escort. And your running mate, Petty Officer Crotty, is in deep do-do. Not only is he the subject of a murder investigation, but he broke the nose of an officer, and a doctor at that. It seems no one can locate the originator of the message that authorized him to accompany you to Vietnam. And those orders didn't come from the Secretary of the Navy's office. I assume you know they are going to lock him away for a very long time. You want to fess up to the orders?" The commander waited. Then he spoke, "I didn't think so. It looks like you have been through a lot. I'll call the hospital and get somebody to escort you."

Laurie came and got me, "You look like Hell. What's going on?"

"I guess I'm caught. Jim and I came over here to find documents that would prove something illegal in the President's re-election campaign. People have been killed over this," I said.

"Did you find the documents?"

"I don't know. I doubt it. One of the SEALs was killed last night and I escorted the body here."

"How did you get to Vietnam in the first place without orders?" Laurie asked.

The way she asked made me suspicious she was gathering information for someone. "I used my White House ID. Jim is a friend of mine. He got orders to escort me." I didn't want to implicate Jim. I figured he was in enough trouble. I needed a favor from Laurie, "Is there a way to keep the deceased SEAL's body here for a few days? It may be important."

"We could order an autopsy. That would give you some time. Things should be slow the next few days. There's a cease fire for Tet, the Chinese New Year. Why do you want to keep the body here?" Laurie asked.

"I don't know. Jim told me not to let the body go to Saigon until he gets here."

"I'll see what I can do," Laurie said as we entered the barracks. The girls gave me a curious look. Some moved away from me. Laurie offered, "You may want to get cleaned upped."

Maybe that was it, I smelled, "Sure." It felt good to take a shower, albeit, lukewarm with no water pressure. There was blood on my hands, forearm, and t-shirt. I felt something crusty around my lips and realized it was Dan's blood from doing CPR. The nurses had seen plenty of blood so there must have been something else that startled them. I took a GI shower which meant getting wet, turning off the water, soaping up, and rinsing off. There was a water shortage even though we were on the Bassac River.

I was getting settled when Laurie came over and said the autopsy was scheduled for tomorrow morning with none other than my friend, Dr. Chip Morgan. I didn't flinch. I didn't care. He couldn't intimidate me. I ate and went to bed early. I was exhausted. I hadn't slept for over 24 hours.

Two huge explosions shook me out of bed. I don't remember the time when the attack started. The building shook violently and filled with dust shaken from the rafters. Items fell off the shelves and people screamed. Someone yelled, "Mortars incoming!" People ran for the exit of the barracks across an open area to a bunker. There were more explosions, some close. The bunker shook and dust trickled down from the overhead. There was constant machine gun fire, a lot of it. A head popped into the bunker, "We need you in the hospital, casualties!"

We filed into the hospital. I don't know what I was more scared of, the unknown, or the unexpected. I didn't want to die, but that didn't concern me so much as how and when. I got busy carrying stretchers and getting supplies. I knew where most of the medical supplies were kept. I went to triage. The room was chaos. One man kept crying, "They're in the wire, they're in the wire."

I caught a glimpse of Dr. Morgan. I don't think he saw me, but I'm sure he knew I was back, the asshole. The room went dark. A nurse turned on a battery powered lantern. It was an eerie scene, blood, dust, moaning, panic among some of the wounded. The hospital staff went about their business professionally. Nothing seemed to faze them. They had a job to do and they were doing it. Maybe by throwing themselves into their work they could block out the bombardment and chaos surrounding them.

Commander Pierce caught my eye as he entered triage helping a wounded sailor. It looked like his yeoman. At the same instant, somebody shoved past him. Even in the dim light and haze I could tell it wasn't an American. For one thing I'd become accustomed to the way Vietnamese moved, and second, he was short, and moving too quick for hospital personnel. He was wearing black pajamas with a backpack and heading toward the main entrance to the hospital. Something took over my body. I wasn't thinking, just reacting. As he ran past I grabbed an M-16 lying next to a wounded soldier, thumb flipped the selector to full auto, stepped toward my target and let go a burst.

176

Then everything went blank. I recalled somebody taking the weapon from my hands. Next I recalled sitting and people asking me if I was alright. Why were they asking, had I been shot? I didn't feel anything. I felt like I was floating. Someone could have lit me on fire and I wouldn't have felt it.

It seemed the attack ended almost as quickly as it began. I kept waiting for the next explosion, but it never came. There were muffled explosions in the distance. The machine gun fire continued but it was outgoing. I could distinguish between incoming and outgoing fire. Isn't that a skill every debutante should master? An Army sergeant told everyone to stay in the hospital, that some VC penetrated the wire and were on base. He said we could be shot by either side if we went running around the base. He didn't need to tell me twice. Every so often there would be a single shot or a short burst of automatic weapon's fire.

The hospital staff settled down and got organized. I told everyone I was alright and went back to triage. Some of the lesser injured started arriving. They were the ones who stayed at their post and fought even though wounded. They described the battle as being a world of shit. I could relate. People came in with rumors that Saigon was overrun. They said the U.S. Embassy was occupied by the VC. Supposedly Dong Tam and Can Tho were hit harder than us. It was sounding like the VC and NVA were attacking the whole country. That was it, North Vietnam had invaded the south for the final battle of the Vietnam War, and here I was caught in the middle. I was going to die in this shit hole of a country and for what? I asked about Rach Gia, but nobody knew. Communications were spotty and only priority messages were being sent or received.

Helicopters started arriving with wounded from outlying bases. I looked for Jim. I was too afraid to go to graves registration. Afraid of what I might find. There was one helicopter from Rach Gia with some wounded black berets. I recognized one of them and asked about Jim. He said none of the SEALs were wounded that he knew of but the camp was torn up pretty bad. He said the situation was still in doubt. The hospital work never stopped. The base stayed on high alert. They expected another attack that night.

When I returned to the barracks that evening the girls acted even stranger toward me than when I returned from Rach Gia. I asked Laurie, "Have I done something wrong?"

"No," she said, "on the contrary. You're a hero."

"What?" I asked.

"Don't you remember shooting that sapper?" Laurie asked.

"I remember something, but it's like a blur. Like a dream, something that's not real."

"Yeah, I wasn't there, but what I heard is you plugged a suicide sapper just before he set off his explosives. He would have killed everyone in the hospital. Where did you learn to shoot like that?" Laurie asked. "People are saying you handled that M-16 like a Green Beret."

"Oh, the SEALs taught me how to shoot an M-16 while I was at Rach Gia. Are you telling me I killed someone?"

"Yes, a VC." Laurie said, "He looked like he was 15." I was in shock. Again my mind was paralyzed. I sat blankly for a long time.

A second day passed with no new attacks. People were still anxious. The base was declared secure, but remained on high alert. I walked around a portion of the base. The damage was extensive. Sides of buildings were blown away, along with vehicles and planes. I think Commander Pierce forgot about me with the excitement. Dan's autopsy was postponed. I was about to call it a day when I saw Jim's silhouette in the doorway. I couldn't see his face, but I knew it was him. I ran over and grabbed him. I didn't care what people thought. My eyes got misty, I squeezed, digging my fingernails into his shoulders. I can't explain my feelings, but they were genuine. He held me tight. We went arm in arm to the waiting room. He looked terrible.

"I got a ride with a medi-vac. The seriously wounded were taken out the first day. They let me come with the dead and some of the lesser wounded. I told them I had to get back here before you got mad and finished off the NVA by yourself. How was it here?" Jim asked.

"Look around. I thought I was going to die. I killed someone. What's going on with you?" I asked.

"What? What do you mean you killed someone?" Jim asked. "Ours or theirs?"

"They're telling me I killed a VC sapper. I just reacted. I can't even tell you what happened." I wasn't bragging, but I wanted Jim to know. The look he gave me.

"We'll have to talk about that. I don't know what's going on. Evidently, the whole country was attacked. I guess it's still bad up north around Hue. It seems the Marines are taking the brunt of this," Jim said.

"I have to tell you something, Commander Pierce checked on us. He knows your orders are bogus. And I no longer work for the White House and he knows my real name. He is sending me to Saigon and then onto Washington, D.C. under armed guard for a public execution. He wants to see you."

"Forget that, we have to get to Saigon before he knows I was here. First we need to go to graves registration," Jim said. He took me by the hand.

It was busy over at graves registration as one would expect. Jim had me wait outside. He told me I wouldn't want to see what went on inside.

He was in there about half an hour. I was starting to get concerned when he reappeared. "Okay, it's all set. Let's go."

"What's all set?" I asked.

"Never mind, get your bag, we're going to Saigon," Jim said. I didn't care for his secrecy.

At the air terminal Commander Pierce was waiting for us. Jim moaned, "Uh oh, this can't be good."

"I want to speak with Petty Officer Crotty alone if you will excuse us Ms. England," Commander Pierce requested. I took the cue and waited. They walked around behind a building. They were gone for a good 15 minutes.

When they reappeared they acted as if they were best buddies. As we walked out of the air terminal Commander Pierce spoke, "Now let me see, Petty Officer Crotty, you are in country on unauthorized orders, you broke the face of an Air Force doctor and I imagine you engaged in armed combat while at Rach Gia with no legal orders. And you Ms. England are also in Vietnam with no authorization. You killed a Vietnamese national. You are not in the military or any government organization that authorizes the use of fire arms in killing civilians in their own country. That's murder. So what am I to do?"

What he did was use his influence to get us on a C-130 flight to Saigon that was ferrying aluminum transfer cases and some of the more seriously wounded. I hoped Dan's aluminum case wasn't on the plane.

During the plane ride I asked Jim, "What's the deal with Commander Pierce? I thought he was sending me back to the States in leg irons for public humiliation," I asked.

"It seems you are a hero. He told me you saved his life. The sapper you greased was wearing twenty pounds of C-4. That much explosive would have leveled the building you were in plus most of the main hospital. He said you put three rounds dead center on the VC's back. A silver dollar would have covered all three entry points. That's good shooting, Ms. England," Jim said, and then added, "I know Commander Pierce had orders to send you back to the States and to put me in the brig, but sometimes the right thing has to be done. Once I explained everything to Commander Pierce he did the right thing. You'll understand."

"Thanks about the shooting," I didn't think I should be proud to have killed a fellow human being. Then I thought, "Oh my God, how come the explosives didn't go off?"

"C-4 is a plastic explosive that needs a detonator. It can be dropped, shot, lit on fire, all without exploding, it's hard to set off. The sapper had a clacker from a claymore mine in his hand with wires running to blasting caps embedded in the C-4. When you shot him, he dropped the clacker. If he'd fallen on it there would be no more cocktail hours for you on the veranda of your country club. They could have mailed what remained of you home in a two penny envelope. EOD said the C-4 was ours of course, probably stolen from the armory right here at Binh Thuy," Jim said.

180

"But Jim, I shot a kid in the back." I was having difficulty coming to grips with that.

"I don't care if you shot him in his sleep. He was going to kill you. He was going die in a few seconds by his own hand. You saved dozens of lives. What do you think we are doing out here, sitting around smoking dope discussing world peace? This isn't college."

"Commander Pierce also had a chat with Dr. Morgan. He told Morgan that if he didn't drop the charges against me he would have every woman he ever took advantage of show up on his wife's doorstep."

"That's blackmail," I accused.

"You are right about that. Also, we recovered the documents."

Chapter 22

Saigon was a mad house. Where there used to be soldiers wearing khaki uniforms I only saw soldiers in full combat gear. It seemed everyone was carrying a weapon. Sand bagged machine gun emplacements were at every corner. There were no rooms at the Victoria. Jim ran into some SEALs in the lobby. They said we could bunk with them. He couldn't wait to tell them about me greasing a gook, as he phrased it. He knew my thoughts about using such terminology. The SEALs were impressed and treated me with a newfound respect. Gosh, now I could go to the country club and have waiters kiss my ass and I could just as easily go to the Trade Winds in Coronado, and knock back a few brews with the boys, and tell them how I greased a gook. How many debutantes can say that?

Curfew was at dusk. Anyone on the streets would be shot. They told us at the airport Saigon was going to be attacked again that night. There was very little food at the rooftop restaurant. The SEALs stocked their room with C-rations and beer. They gave me the lima beans and ham. They said everybody fought over the lima beans. It was better than salamander, but not by much. While the other SEALs were there I never got the fruit cocktail or pound cake. C-ration was actually a term held over from World War II and the Korean War. The correct name was MCI or meal combat, individual. There were 12 meals to a case. The entrée, if that's what it could be called, came in a small tin can. Each case came with one P-38 can opener. Every GI in the bush in Vietnam carried a P-38 on his dog-tag chain. The meals ranged from the delectable ham and lima beans to beef with spiced sauce, beans with meat balls in tomato sauce, pork sliced cooked with juices, and so many other yummy meals. Dog food smelled and tasted better and I doubt any self-respecting dog would touch a C-ration. In addition to the main course there were matches, four cigarettes, chewing gum, instant coffee, salt, sugar, fruit jam, fruit cake, crackers, cocoa, a spoon, and one square of toilet paper. No thank you, I don't even sneeze into one square of tissue paper much less...... never mind.

The night sky was filled with parachute flares, intermittent bursts of machine gun fire, and the H&I artillery fire. It was all outgoing.

The next morning Jim and I went to Ton Son Nhut airport to arrange a flight to Hong Kong. Normal commercial traffic would not be restored until Saigon was declared secure, and they didn't know when that would be. The first few flights were booked. We got tickets on the fourth flight to Hong Kong, and we were lucky to get those. There was no telling when the flight would be scheduled.

When Jim and I were finally alone in our room he pulled out a plastic bag. "These are the documents we found under the pier. Except it wasn't a pier. It was a bench hanging over a canal used as a toilet seat. The documents were buried in shit. Ski tripped over one of the shoulder straps. There must be a dozen knap sacks in there. We grabbed one. The documents are MPC. When I see a lot of freshly minted MPC I smell black market."

I was confused. I thought the money captured would be American dollars, "Who knows about this?"

"Ski, Joe, and Henderson are the only ones who know and they know what happened to the four SEALs so they're keeping quiet. No messages are going out saying documents were found. They stayed behind in Rach Gia until we find out a few things," Jim said.

"Like what?" I asked. I didn't want to admit that I'd known all along the money was being used by the President's re-election campaign.

"Like where this MPC came from, and how it has cost more than a few people their lives. Come on, we're going to the MAC-V disbursing office. Commander Pierce told me to look up LtCol. McKenzie. He'll help us find out where this MPC came from. You still got your White House ID?" Jim asked.

"Yes, but I'm afraid it's of no use. I'm in enough trouble as it is."

"You have more support than you can imagine. And besides, you can't get into more trouble than you already are," Jim said as he got ready. "What are they going to do? Send you to Vietnam."

MAC-V's disbursing office was in chaos. During the Tet Offensive records were destroyed at various bases and money was stolen by either the VC or American soldiers. The disbursing personnel looked to be of the geek variety. They wore new greens, flak jackets and helmets. Some wore side arms and their M-16 rifles were leaning in the corners. There were no magazines in the weapons or signs of ammunition. The weapons looked new. Possibly they'd never been fired, and if they had, probably not by this bunch.

Jim asked to speak with LtCol. McKenzie. While we waited I looked around the office. I asked a nervous private, "Where are your magazines and ammunition?"

"The Army has it all. They said we can have a bullet when the danger passes," the private answered. I wanted to remind him it was a round, not a bullet, but what was the point?

The colonel showed up and escorted us to his office. He gave me a quizzical look, like he didn't believe who I was. Jim showed him the MPC. The colonel opened a thick book of tabulated numbers. "I got a message from Commander Pierce. Seems you guys have been through a lot," the colonel said as he thumbed through the pages. "This book has all the blocks of serial numbers of printed MPC and to whom it was distributed." He came to an abrupt stop. "I don't believe it."

Jim asked, "What is it?"

"This money was printed for SARA," the colonel stated.

"What's that," I asked.

"SARA is the Strategic Action Reserve Account. It's an account for special operations, black ops, and such. The money is used for paying informants, buying unauthorized equipment, things like that," the colonel stated.

"Could it be used to hire a special helicopter for prisoner preparation for interrogation?" I asked. Jim gave me an exasperated look.

"I suppose so, what's that?" the colonel asked.

"Never mind her," Jim asked a more practical question. "Do you have any paper work showing who authorized the MPC to be printed and distributed?"

"Well, who it was distributed to is always a secret. But let me see if I can find the work-order for the printing." The colonel left for about 10 minutes.

The colonel returned with a form, "This is the work-order. It came from the Defense Department. Once they get funding for the MPC they send us a work-order and the MPC is printed here in Saigon."

He passed it to Jim. I looked over his shoulder. "Give me that," I grabbed the order. My name was signed as the authorizing authority, but it wasn't my hand writing. "That's my name."

"You authorized the printing of this MPC? Who gave you authority to print MPC for the Defense Department?" Jim asked.

"No, of course I didn't have authority to print MPC, but I recognize the hand writing," I stated. "I'm sure I know who signed this."

"Well, who is it? Don't keep us in suspense," Jim asked.

"My boss; I would recognize his hand writing anywhere," I said.

"Do you need anything else?" the colonel asked.

Jim answered for the both of us as I was still in shock. "No, you've been a great help."

The colonel got the duty driver to take us back to the Victoria Hotel.

Back at the hotel we took a warm beer to the roof top. Nobody was around except a Vietnamese waiter who was sleeping in the corner. With little to offer in the way of food, business was slow. And besides, everyone was at their duty station standing by for the next attack. My presence discouraged the working women from soliciting Jim for a 'numba one boom boom.'

"I suspect a black market. I'm sure that's what's going on. Think about it, Susan. There are dozens of packs of MPC buried in that pile of shit. This wasn't to pay off some informant. There must be a million dollars' worth of MPC buried in there. And what has your boss got to do with this? He's not involved in covert operations over here. At least I wouldn't imagine he would be, and the Presidential election is this year. He's raising money for the President on the MPC black market, isn't he? If the Republicans got hold of this information or the press, the President's campaign would be toast," Jim stated. "That's why they are killing everyone who could expose them." I guessed Jim wasn't so dumb after all. He figured it out.

"You're losing me. Okay, let's say you're right. Explain to me how the President's campaign can make money in Vietnam in a black market using MPC?" I needed to understand this.

"The MPC black market has been going on for years." Jim started, "The military uses MPC in Vietnam and Korea to keep American currency from the Communist. Servicemen aren't allowed to have American greenbacks in-country. When entering Vietnam we exchange our American dollars for MPC, and our monthly pay is in MPC. When we leave Vietnam we exchange our MPC back to American dollars."

"I know all that," I said to keep the explanation moving.

"Okay, MPC is what we use to buy cameras, liquor, and stereos at the exchange. But Communists understand capitalism better than we do. They accept MPC as payment for prostitution, drugs, black market alcohol, etcetera. Then the VC turns around and exchanges the MPC that prostitute Ay Suc Yu earned, back to the servicemen for the soldier's American dollars at a rate of two MPC for one U.S. greenback."

I interrupted, "How does the VC exchange money with servicemen. Aren't you guys shooting at each other?"

"The cleaning lady, the bartender, the waiter, there's a lot of contact between the VC and Americans that doesn't involve shooting. Prostitution is a good example except it usually results in a shot of penicillin in the ass with a large bore needle. Hey, didn't you buy a party pack of marijuana?"

"I may have, but I will deny it in court?" I mentioned.

"See, you have contributed to the Communist effort to overthrow the Capitalistic pigs. By the way, since your money may get back to the President's re-election campaign you can take it as a tax deduction. Of course you got a receipt for the pot, didn't you?" Wasn't he funny?

186

"She couldn't have been a Communist," I declared. "And besides I paid her in American dollars."

"Then you should have gotten twenty marijuana cigarettes, two party packs. You're an easy touch," Jim smirked.

"But she was so nice."

"Forget it. The President's black market must be making millions. With a free source of MPC from the secret SARA account all they needed was somebody to manage the show. It is pure profit."

"So let me get this straight. The men and women the President sends over here to fight his war, based on some dubious Tonkin Gulf Resolution, are sacrificing their lives while inadvertently financing his re-election," I stated.

"That about sums it up," Jim said.

"One more question, how do servicemen get American dollars to exchange for two times the MPC if you exchange all your dollars for MPC when entering Vietnam?

"There are a lot of ways. The most common is to buy a friend a watch or camera at the exchange using MPC and send it to him in the States. And have him send back American dollars. The friend gets a good deal. Nikon cameras, Sansui stereos, Rolex watches are a lot cheaper over here than at home. There's a risk when mailing cash, but the payoff of getting twice the MPC in return for the American dollar makes the deal worthwhile.

The serviceman goes to his friendly VC contact, who may be inadvertently working for the President's re-election campaign, and exchanges the American dollars for twice the MPC. With the extra MPC the serviceman can either keep buying items for friends or go to the airport and exchange MPC for American dollars with newly arriving servicemen. The new guys don't know about the MPC black market yet and how valuable their American greenbacks are. The FNGs are standing in line at the bank, about to pass out from the heat, when a GI comes up and offers to exchange his MPC for their American money. The GI says he is going home and doesn't want to stand in line to turn his MPC back into

187

American dollars. So the stupid FNG exchanges his American dollars for MPC, one for one." "And an FNG is?" I knew I shouldn't ask. Think Susan think, there must be a dirty word in there somewhere.

"Fucking new guy," Jim said. Of course, how obvious.

"Did you ever exchange MPC on the black market?"¬

"You said one more question. Besides, that's not important. What's important is we get our sample of the captured MPC back to the States and get it to the proper authorities," Jim said. "They can investigate the serial numbers, track down who really authorized it, and put your boss, and TJ in jail. Does that upset you, I mean about your boss?"

"I'm surprised about him and I suppose disappointed. This was going on right under my nose. It just goes to show, we have to question authority. By the way who are the proper authorities? The President could be involved," I said.

"We have to think about that."

Chapter 23

The next attack on Saigon never came. There was still sporadic street fighting and tensions ran high. For three days we were cooped up in that hot hotel eating C-rations and drinking warm Black Label beer with the formaldehyde aftertaste. The SEALs rooming with us left the second day. They were heading to Nha Be in the Rung Sat Special Zone, a hot area according to them. The boys called it Knobber Be because of a certain acrobatic sex act a girl performed. One of the boys described the act to me. Conceptually I thought it physically impossible. There's no way I could have gotten into that position without dislocating my hips. Anyway, I found it vile and disgusting, and I don't know why I'd digressed to the point of getting into conversations with those boys about such subjects. It must have been the boredom and beer.

After the Nha Be boys left I found the beans with frankfurters chunks in tomato sauce to be the best C-ration along with the fruit cocktail. And all the while the SEALs were there all I got were the lima beans and ham, tuna fish, and ham and egg chopped.

We finally got on the plane for Hong Kong. I was beginning to believe I would never leave Vietnam. "Do you feel that?" I asked Jim.

"Feel what?"

"Air-conditioning, American made air-conditioning. Have you ever felt anything so lovely?" I swooned. I don't think I'd ever paid attention to air-conditioning until I lacked it. I never wanted to leave that plane. Everyone on the plane told their story of Tet, about how they cheated death.

Upon arriving in Hong Kong, Jim made flight reservations for San Francisco, continuing on to Detroit. It would be two days before we could fly. My trust fund was taking a serious hit buying airline tickets at the last moment.

"Why Michigan?" I asked.

All Jim would say was, "For Dan's funeral. We need to be there."

"We have to be in Michigan before they inter the body," Jim said. It seemed mysterious to me.

We got quite the look when we walked into the Peninsula Hotel. It took me some time to convince them who I was and that I'd stored my luggage with the Bell Captain, and some tailored clothes should have arrived. Reluctantly they gave us a room when I paid cash in advance. The first thing I wanted to do was take a warm bath. Hot water as hot as I could stand, another luxury I took for granted from my previous life.

When I walked into the bathroom I gave a casual glance in the mirror. I froze and looked again. I hadn't seen myself in a full length mirror in Vietnam. There were no such mirrors in Saigon, Binh Thuy, or Rach Gia. I looked behind me to see who was in the mirror. I didn't recognize myself. I was a lot tanner. I wasn't surprised by that, but I looked 10 years older. And then I realized why, it was my eyes. The eyes I saw on those boys when I first arrived in Saigon. I was one of them. I'd seen the shit as they liked to say. That's what alarmed the nurses in Binh Thuy when I returned from Rach Gia. I wasn't Susan England, St. Louis debutante. I was a creature of war, of combat. Those words are so casually tossed about by people who don't have a clue of what combat does to people.

The bath felt wonderful. I put on one of my new skirts and blouses. They were two sizes too large. The fittings at the tailor had been perfect. The bit of flab around my waist and thighs was gone. I should also mention my boobs were smaller, the first thing to suffer with weight loss. Not that there was that much to lose in the first place. My legs showed svelte muscle definition. My skin was smooth and tight. I didn't need lotions and only a little lipstick did the trick. I wouldn't recommend combat in Vietnam and a diet of salamander for a health spa, but it worked wonders for me. My face looked 10 years older, but my body looked and felt 10 years younger. You can't have everything.

Jim gave me an engaging smile. He was wearing one of his new sport jackets I had picked out for him. He looked great. For the last month he'd seen me in blue jeans and t-shirts. He'd washed out my soiled clothes, cleaned out my bucket when I was sick, and bathed me. I won't describe the smells he endured. I accepted his smile as him forgiving me. I got the impression he wanted me. I wanted him. I didn't want him to realize that.

Jim asked, "You want to get something to eat?"

I answered in the affirmative, "Yes, a steak and baked potato and fresh milk and chocolate cake and three vodka martinis and……."

"Okay, okay, let's go to the San Francisco Steak House and see what they can do," Jim said as he took my arm.

My eyes were bigger than my stomach. I ate half of what I ordered except the martinis. After drinking one of those and I was blitzed. For the first time in a long time I felt relaxed. The martini must have drugged me because I started asking Jim questions I normally wouldn't. Questions like, "Why don't you ever talk about a girl? Your friends never seem to talk about anything else."

"That's easy, I don't have a girlfriend," Jim answered.

"Are you married?" I thought I should get that out of the way.

"Hardly, do I look married?" Jim answered.

"What does a married man look like?" I slurred.

"Compromised."

"We can discuss that later. So what's the deal? You're not that bad looking. You are no weirder than the average guy. What about Emmy Lou or whatever her name is? When she's old enough to drive I'm sure she'll be over all the time." I was getting a little mean, but it was all in fun.

"Emmy Lou, get serious." A couple of scotches got Jim confessing. "I don't like getting close to people."

"You want to explain that? You don't have to, but I would like to know."

"I had a girlfriend in high school and one or two in college. I thought it was serious, and I think it was for them as well. I don't know, what's love at that age? When I became an enlisted puke the kind of girls I liked wouldn't date me. There's a stigma about being enlisted," Jim said. "I don't care for the tattooed, sluttish type of gal that hangs around sailor bars like the Trade Winds. Not that I'm crazy about debutantes either. Believe it or not, there is an in-between, and if you're not careful you'll

191

slip into that in-between category. It's like a bell shaped curve. Five percent of women are on one end with stuck up noses, and five percent of women are at the other end which are trash. Then there's the 90 percent between each extreme that are decent. It's the same for men."

That was the nicest compliment anyone ever paid me, that I was a decent person. "Before you go on, let me clarify something. I didn't know you went to college."

"I graduated from the University of Missouri. I was soon to be drafted into the Army. I was afraid they would send me to Vietnam so I joined the Navy."

"Why didn't you become an officer?"

"The Navy recruiter told me I had to enlist first and then I would be picked up for OCS or Officer Candidate School. Of course that was a lie. The recruiter was filling his quota and couldn't have cared less about a college graduate becoming an officer. He probably delighted in the fact of screwing a college grad," Jim explained.

"Yeah right, well you showed them about going to Vietnam, didn't you?" I goaded. "Go on about the not wanting to get close to people."

"You saw it in Rach Gia with Dan being killed. When somebody close gets killed it tears you apart. The closer you are the more it hurts. If you're in a serious relationship, and it falls apart it's the same thing, something dies inside you. I don't like that feeling so I don't get close to people," Jim reasoned.

"But then you lose your sense of feeling, your capacity for love," I argued.

"I know, but the last couple of years there have been a lot of feelings dying, maybe all of them," Jim said.

I didn't know how to respond to that so I didn't. I nursed my drink. We sat in silence for what seemed a long time. Eventually Jim said, "I guess we ought to go."

There was one more subject I wanted to broach. The girl-boy relationships were easy compared to what was really bothering me. I wanted to talk to Jim about taking another's life. There was a Vietnamese boy who would never be with his family again, he would never go home to his mother, he would never enjoy the warmth of a woman, have the satisfaction of raising a family, growing old, and it was because of me, because I killed him.

On the walk back to the Peninsula I took Jim's arm. I wanted to be close to him. I hoped it wasn't out of pity. Maybe I was challenging myself to see if I could restore feelings to his life and redeem mine. And worst of all, I hoped I wasn't trying to rectify my own failed relationships. I knew my relationship in Washington, D.C. was finished. I wasn't jumping from one man to the next. After Vietnam I was a different person. I planned when we got into bed I was going to get close to Jim and we were going to have that serious talk about life and death, and love and hate, and then we were going to make love.

Chapter 24

As I entered the room I noticed my suitcase was on the bed. It wasn't there when we left. Then I noticed my clothes on the floor. I got a sinking feeling. Jim was also looking around when he was shoved from behind, and the door slammed. The lights flashed on. I turned to stare down the barrel of a very large hand gun. I backed into the room hiding behind Jim who was also backing away from the weapon. All I could do was stare at that gun. Then I looked up and recognized TJ. "Sit," he ordered.

Neither of us spoke. The room was a mess. All of our clothes and personal belongings were scattered. TJ motioned with his weapon for us to sit on the chairs by the window. Jim looked scared and confused. "So you two have been to Vietnam? And found this." TJ was holding the MPC. Jim had brought two thousand dollars of MPC with us to use as evidence. Now TJ was holding what I needed to vindicate myself. I don't know what I was more despondent over, TJ holding a gun on me, or him holding the MPC. Then I thought about dying. I was going to die in a hotel room in Hong Kong.

"Now what I need to know is where you have hidden the rest of the MPC? I'm not a patient man. I'm not here to play games. If you tell me, it will make my life and yours easier. If you don't, I'll find it eventually and you two can say your goodbyes to each other right now." I took that as a threat.

"It's about 10 klicks from the MAC-V base at Rach Gia. Chief Petty Officer Henderson is down there. He can show you where it is," Jim volunteered. I glared at Jim. How could he tell TJ where the MPC was?

"I'm going down there. If I don't recover the rest of the MPC I'll hunt you two down like the dogs you are. Once I made the mistake of eliminating some people before I knew where the money was. I'm not making that mistake again. There's nowhere on earth you can hide," TJ stated. He got up and walked backwards toward the door, keeping the weapon trained on us. "Oh by the way, your friend the nurse in Salinas,

Kansas, it seems her memories of Vietnam were too much to cope with and she overdosed on sleeping pills. Don't go far now, I'll be back. SEAL Team, what a bunch of pussies." TJ smirked at Jim as he left.

"How could you tell him where the money was? Why didn't you stop him? Your buddies keep talking about how tough you SEALs are. Why didn't you jump up and karate kick him in the nuts or something?" I screamed. "You didn't mind picking on a drunk, weakling doctor in Binh Thuy."

Jim was chaining and bolting the door, "Was that TJ?"

"Hell yes that was TJ. Who do you think it was the Easter bunny?" I mocked. "How did he find us?"

"Passport control, you signing traveler checks, credit cards who knows? When you disappeared he figured you were going after the money. He's been tracking us. He followed us to Kansas. We need to get to Michigan before he gets back from Rach Gia," Jim said as he started picking up our clothes.

"What's in Michigan?" I asked.

"Dan's funeral, I told you we have to get there before he's interred," Jim repeated. "Once TJ recovers the MPC he'll be after us. He left us alive in case he doesn't recover the MPC. We are his insurance. That's the mistake he made with the four SEALs. He assumed the SEALs brought the MPC back to their hootch. He probably didn't have time to search their hut so he booby trapped it. After he killed them he thought he would find the MPC among the ruins. When the MPC wasn't there, he couldn't get the intelligence or the support to go looking for it like we did. He let us do his work for him. Once he has the money we are dead meat."

"I got Emily and her baby killed, didn't I? And now Dan and Teresa."

"Don't dwell on that. That's past history. TJ lucked out with you tracking down the MPC for him," Jim said.

As one could imagine, there was no love making that night. TJ ruined the mood. I was so upset I couldn't sleep. I couldn't stop thinking about Teresa. She was dead because of me. TJ was tracking us the whole time. He knew our every move and let us do his dirty work. This whole trip was to recover the documents and now they were gone. Not only were they gone, but a crazy man possessed them, and someday he was going to hunt me down and kill me. Even if I got back to the States alive without the evidence, who was going to believe me? And Jim wanted to go to Michigan. I didn't know where I wanted to go, someplace where TJ couldn't find me. I wondered if I could become a cloistered nun in Switzerland. What was their policy on virginity?

I calmed down. I was still mad at Jim for not stomping TJ's ass and upset about Teresa and Dan. For the next couple of days, Jim and I toured Hong Kong and Kowloon. We had more clothes made by Indian tailors. Believing that TJ was in Vietnam, we were able to relax. We were the consummate American tourists, shopping, eating out, and sightseeing.

In the evenings, after dinner, we would go to touristy night clubs for a few drinks and dancing. Jim didn't like to dance. I never lacked partners with the American, British, and Australian sailors in port. What was it with men that they think embellishing on war stories will impress young ladies? I mean okay, they've been to war I was impressed with that, and I appreciated their service to their countries. But hearing endless tales about an aircraft carrier on Yankee Station for 90 days and loading bombs on planes 16 hours a day gets a bit boring. Convince me you own a 150 foot yacht, a private jet, a chalet in Provence, and a 100 acre horse farm in Maryland then maybe we can chat. Every sailor asked me to go back to his hotel with him and more than once a fight nearly broke out with Jim having to intervene.

I should have started off every conversation with, 'I greased a gook last week. What did you say you did on your ship?'

He held my hand when we walked, but I could feel a hesitation. I knew he wasn't ready to start a relationship. Once we got back to the States I needed to find employment. I doubted I could get a favorable reference from the White House. Whatever job I got most likely wouldn't last long with TJ on the prowl. I keep mentioning TJ because that was all I could think of, him and Teresa.

196

I was anxious to get back to the States. I would feel more in control. There was still so much unknown. How could I make all this go away?

If TJ recovered the money and I dropped out of sight and never mentioned the word black market, wouldn't that be enough? I knew now I would never live the life I'd envisioned for myself. I wouldn't be able to see my friends or go home. I was going to start a new life. Maybe I could become a Buddhist monk in Tibet. I liked the mountains. Did they ski? What were their views on alcohol?

Jim startled me, "We have to fly to Toronto. TJ gave us the answer, passport control. They'll be looking for us at a U.S. port of entry. If we fly to Canada we stand a better chance."

Chapter 25

We landed in Toronto. I slept most of the way. I didn't want to face reality. We rented a car and started driving toward Windsor where we planned to cross the border late at night, hoping the person on duty wouldn't be attentive.

I could tell Jim was anxious. While in Vietnam I only wanted to stay alive. I cared for, and worried about the men I was with, and they cared for me. I came to understand they would do anything for each other. Flag, country, whatever didn't matter; they were fighting for each other.

Survival was all that was on my mind while being mortared in Binh Thuy during the Tet Offensive. That's what the news was calling the country wide attacks during Tet. Now that I was back in North America I started thinking about the mess I'd left behind. Like where was my car, and what happened to my townhouse and personal belongings? It struck me that when I was close to death I didn't fret about the material things. I was grateful to have a warm beer and a C-ration, even if it was the lima beans and ham. Before I left the States I would send back a drink or salad if it wasn't to my liking. Now I realized how unappreciative I'd been.

I always wanted to be safe and secure like anyone else. The safer I was when cloistered in Ladue, the bitchier I got. With death surrounding me in Vietnam the more helpful and cooperative I became. Maybe that was my problem. Maybe that was everyone's problem; security breeds a intolerance, a 'me first' attitude, and indifference.

With a sense of security one lets down their guard, becomes complacent, and lacks situational awareness. Ideological wanderings give rise to a sense of entitlement and elitism. With little real stress in one's life, one creates artificial stressors. For instance, what shoes to wear, or a stain on a new blouse, or a bad hair day. Worrying about being killed, or if you'll be able to get food and water is stress. In the U.S. idle people worry about the environment and if the air is clean enough. In Vietnam people worried if they had seen their last sunrise.

Jim asked me, on the slim chance we survived this, what my plans were. I told him I hadn't given it much thought. "Before all this started I planned to go back to graduate school for business, or maybe even law school. Lately I thought I was going to get married first. But that's out of the picture now."

"Why's that?" he asked.

I didn't want to tell Jim this, but it was going to come out sooner or later. "Remember in Saigon I told you I recognized the handwriting that signed my name on the work orders to print the MPC? That it was my boss's writing."

"Yes, what about it?" Jim asked.

"Well, he wasn't only my boss." Now I'd done it.

"Okay, so you were sleeping with the boss. Was this the guy you thought you were going to marry?" Jim had a disappointed look on his face.

But he deserved to know the truth. "Yes, and that's not all. Not only was he 10 years my senior, which isn't terrible, but he was married with children." Jim didn't respond. I knew he hated me. I got as far from him as possible. I squeezed against the car door. Should I just open it and end it all?

We made it across the border with just our driver's licenses as proof of citizenship. We drove towards Dan Beck's farm in silence.

Before I killed myself I thought I should ask, "What are your plans after serving 10 to life for killing innocent civilians in Vietnam and going AWOL?"

"I've been accepted to UCLA's Anderson School of Management for graduate school," Jim answered.

"You have? I'm sorry. I don't mean to sound so shocked, but you never told me you planned to go to grad school."

"The acceptance letter was in the mail just before we left San Diego. I hope to get out of the Navy in April. I was going to travel a little then go to school and then who knows. I still have the bogus murder rap to face and explain why I went to Vietnam with a crazy lady."

So he had a plan. I felt envious. My life was in ruins and he was going to grad school. I didn't know where I was going. I sat in silence. Once we were out of Detroit it got pitch black driving in rural Michigan.

"What are our plans now?" I asked.

"The funeral first, then we'll make plans. We'll know in a day or two. I don't want to get your hopes up, but there may be a chance of stopping TJ from killing you." That's all Jim would say. Any hope, even if it was false hope, was welcomed after Vietnam.

Chapter 26

Even with the car heater on full blast I was cold. It got cold in St. Louis and it got plenty cold in Northampton, Massachusetts in college, but Michigan in February was ridiculous. Once we cleared Detroit we drove about another hour then pulled into a cheap motel. The room was cold and smelled. I didn't dare take a shower in the morning. The water never got close to being warm. I promised myself to never complain again after Vietnam, but here I was complaining.

It's stereotypical to say that people who live in the country give confusing directions, but it took us over half a day to find Beck's farm. I could tell Jim was irritated and to the point of punching out the next schmuck who told him to turn right where the old school house used to be. It was getting dark when we drove up to the two story white wood framed farmhouse. A bare light bulb dimly lit the front porch.

When Jim knocked on the door, a dog started barking. A slight middle aged woman opened the front door while wiping her hands on an apron. She wore a simple house dress. Her graying hair was pulled back in a bun. Jim introduced us, "Mrs. Beck? I'm Jim Crotty, one of Dan's teammates, and this is Susan England, one of Dan's close friends. We were with him in Vietnam and the Teams sent me to be an honor guard. I'm sorry we didn't call ahead and for arriving at such a late hour, but we got lost."

There was an awkward moment of silence. I stood behind Jim freezing. I didn't know what Mrs. Beck's reaction would be. Would she go berserk and yell at us to leave, or would she collapse in a heap? Instead she stared at us for what seemed a long time. Then her eyes began tearing, she opened the storm door and pulled Jim in by the hand. The black Lab sniffed us to make sure we didn't have any hostile intent or maybe he was looking for food. "Come in out of the cold. Robert some of Dan's friends are here."

Dan's dad, Robert, was a big man wearing a flannel shirt under his coveralls. Jim shook his hand saying, "I'm sorry for your loss, sir. Dan was a great teammate."

Dan's dad said in a husky voice, "Come in the living room. Have a seat. I want to talk to you. I want to know what really happened. The officer who came to notify us of Dan's death didn't know squat."

We walked into the living room where there was a television and a comfortable fire. Mrs. Beck said, "Now Robert, you promised not to get excited." She turned to us, "It's his heart. The doctor told him not to get worked up."

"Never mind my heart. I want to know how my son died. Were you with him?" Mr. Beck went over to a desk and pulled out a few envelopes. "This is all we've gotten," he said while shaking the envelopes at Jim. "A letter from a Lieutenant Commander Pierce saying Dan died while supporting an operation fighting Communist insurgents in South Vietnam. That sounds like bureaucratic bullshit to me. Here's a letter from the President of the United States with nothing about Dan. I'm sure it's a form letter. With 200 boys dying every week in Vietnam I doubt the President sits down and writes 30 some letters a day. He probably hears the body counts and yawns. I tell you if I ever got my hands on that son of a bitch."

"Now Robert, your heart," Mrs. Beck interrupted.

Mr. Beck waved her off, "Shush woman."

Jim spoke, "I was on the operation with Dan when he died. We had intelligence about secret documents the enemy was holding. The operation was to recover those documents. We captured them and were being pursued by the Viet Cong as we extracted. Dan was our rear security. He kept the enemy pinned down until we were all safely aboard the boat. As he was getting on he got shot in the back."

"Weren't you guys covering Dan getting on the boat?" accused Mr. Beck.

"Yes, of course we were. The boat took over twenty hits on our extraction," Jim said. Mr. Beck looked down.

"Would you two like something to drink," offered Mrs. Beck.

Jim shook his head, but I said, "Water would be nice."

"Have you had your supper?" Mrs. Beck asked.

I said, "We didn't have time to stop and eat."

"I'll fix you a little something." Mrs. Beck got up and left.

Mr. Beck still had his head bowed. Jim said, "Dan died fighting. He didn't suffer. You can be very proud of your son." It seemed Jim was saying things he thought Mr. Beck would want to hear.

"Dan was my only boy. Do you understand what that means out here? Of course you don't. They won't even pay his death benefits or serviceman's life insurance. They say his pay records have been put on administrative hold. Something about him owing money to the government." Mr. Beck got up and without looking at us went upstairs. Jim and I looked at each other not knowing what to say or do.

I asked Jim, "Do you think they are holding up his benefits because of the barroom brawl in Binh Thuy?"

"I'm sure that's it. That's the way the government works, always nickel and diming the little guy, even somebody who gave their life for their country," Jim answered.

"I recall a Senator's brother getting a half million dollar grant to study air quality in Buzzard Breath, Wyoming or someplace. There's never a hang up with those people getting money." I was so disappointed with my government.

After a few minutes Mrs. Beck called us to the dining room. She'd warmed up meat loaf, string beans, and mashed potatoes. There was homemade bread, butter, and a pitcher of milk. "You'll have to excuse Robert. This has been very hard on him. It's getting towards his bed time. He needs to get up early and get busy with the chores."

We ate in silence. Jim said, "Thank you for dinner. I hate to bring it up, but have Dan's remains arrived?"

"The funeral home called and said Dan should be here tomorrow. The body has been in San Francisco. There was a mix-up of some sort, but everything is straightened out now," Mrs. Beck said.

"Do you want him dressed in his uniform?" Jim asked.

"Yes, if you think it would be alright. He was so proud to be a SEAL. That's all he talked about," Mrs. Beck said. "I'll give you directions to the funeral home if you want to go over there tomorrow."

Jim said, "Yes, I would very much like to go over there. We should get going. I know you have to get up early."

I added, "Yes, the dinner was wonderful. Let us help with the dishes. Can you give us directions to a motel?"

"I will not hear of it. You two are staying here," insisted Mrs. Beck.

"We couldn't impose. You didn't know we were coming," I said.

"Nonsense, Susan you'll stay in Dan's room and Jim we'll put you down here on the sofa," Mrs. Beck said. "In the morning you'll meet Sally, our 18 year old senior in high school. Come with me and I'll show you to your room and where the bathroom is." Mrs. Beck got up. "I'll find some clean towels for you."

'The bathroom, as if in one,' was I going to have to share a bathroom with four other people, three of them total strangers? In Binh Thuy I shared a bathroom with a lot of nurses. In Rach Gia I shared an outhouse with over twenty guys. In Saigon I shared a bathroom with a bunch of SEALs in the hotel. Somehow that seemed more appropriate. "Let's get the table cleared." I started picking up dishes. Jim got the hint and joined me.

"Leave it, we'll come back down and have pie," Mrs. Beck said. 'Have pie,' I couldn't eat another bite. We went up creaky stairs and down a narrow hardwood floor hallway. Dan's room consisted of a single bed against a wall and a small dresser, and mirror that looked like they came by covered wagon. There was space for one straight backed chair. The one window had venetian blinds. And the closet was the width of the door. I soaked it in.

I walked over to the dresser. There was a picture of Dan and a girl in formal wear, probably a high school prom.

Mrs. Beck caught me looking at the picture, "That's Kelly, Dan's girlfriend at their senior prom. You'll meet her soon."

Dan looked so young and out of place in a tux. I'd only seen him in combat gear or the khaki shorts. There was a varsity letter with a football embroidered on it along with other pictures. One was of a pig, one of a car, and several of small groups of kids holding beer cans. Across the top of the mirror were labels of various beer brands.

I remembered Dan talking about training and the crazy things these guys did to make the Teams. I'm sure he felt he'd accomplished something worthwhile. And if one died doing something they thought worthwhile then they had lived an honorable life.

It was eerie being in Dan's room and looking at his personal life. There had been many a night we sat up playing cards talking about home. He told me about the farm and his girl and goals in life. Coming face to face with Dan's life made it that much sadder.

Jim got our luggage as I couldn't face the cold one more second. We did have a piece of cherry pie. I got the impression it was a misdemeanor in Michigan if one didn't have pie after every meal, same with Kansas.

The next morning, well before sunrise, I was awakened by the commotion of early risers. The bare wood floors creaked with Mr. Beck's heavy foot falls. I smelled breakfast, sausage, coffee, biscuits, and pancakes. I was so cozy I didn't want to get out of bed. "Get your lazy ass out of there," was the morning greeting from Jim.

"It's dark outside, the wind is blowing. Come back in an hour." I rolled over.

Jim came over and sat on the edge of the bed. He started rubbing my back, "Mrs. Beck wants to clean up."

"Oh, alright," I said, kicking off the comforter. I was wearing Jim's SEAL Team blue sweatpants and hooded sweatshirt. The bathroom was available since everybody else was long gone. I could not believe how cold my feet were on the bathroom's tiled floor. I missed meeting Sally who had already left for school.

After an enormous breakfast and a small sliver of pie we went searching for the funeral home. It was 10 miles to town with a lot of twists and turns on country roads. The funeral director told Jim that Dan's body had arrived the evening before. Jim asked if he could help with Dan's uniform. The director said no, his staff would prepare the body. Jim said there was a certain way the uniform was to be worn. The funeral director assured Jim he could inspect the body before the family viewing. Then Jim told the funeral director that there was a knapsack with personal effects in the transfer case that he would like to take back to the Becks. I could tell by Jim's uneasiness that there had been ulterior motives for seeing the body.

Jim was very anxious. It must have been over half an hour before the funeral director came out with the knapsack. I knew something wasn't right. Jim seemed relieved when the director gave him the knapsack.

The director told us there would be a private visitation for the immediate family that evening and there would be a visitation for friends and family the next evening with the funeral the following morning. Back in the car Jim asked me if I wanted to eat lunch in town so as not to bother the Becks. I was curious about the knapsack, "What's in the bag?"

Jim was hesitant, "You might as well know. I hope it's what I put in there." He pulled the knapsack from the back seat and opened it. Out came hundreds of 20 dollar MPC notes. "Dan had one last mission, and that was to bring home the evidence."

"That's why you didn't want Dan's body shipped out of Binh Thuy until you arrived?" I asked. "And that's why you insisted on coming to Michigan."

"You got it," Jim said.

"I don't know what to say," I said. "On one hand I'm glad all is not lost, but on the other hand I feel terrible. You used Dan's coffin to smuggle evidence."

"I paid the guy at grave's registration 1000 MPC to let me hide the money in Dan's aluminum transfer box." I thought that was terrible. Jim said the graves registration guy would turn the MPC into 500 U.S. dollars on the black market at the two MPC for one American dollar rate. He would buy five Rolex watches from the Gook who steals them off the pier in Saigon. Then he would sell them to a fence in Detroit for 500 dollars apiece. The fence sells them for 900 bucks and the buyer still gets a good deal. He made $2,500 of tax free money for turning his back for a moment. That's a lot of moolah for an E-1 buck private. No telling how much stuff he's taken off dead bodies.

"You're a cynic," I said

"I'm a realist," responded Jim.

"Don't tell the Becks. I hope the funeral director didn't look in the knapsack. If he did, we could be in trouble. This business is going to get a lot uglier before it gets better," Jim said.

"Please don't remind me," I responded. "Let's get something to eat." We found a diner. If I ever felt like a creature from outer space, it was in that diner. Was it what I was wearing? I didn't know, but those people made me feel more uncomfortable than the men in Vietnam. They should put a sign in the window, 'outsiders not welcome.' We ate pie so as not to offend anyone.

Jim and I didn't go to the immediate family viewing. We didn't feel it was our place. The way Mr. Beck reacted the previous evening we felt it was best to let him have a private moment with his son.

The next evening was the visitation or wake for family and friends. Mrs. Beck introduced me to Kelly, Dan's girlfriend. She wasn't what I expected. She was cute enough and dressed like she thought a city girl would dress with her makeup and hair being overdone. But, what bothered me was that she had a prickly edge. She wasn't grieving like I expected, but rather gave an attitude of, 'I've got better things to do.' In Vietnam when speaking with Dan I got the impression that he and Kelly hadn't done the dirty deed, but this little tramp looked like she'd done plenty of dirty deeds.

Women can tell these things. I didn't like her and wanted Dan to know she was no good. What was I talking about? Dan wasn't going to know anything ever again.

Before the public entered, the family held a memorial service. There were a lot of uncles, aunts, and cousins. A minister talked of Dan's childhood, his 4-H activities, hobbies, athletics, church, and I cringed when he mentioned Kelly. He acknowledged Dan died serving his country and that he was a Navy gunner's mate. That was his Navy rating, but that's not who Dan was. He was a Navy SEAL, and people should know that.

I could have done a better job having only known Dan for a short time. I would have spoken of his goals in life, his apprehensions, his wanting to marry Kelly and start a family. I would have talked about his quirky personality, gullible to say the least. But mostly I would have dwelled on his character, his trustworthiness, his willingness to sacrifice his life for his teammates, which he did. When I was sick, he and Jim were the ones who stood by me. Nobody could have asked for a better or more loyal friend.

Jim stood next to the open coffin and shook people's hands as mourners passed. I could not look at Dan. I may have been the last person to touch him while he was still alive, my lips on his. People asked Jim questions like what were we doing in Vietnam, and why were our boys dying in vain. Jim gave the party line. Up to that point I hadn't talked to Jim about his views on the war, but I don't think he was convinced our nation was doing the right thing. I certainly wasn't.

But after being over there, I understood the sacrifice the men and women were making to their comrades. I blamed the self-serving politicians for the Vietnam fiasco. And to think the President was using the Vietnam War to make money on the black market to finance his re-election campaign, and murdering anyone who got in his way. That included my best friend from work, and poor Dan Beck, a young kid.

I met Sally, Dan's sister. She was a pleasant enough girl. She seemed bewildered that her only brother was dead. She looked lost. Everyone was nice. Homey would be the proper adjective which wasn't meant to be a slight, it's just the way those people were. I saw people who were in the diner the day before. Now that they understood who Jim and I were they couldn't have been nicer.

The crowd started dwindling after an hour or so. The funeral parlor was still packed, but more people were leaving than arriving. I felt conspicuous being introduced by Jim as representing the administration. People treated me nice, but suspiciously. I asked Jim if I could take the car and go back to the farm. I believed I could find my way. I was tired and didn't know anyone. He gave me the keys. Walking to the car I noticed another car's windows were fogged. I thought no one could be making out in this freezing weather, and at a wake, no less. What kind of cretin would do that? As I walked past the car there were two bare feet pressed against the window. The car was rocking rhythmically and I'm sure I heard the appropriate groans that go along with unbridled sex. I rushed back to the wake and asked Mrs. Beck if she'd seen Kelly.

"The poor dear has a terrible headache from all the emotion. She left a while ago." As I passed the passion wagon on my way back to our car I recognized the profile of Kelly's face lighting a cigarette. I hated that little bitch.

Daniel F. Beck, United States Navy, 1948-1968 was chiseled into the headstone. It was a crystal clear, bitter cold morning in central Michigan. A color guard from the local Marine reserve unit was standing by in their dress blues. The rising sun glistened off their brass buckles and buttons. I'd never been to a military funeral. Emotions welled inside me. This seemed more than I could handle. Dan Beck died because he got into a barroom brawl in Binh Thuy, resulting in him 'volunteering' for a special operation in Rach Gia that was ordered because of my suspicions. We possessed the evidence that may never see the light of day. Even if it did, was it worth Dan's life? Of course it wasn't.

There was a row of folding chairs along one side of the grave. Mr. and Mrs. Beck sat center with Sally next to Mrs. Beck. Kelly, the whore, got the place of honor next to Mr. Beck. Other family members sat on chairs behind the immediate family. Close friends etcetera, stood on the other side of the grave. I stood in the back, behind the family. I looked for a creep giving Kelly the jealous eye because she was sitting with her dead boyfriend's family. Jim stood at attention at the foot of an American flag draped coffin perched above the grave.

The minister performed a short service. The next events overwhelmed me. The Marines folded the flag from Dan's coffin with crisp military precision. Young Marines with ram-rod straight backs signified, "I will give my life for this flag." They handled the flag with such reverence. A Marine Corps Captain presented the flag on bended knee to Mrs. Beck, "On behalf of a grateful nation." I couldn't hold back the tears.

The gun salute startled me. The rifle shots' echoes crackled through the hills and valleys and as the sound faded, a lone bugler played Taps. There is not a more haunting tune. I don't care what people think of this country, but if they are not moved by the sight of a person being buried who served them, who gave their life so they could live the life they live, then they have no business living here. War is so horrible, so many young lives cut short.

Jim shook hands with the Marines and chatted a while. The camaraderie among combat veterans runs deep. Veterans of previous wars shook Jim's hand, thanking him for his service. I stood in the background. Finally it seemed appropriate to go to his side. I slipped my arm in his. Jim patted my hand. As we left, Jim introduced me to the Marine captain. On the way to the car I buried my face in his shoulder. In the car he took my hand and I scooted next to him. We didn't speak. There were no appropriate words.

The reception was at the VFW hall. A lone bagpiper, in full Scottish regalia, piped the guests in with 'Amazing Grace,' and after everyone downed a few drinks a lady with a beautiful Celtic voice sang, 'Oh Danny Boy'. That was it. Everyone was an emotional wreck after that. There was more drinking, pie eating and stories about Dan. Some laughter broke out. Dan was of German decent, but Scottish bagpipes and Irish whiskey seemed appropriate.

I talked to several people. One man told me the Becks couldn't afford the funeral. The VFW took up a collection and paid for the whole service along with donating their hall for the reception. These were good people.

I looked around; it seemed Kelly was so distraught she couldn't make the reception. She was probably in the backseat of some car doing something to get her mind off her great loss.

Jim and I planned to leave the next morning. I assumed we would fly to St. Louis and I would face my fate. And Jim would continue onto Coronado with the MPC evidence and face his fate.

Back at the farmhouse, after everyone went to bed, I talked with Mrs. Beck. Since I'd arrived it seemed she wanted to speak with me. She appeared to be the strong one. Sally was overwhelmed and Mr. Beck was distraught to the point of being nonfunctional. "This is my fault," Mrs. Beck said. I wanted to let her know it was actually my fault.

"This farm has been in the Beck family for over a century. With Dan taken from us, it will be sold when my husband dies. After Sally was born I couldn't have any more babies. That's why it's my fault."

"You can't blame yourself."

"You don't understand life out here," Mrs. Beck said.

She was right, I didn't. We talked on, but that was the crux of the conversation. I was thinking, in this week alone more than 200 families across the nation would bury a son or daughter, a husband or wife, a brother or sister. Two hundred sons and daughters, each with 1,000 memories, 200 brothers and sisters with hopes and dreams would give their lives in Vietnam. I must have looked distracted when Mrs. Beck asked, "You all right?"

"Yes, I'm sorry. I was thinking of Dan."

"He was a wonderful boy. He got into his share of mischief, but he was my boy," Mrs. Beck said. "You hang onto that man of yours."

"What man?" I asked.

"Don't try to fool me," Mrs. Beck said. "I've watched you and Mr. Crotty."

Up to that point I didn't think of Jim as a long term relationship. I liked him. I wanted to be with him. Well, maybe more than just be with him. We'd become trusting friends, but he didn't fit my mother's drummed in profile of the man I was supposed to take as a lifelong mate, which was rich, important, and socially acceptable.

Jim wasn't close to any of those criteria. But when Mrs. Beck said she saw something between Jim and me it made me realize I had changed in the last four months. Could I, Susan England, beautiful, desired (my words) debutante from St. Louis, Missouri, accept a commoner into my bedroom? Horrors, what would people say?

The next morning at breakfast Jim told the Becks we were leaving for Washington, D.C.

"What?" I couldn't swallow.

Chapter 27

On the plane to Dulles International Jim and I formulated a plan. Well, it was Jim who came up with the original ideas. My responsibility as a woman was to find fault in everything he said. We spoke in hushed tones. No telling who could overhear us. "We need to know where your boss/lover fits in with this black market scheme. I suggest we do a little reconnaissance work before we confront him. We'll watch his apartment for a day or two and see who comes and goes."

"Don't you ever refer to him as my lover again if you know what's good for you." I hoped I made myself clear. "But don't you think we should be upfront about what we know? You know, put him on the defensive." Jim ignored me as men have a proclivity to do. He was going to do it his way and I was being a nuisance, a perfect female/male relationship.

"Once we know who he meets with afterhours we'll know a little more about who is working with him. After that I think you should call him and act as if you know nothing about his involvement. Tell him you have the MPC. Tell him you know it was being used on the black market to raise money for the President's re-election campaign. Say this confirms what Randy told his sister last fall. He'll act concerned like he wants to help catch whomever is illegally raising money. Tell him you are turning it over to the FBI," Jim said. "If he's running the black market he'll want to meet with you privately. If he's not involved he'll want to meet you at the FBI headquarters."

"You think so? I don't know if I feel comfortable with this. I know he's involved. He was signing my name on the MPC printing work orders. He was going to leave me holding the bag if the MPC black market was revealed." I gave the standard female response to let the male know he wasn't so smart. I didn't have a better idea, but if everything went to hell I could always say, 'See, I told you so.' Just like the bureaucrats.

We checked into a motel in Bethesda, Maryland. I didn't want to stay in Washington, D.C. on the off chance of running into somebody I knew. I wanted to call home, but Jim vetoed that idea.

That evening we spied on Mr. Williams' townhouse. It was the middle of February and cold in Georgetown. I wore a winter coat I bought in Michigan. I couldn't have survived there without it. There wasn't much to choose from so I looked like a lumberjack. I had all my Hong Kong clothes to wear which were really nice and up to date.

By the time we got to Bob Williams' townhouse it was dark. We couldn't find a parking place in front of his townhouse which wasn't surprising in Georgetown. We found a spot a few blocks away and took turns watching his front door to spot anyone coming or going. Jim came back from one sojourn saying he spotted a male and female going upstairs. I wondered if his wife was in town.

A parking spot opened up on Bob's street so we moved the rental car. It was a lot more comfortable sitting in the car. We planned to wait until midnight and if there was no activity we'd call it a night. About 11 o'clock the front door opened, a female appeared and headed toward a car. I should have recognized her car when we first arrived. I'd walked by it hundreds of times when going to my townhouse, but that night it didn't register it was hers.

"Are you alright? What is it?" Jim asked.

"No, I'm not alright. Can we go?" I was crying. So many memories came rushing back, so many ugly things. I just wanted to die. We drove back to the motel with me sobbing like an idiot.

Once we got in the room Jim wasn't going to take my mood in stride. "We've been through a lot, you and me. We're not stopping here. What is it? That girl leaving his townhouse upset you. There is something you haven't told me."

"Nothing that concerns you, it's a private matter," I was trapped. I had nowhere to escape, no one to turn to. What was I going to do? Throw Jim out and kill myself. Instead I opened up, "That girl was my roommate." There I said it. Now the recriminations would start and eventually everything would come out, and I would be made to look like the fool I always knew I was.

"So your old roommate is involved. Why does that upset you?" asked Jim.

"Are you blind? Can't you see they're involved? You said they went upstairs," I yelled.

Jim contemplated for a moment, "So both of you were having an affair with your boss?"

"Brilliant Jim, you are so smart. How could I be so stupid?" I just wanted the world to stop. He sat there. Why didn't he speak? I guess he didn't have to. "Okay, but it's not what you think."

"Oh yes it is, the cute girl right out of college getting an important job in the White House. There you are working long hours with the handsome Presidential advisor. Him impressing you to no end with inside knowledge of the President's administration. He was probably going to leave his wife and marry you. Am I leaving anything out? Maybe he drove a Corvette and made you laugh." Jim was going to go on until I screamed.

"Stop it, it was a Mercedes. And yes, he was leaving his wife and we were going to be married after the President was re-elected. Of course I believed him, why wouldn't I? I'm a gullible tramp. There, does that make you happy?" I couldn't look at him.

"No, that doesn't make me happy. I love you." What did he say? "Let me clarify that. I love you as a friend, as a person. I don't want to see you hurt. Now get yourself together, we have work to do." I knew it was something like that, 'I love you as a friend.' But he was right. I needed to get my act together.

I wiped my eyes, blew my nose on more than one square of tissue, and sat down on the bed next to him. "Okay boy genius, what do we do now?"

"For starters will you be my Valentine?" That came out of the blue.

"Whatever made you think of that?" I'd lost track of time.

"It's February 14th so Happy Valentine's Day," Jim said.

We kissed. It was very innocent. It didn't go farther than that, not that I wanted it to, but I could sense something holding Jim back. I guess there was more torn out of him than I realized. I could have been more encouraging, but it didn't seem appropriate at the time. I let out a big exhalation. The kiss seemed to erase a lot of my stress. I felt somebody cared about me. That meant the world.

"I would like some background. There has to be a lot more you haven't told me. You came to me last fall claiming a friend of yours was killed because he knew something about documents that lead to four SEALs deaths. And you implicated the government. So we go traipsing half way around the world and find this MPC, and now we know your boss ordered the MPC printed by using your name."

"From that we surmise the President's re-election campaign is involved in a black market to raise money. We've come back here and now you're pretty sure your boss is not only involved in the black market, but in bed with your roommate, and maybe he's not waiting for you to return so he can leave his wife and marry you. Did I forget anything?"

"Yeah, that TJ is trying to kill me. That's why we are here, to stop TJ from murdering me." I thought that was important to mention.

We talked well into the morning. "Okay, you're right. I came here right out of college. My father knows some people in Washington, D.C. He landed me a job as a secretary in Mr. Williams' office who at that time was an administrative aide to the Vice President. I knew a few people from Smith College and Boston who worked in the Washington, D.C. area, but none of them needed a roommate. One of my college friends suggested Mary Jo, who at the time was a secretary for Senator Smathers of Virginia. Everything in Washington, D.C. is calculated. There is no such thing as random luck. I didn't know that at the time."

"Mary Jo and I never became close, but she volunteered a lot of information that I should have questioned, but instead I was impressed. For instance back in 1963 she said the President was considering dropping his Vice President and choosing Senator Smathers for his running mate in the 1964 presidential election. She said she overheard this in Smathers' office. This was just after I started working. I thought she was giving me a heads up to start looking for another job because the current Vice President was going to be dropped. Meaning Mr. Williams was going to be out of a job. I didn't know Bob Williams that well at the time. It was before we started, you know, seeing one another."

Jim interrupted, "Is seeing one another the same as screwing?"

"You know what I mean. Don't make this harder than it is." I continued, "I thought Mr. Williams should know that Senator Smathers was replacing the Vice President on the ticket. Bob laughed it off as political gamesmanship."

"Then all of a sudden, I'm in the middle of a political controversy. The President's consideration of dropping his VP was leaked to the press. Mary Jo and I were blamed for the leak because we were roommates and worked in both the Vice President's office and Smathers' office. I never said anything to the press. How the press found out I will never know. Here I am, my first year in Washington, D.C., and the press was hounding me everywhere I went. It must have been Mary Jo, and I believe her motive was to sabotage Senator Smathers' chance of becoming the Vice Presidential nominee. But why would she want her own boss not to be Vice President?"

Jim piped in, "You were set up by Bob and Mary Jo. Mary Jo told you so that when it was leaked to the press they pointed to you as the source. I hate to say it but they were using the FNG. They may have already been involved in their affair before you arrived. Mary Jo was preventing her boss from becoming Vice President, so her lover Bob Williams could keep his job as an aide to the current Vice President."

"You're probably right. God, what a fool I was, so ambitious, so enthusiastic, and so naive. Mary Jo always asked about Bob. How could I have been so blind to the reason? She always suggested I look for a better job probably so I wouldn't be working close to her adulterous lover. Look who I'm calling an adulterer."

"Then low and behold a couple of months later the President was assassinated and Bob's boss became President. So, miraculously the Vice

President wasn't going to be dropped from the ticket, he was now the President. In case you haven't noticed there are no accidents in Washington, D.C., it's all calculated."

"One of the conspiracy theories flying around Washington was Williams and the Vice President had the President assassinated because of the commonly held belief that the Vice President was going to be dropped. The more popular theory was the CIA pulled the trigger because of the Bay of Pigs fiasco. So today we have this asshole President escalating the war in Vietnam on a faux resolution and escalating class warfare with his so called 'great society.'"

"After the assassination, I'm part of the President's administration as Bob's administrative assistant. There was a lot of staff shuffling at the time, people losing their jobs, and new people coming on board. Looking back I'm sure Mary Jo was frosted that she didn't get my job."

"Another curious job switch after the assassination was Mary Jo moving from Senator Smathers' office to the United States Attorney General's office who at the time was none other than the brother of the assassinated President. With the Vice President taking over his brother's presidency the Attorney General knew he wasn't going to be the Attorney General for long. So he ran for the U.S. Senate from New York in 1964. Mary Jo stayed on as his secretary when he became a Senator which is the office he holds today. You can't make this stuff up. Why I didn't start questioning authority at the time I don't know, but I was star struck by the intrigue and glamor of D.C."

"Washington, D.C. is a mesmerizing place, that doesn't deal in reality, which explains how I got involved with a married man. One more thing I just thought of, do you think Mary Jo seeks jobs with Bob Williams' enemies? I mean Senator Smathers was a political rival of the then Vice President. And now she works for the assassinated President's brother who is rumored to be considering a run at the incumbent President for their party's presidential nomination. And do you think she suspected I was also sleeping with Bob?"

"Possible, as you said everything is calculated. So what's your infatuation with married men?" Jim asked.

"That's not fair. I didn't know the doctor in Binh Thuy was married." Why would Jim ask me such a question? "You are just like all the other men. All you want to know is the sordid details?"

"It's a matter of curiosity. Since I've gotten to know you, I can't imagine you falling for a slime ball like Williams. I understand Dr. Feel Good in Binh Thuy with you being lonely, and his line of bullshit and drugs. I should have broken more than his nose."

"You have no idea what's it's like to work in D.C. as a young impressionable woman. We worked 12 hour days, ate a lot of meals together. That went on for over two years. We got chummier talking about intimate things. He knew I was involved at the time, but that didn't stop him. He talked about his rocky marriage. His wife came to Washington, D.C. a couple of times a year. She seemed snotty, like she didn't approve of the Washington, D.C. crowd or the people working for her husband. She would rather be in Virginia socializing with her horse people, you know the mink and manure crowd. I didn't like her."

"So one weekend, he proposed we take our work to a hunting lodge he belonged to in Maryland. We could have a cabin to ourselves and get a lot done. We got a lot done alright. I knew it wasn't right, but I wanted to believe so badly it was going to work. Bob is very convincing and very controlling. We didn't tell anyone, dare we lose our jobs. I would see him once or twice a week. Do I need to explain, 'see him'?"

"I'm sorry. Forgive me. I have no right to ask." That was nice of Jim to say.

"Yes, you do have a right." After all we've been through I wanted Jim to know about me, and if he was okay with my past then maybe there was a future.

"Well then let me add this, I'm convinced he was doing you and your roommate at the same time, and you were both sworn to secrecy. He must have been worn out by the time he went to see his wife. Maybe

219

that's why she was unhappy with him. You didn't tell your roommate you were seeing Bob, did you?" Jim asked.

"Lord no, I never told Mary Jo anything, and she never told me who she was seeing. Is this the most bizarre thing you have ever heard?" I asked. "He didn't love me. Why would he treat me that way?"

"Because he could," Jim said. "He probably loved playing the two of you. Mary Jo is in for a big fall."

"What is it with me and men? High school never happened. My college boyfriend turned out to be a philandering, lying Casanova. Then Bob the jerk and almost the doctor if you hadn't intervened. I'm going to be twenty-seven next month. I invested over three years falsely believing everything was going to be wonderful. Life isn't wonderful."

"You said you were involved when you started up with Bob. Who was he?"

He would ask that, "It was somebody I met when I first got to D.C. He was actually the only decent boyfriend I've ever had, but I messed that up royally so it's not important."

"By your approach life never will be wonderful." Jim explained, "You're looking for the perfect man, socially prominent, wealthy, prestigious position. You can find that man and even marry him. You get the big house, the club memberships, the clothes and all the other shit that goes with it. Then what? You don't know him. He may have a wandering eye, ignore you or worse beats you. He may drink, gamble and do drugs, or maybe he would rather go on trips with the boys than be with you. Is that what you want? And not out of the realm of possibilities, some rich, important men marry women to hide relationships they have with other men."

"I know, it's my upbringing. Okay, let's get back to reality. A lot of things are starting to make sense like how TJ found out I was snooping around about the documents which turned out to be the MPC. When this all started I called Bob and told him that Randy's sister told me that Randy suspected something was illegal in the campaign. I didn't tell him what

Randy's sister told me about the SEALs being killed. Bob probably ordered TJ to keep an eye on me. I don't think they wanted to kill me at first. When I told Bob about Randy's suspicions I could tell he was tense, like he was calculating. The way he blew me off about Randy's mental status gave me a bad feeling that something wasn't right."

"Where I made my mistake was contacting you. You remember we met in St. Louis at Busch's and Franci told me you were a SEAL? I thought you were in some kind of circus act. Anyway, I was assigned to a trip to California so I contacted you and told you about the SEALs, and the documents. If I hadn't contacted you, none of this would have happened. But at the time I felt obligated to find out what had happened to Randy. By the way, why didn't you try to kiss me? A girl comes to California, calls you and takes you out to dinner is a come-on for most men."

"I told you, I'm immune to your type."

"Well, I'm not my type anymore," I reminded Jim. "I called Bob from California and mistakenly told him I'd talked to some people about what Randy knew. I think that is what got me on TJ's hit list. When I returned from California TJ was waiting for me. I recalled what happened to Randy so I escaped, found you in California and as they say, 'you know the rest of the story.'"

"We need to contact Mary Jo. Are you up for that?" Jim asked.

"You bet. I can't wait." I kissed him on the cheek. "We should get some sleep. It's past three."

Chapter 28

The next evening we waited until supper time to call Mary Jo hoping she would be home from work, and before she went to visit the slime ball of the world Mr. Bob Williams. "Mary Jo I bet you are surprised to hear from me."

"Susan, is that really you? Where have you been? Where are you now? What's going on?" She sounded surprised.

"A lot has been going on. I wonder if we could meet someplace and have a talk," I requested.

"Yeah sure, why don't you come over here? There's a new roommate. I didn't know if you were coming back. I hope you are not mad," Mary Jo said.

I responded, "No, of course not. I didn't give you much warning I was leaving. I won't be working in D.C. anymore." Jim gave me a curious look. "How about meeting at the deli around the corner? Let's say 10 minutes."

"I guess that would be okay," Mary Jo said.

We waited in the car outside the deli. We picked a place to meet that Mary Jo could walk to so she wouldn't have to park. I've mentioned before that parking in Georgetown was a nightmare. As she walked up I called to her, "Over here Mary Jo," she seemed startled. "We've decided to get a pizza."

Mary Jo walked closer to the car and hesitated, "Is that you Susan? You look different." After a double take she said, "I'll have to make a phone call first."

"No you don't. We're calling Bob tomorrow. We want to talk to you alone." Jim was correct in thinking Mary Jo probably called Bob to let him know I was in town and where to find me. I wondered if Bob was sending TJ to finish the job.

"What do you mean talk to Bob? Bob who?" Mary Jo wasn't convincing.

"We know all about you and Bob Williams. We'll discuss it. i want you to meet Jim Crotty, a friend of mine." I got out of the car so Mary Jo would be seated between us. As we drove off a car came in the opposite direction screeching to a stop. A man in a trench coat jumped out and ran into the deli. I hoped he didn't recognize Mary Jo in our car.

Jim ordered a 12 inch with a pitcher. Mary Jo was guarded at first, but with a few pitchers of beer she started to loosen up and talk like she'd never talked before. "Yeah, I'm fucking Bob Williams, but I'm using him, and I hate to say it Dearie, he was using you."

"You knew about us?" For some reason the fact that the two of us were involved with the same man didn't bother me. I no longer had any feeling towards Mr. Williams except to see him eviscerated.

"Of course I did, you ninny. What do you take me for?" I had an answer for that, but maybe that wasn't the best time.

"How are you using him? What's the game?" I asked.

Mary Jo was slobbering by then, "The game is I'm going to have that son of a bitch junior Senator from New York that I'm working for killed, just like I had his asshole brother the late Mr. President assassinated. And by the way, I'm fucking the Senator too, but don't tell Bob. It could complicate things."

Jim looked at me like, 'this gal has gone around the corner.'

I asked, "Why, what's the point of all this?"

"Because that family ruined my family, that's the point. When the stock market crashed in November of 1929 my grandfather had everything invested with my New York Senator's dad, the patriarch of that horrible family. They called him Papa Joe and he promised my grandfather everything would be fine. Well, things weren't fine and my grandfather lost everything. My grandfather was a wealthy banker on Wall Street and should have known better. Our family owned a large estate on Long Island and a three thousand square foot apartment on Fifth Avenue overlooking Central Park. He lost it all."

"My father ended up living with an uncle in Pennsylvania and never got the education he should have. He committed suicide when I was 12. Not as dramatic as my grandfather who made the papers by shooting himself at his desk when the market crashed. No, my father walked into the living room on Christmas Eve, and in front of me, my brother, and my mother put a shotgun in his mouth and blew his brains out. That leaves an impression on a young girl. And it was all because of how the Senator's family screwed my family."

"I worked my way through college and landed a job in Senator Smathers' office. Smathers was a good friend of that family. That is where I wanted to be, close but not too close. The reason Smathers wasn't picked for the VP nomination in the 1960 presidential election was that the horrible family needed to balance the ticket. So where the presidential candidate was a Harvard educated New England establishment type they countered with the Texas rancher with cow poo on his boots and the 10 gallon hat with the pint size brain; the clown who is now President."

"In 1963 the strategy was to drop the hick from Texas and bring Senator Smathers on board as the 1964 VP nominee. The now assassinated President found out that the dickhead Mr. Bob Williams was involved in a black market while working in the then Vice President's office. I got wind of it in Smathers' office and passed it on to Bob. That's when Bob and I started up. There was no love there, never has been. I knew Bob worked for the Vice President. I met him at a lobbyist function and told him I worked for Senator Smathers, and that he and the Vice President were about to lose their jobs.

That got me an immediate meeting with Mr. Williams. The meeting took place in his bed in Georgetown. That's where all our meetings took place. There are more important decisions made in beds in this town than in all the government buildings combined. For some reason men think whatever they say in bed is confidential and will never leave the room. They blab about everything. What makes them think sex makes everything secret? I'm sorry I involved you in leaking the information of

Senator Smathers being considered for VP back when you first moved in, but Bob and I needed a scape goat and he insisted."

I interjected, "I seem to be Mr. Williams' favorite scape goat, but go on."

"I use sex like most women use sex in this town, to get what I want. Well low and behold a few months after I told Mr. Williams he was losing his job, the President was assassinated which made Mr. Williams' boss the President. And in 1964 instead of the former Vice President being dropped from the ticket, he was elected President, and Mr. Williams became a big shot in the new administration. Banana republics have nothing on this country. All these conspiracy theories about the assassination came out. What I learned from pillow talk was that there were three shooters, all mentally unstable activists. One panicked and never got off a shot. The one the police caught was shot to death while handcuffed in their custody. He was shot in front of the news media while they were taking pictures. Believe what you want, this is America. The other two were eliminated a short time later."

I looked at Jim and he looked at me in disbelief. "Oh, you think I'm making all this up?" Mary Jo accused us. "Everyone wants to believe our government is so righteous and working hard for the American people. Let me tell you, these men and women in government wouldn't be here if they weren't the most backstabbing, power hungry, greedy people in the world. That's what got them here and that's what keeps them here. It's all money, power, and sex. Nobody leaves here without becoming 10 times wealthier than when they came."

I knew our government wasn't all goody two shoes after witnessing the prisoner interrogation method in Rach Gia. I wanted to calm Mary Jo down. "So in your roundabout thinking you take credit for the President's assassination?"

"Damn straight I do," was Mary Jo's short answer.

"How do you plan to eliminate your boss?" This was getting interesting.

"I haven't figured that out yet, but I'm patient. I work for him now and share a bed with him occasionally. He blabs like all the rest. That family of his is so fucked up I almost think it would be better to let him live in misery. They put on such a good show for the public, the sailing, and touch football, and the horses. What a bunch of hypocrites," Mary Jo responded.

"Well, I have something that may help." Jim gave me a disconcerting look. "The reason I've been gone for the past four months is because I discovered the President's re-election campaign is raising money by running a black market in Vietnam. Or to be more precise, your bed mate Bob Williams is running the black market. It seems Bob's corrupt black market activities never stopped." Mary Jo sat there stunned. I got the impression that in all their pillow talk Bob neglected to mention his black market in Vietnam.

That pretty much finished the evening. When we got back to Bethesda Jim wasn't happy with me. "Why in the world would you tell her that? You know she's on the phone or in bed with your former fiancé at this very moment telling him what you said."

"I know. Tomorrow we'll call Mr. Williams and see what he has to say about all this. And as I told you before, if you value hanging onto your man parts you will never refer to that creep as my fiancé again. Understood?" I hoped I'd made my point clear.

"Fine, one more thing, I thought you said Mary Jo never opened up to you. She wouldn't shut up. I can't believe some of the things she said."

"Yeah, I forgot to tell you what Dr. Morgan drugged me with in Binh Thuy. That's how he got me to his room. When I returned to Binh Thuy, after Rach Gia, I asked Laurie to get me a vial of his drugs, just in case I might need them one day. When Mary Jo went to the bathroom I put the drugs in her beer," I explained.

"What's the drug?" Jim asked.

"Benzodiazepine and amphetamine, it's not a truth serum, but it breaks down inhibitions. What she said I would imagine is true."

"Well I guess you have something to thank Dr. Morgan for after all."

"Yeah, I'll thank him right after I kick him in the balls." I thought that was only fair.

"You know, if you had a sex change you would make one hell of a SEAL," Jim said.

"You want me to have a sex change?" I asked.

"No," Jim stated.

Chapter 29

The next morning we slept in. Once we got up we went for our run. Jim had this thing about running and staying in shape. We'd run everywhere we'd been, except Michigan and Vietnam. There was no way to run in those places and survive. I'd worked up to 30 or 40 minutes, depending on my mood, weather, and such. We would start off at a conversational pace. Well, it was a one sided conversation with Jim doing all the talking and me huffing and puffing alongside. After 15 minutes or so I would turn around and beat him back to the motel. He usually ran about an hour. After getting cleaned up and eating Jim said, "Today's the day, it's time to call lover boy."

"I told you about that lover boy stuff. What should I say?" I was nervous calling Bob. However, I felt I held the upper hand and was excited to hear his response.

Jim told me I should tell him I recovered the MPC that was being used in a black market in Vietnam to finance the President's re-election campaign, and this character TJ was trying to kill me. And that I was going to turn the MPC over to the FBI so they could investigate and arrest my potential killer. He also gave me a few ground rules, "Remember, he probably talked to TJ after he visited us in Hong Kong and by now he has probably talked to Mary Jo. Don't tell him where you are staying, sound positive, don't get choked up, and tell him you're still madly in love with him and want to please him in every way possible."

I'm sure Jim was joking about the last part. We waited until evening to call Bob's townhouse from a pay phone in Georgetown. It seemed less likely he would be able to trace a call from his home as opposed to a call to his office at the White House. I hoped I wasn't interrupting any personal endeavor he was having with a member of the opposite sex, "Hello Bob, long time, no see."

"Susan, is that really you?" Bob sounded as if he expected my call.

"Sure is. Haven't heard your lovely voice for months," I was having trouble controlling mine. Jim squeezed my arm as he listened in.

"Where have you been? Why did you leave? There is so much I need to talk to you about. Where are you? I'm coming over right now. Are you alright?" Bob rattled off one question after another not allowing me to answer.

"Well, last fall when I returned from my assignment in California a fellow calling himself TJ was waiting for me in my townhouse. I panicked. There was something frightening about him. I fled and ended up locating the money Randy told me was financing the President's re-election," I explained. "I have it with me. I'm going to the FBI to turn it over and see if they can arrest this TJ character before he catches me."

"Whoa, hang on, that's quite a mouthful. You're losing me. Before you do anything, we need to get together. I can help with whatever problems you are having." I just bet he could.

"If you could get TJ off my tail that would be a big help."

"First, I don't know what you are talking about, and second, I don't understand the connection between this fellow TJ and money you found and Randy. If it's the TJ I knew I think there is a terrible misunderstanding. There was a TJ who used to work for a private security firm contracted by the re-election committee. Sometimes he got over zealous with his assignments," Bob said.

"You said he used to work for the re-election committee, was he fired?" I asked.

"No, TJ was killed in Vietnam several days ago on a special security assignment. It was very tragic. The administration is still in shock. TJ was a Vietnam War hero. He was a Green Beret and was involved in secret missions in Cambodia and Laos." Of course you're in shock you asshole, you weren't upset when Randy disappeared. When Jim heard TJ died, he shook his fist in the air and smiled like he just won an Olympic race. I frowned at Jim like, 'have a heart.'

All of a sudden I had second thoughts, what if I misunderstood TJ's intentions? Then I remembered Hong Kong. No, I was doing the right thing. "I'm sorry to hear that. You can meet me at the FBI's headquarters tomorrow if you like. Afterwards maybe we can talk."

"I think we should first meet alone. You can't just waltz into the FBI's headquarters with some cockamamie story about money from Vietnam supporting the President's re-election campaign and expect to be heard. I can help you prepare your case; I can get you in touch with the right people. How about my place? I don't understand what you are saying about money and re-election," Bob lied.

You don't understand, how about the MPC you ordered printed in Vietnam using my name, you jerk? "Well alright, but let's meet in Fort Marcy Park. I don't feel comfortable at your place. There are too many people coming and going around your place. I don't want to be seen. You'll come alone, right?" I thought asking him to meet me where Randy was incinerated would be an appropriate spot. "Say 10 a.m. Sound good to you?" I asked.

"I think my place would be more appropriate, but if you insist then 10 o'clock by the second cannon. You know where that is?" Bob asked.

The second cannon must be his killing spot. "I'll find it. I'll take a cab. The cabbie should know. Well, I'll see you tomorrow." I began to hang up.

"Wait, don't hang up. We haven't talked. Are you alone?" Bob asked.

"Yes," was my answer.

"You sound different. You sound, how should I put it, more confident. Where are you staying?" Bob asked.

I looked at Jim, "In a Virginia motel." Jim nodded his head in approval.

"That's silly," Bob said. "You can stay here. I've missed you. We have a lot of catching up to do." I could feel Jim's body tense. Bob was with Mary Jo two days ago. Maybe she was in the other room at this very moment. Didn't this guy ever get enough? I wondered if he ever did the two of us in one day. There were a few lunch hour quickies as I recalled. One was even in the White House. I should get a commemorative certificate saying, 'From the Office of the President of the United States of America, I screw 200 million people every day, but today you got screwed in the White House.' To think of an unmarried woman having sex with a married man, a member of the administration no less, in the White

House. I know I wasn't the first and I doubted I'd be the last. Of course it all depended on one's definition of sex and what is, is.

"You may recall we are lovers. I feel there has been a huge misunderstanding on your part. There are things you misinterpreted. Government things I can't talk about over the phone. I shouldn't be telling you this, but there is a lot going on, secret things. I love you. I want you to understand that. I've been worried sick ever since you disappeared. I'm willing to go back to the way things were. All is forgiven. Everything can be explained. I can get your old job back. Your parents hired someone to take your car and personal belongings back to St. Louis. I've been in touch with them. They are as worried as I am. Mary Jo has been great." I bet she has. "She has another roommate, but everything can be straightened out," Bob said. "You can live here for a while." Oh yeah, how long would I be alive staying at your place? And, by the way, are you screwing Mary Jo's new roommate?

"We'll meet tomorrow and discuss it, 10 a.m.," I stated.

"Alright, 10 o'clock by the second cannon. But I think you should reconsider and come over here right now," Bob resigned. "Don't forget to bring the money. If I'm going to help you I need to know everything, where you've been, who you've talked to, everything. I remember you telling me Randy was suspicious of a few campaign donations. I have no knowledge of money being raised on the President's behalf in Vietnam. We'll straighten all this out tomorrow and then see if we need to involve the FBI. Tomorrow night after a nice dinner you are coming back here and we are picking up where we left off."

I hung up. I looked at Jim. He looked at me. I could tell he was pissed.

"I think he sounded scared or he wouldn't have been so nice. I'm sure he's talked to Mary Jo, don't you agree?" Jim wouldn't move. He kept me pinned in the phone booth. "What is it? Let me out of here!" I raised my voice. I knew what it was. It was Jim hearing Bob saying, 'We are lovers,' and 'I love you,' and 'We are going to pick up where we left off.' I was gratified Jim was jealous, but I was getting claustrophobic. I pushed toward the door.

Jim opened the door grudgingly, "You going back to him?"

"No, I hate him. He was two timing me. He had my best friend killed. Are you nuts? Why in the world would I go back to him? Grow up!" Were all men so stupid?

"I don't know. Maybe hearing his voice made you all gushy inside." Men, why doesn't he tell me how he feels? But he can't. Not with his big bad SEAL ego.

"You didn't seem surprised to hear TJ was dead," I inquired in an effort to change the subject.

"Ever hear of an anti-disturbance device?" Jim asked.

"Of course not. What are you getting at?"

"We couldn't haul all of the MPC we found. Besides, we were already taking sporadic fire from the VC. We had to get out of there fast. So we placed a hand grenade with an anti-disturbance device. That way if anybody disturbed the MPC, they were going to get blown to Hell with all the shit and the MPC."

"You booby trapped the MPC knowing TJ was following us and would go down there after it?" I accused. "That's why you didn't put up a fight in Hong Kong and you told him where the MPC was."

"You're making some big assumptions. And how do you know TJ died in a pile of crap with the MPC?" Jim asked. "Vietnam is a dangerous place."

"You know what happened. That's why Henderson, Joe, and Ski stayed in Rach Gia. So if TJ showed up they could show him where the MPC was."

"It could have happened that way," Jim said with a wry smile. "I'll ask them next time we get together." Jim was so smug I wanted to rip his eyes out. Those damn SEALs. They don't just kill their enemy. They kill when the enemy thinks he's winning, when he's secure in his own environment, when he least expects it. What a bunch of sadistic sons of bitches. On the other hand, I was relieved TJ was out of the way.

I took his arm and put my head on his shoulder. I didn't know why. How could a woman be attracted to such a man? God, I wanted him to take me right there on the sidewalk. "I'm sorry I'm such a bitch."

"I wouldn't have it any other way." We walked to the car and headed back to our motel in Bethesda.

"Do you think we are on the wrong side? I mean we are accusing the President of the United States of illegal activities. And TJ was a war hero. I feel traitorous. Maybe TJ did just want to ask me some questions the night I returned from California."

"They are trying to kill you; make no mistake. These people are the scum of the earth. Don't get any guilt feelings. We are doing the right thing. You'll see tomorrow," Jim assured me.

Chapter 30

We were up early to run and eat. Was he going to run every day of his life? Jim briefed me on what he planned to do. He didn't want me getting close to Bob. It may have been jealousy, but I think he was worried that Bob was dangerous. He planned to hire a female escort to take a package to Fort Marcy. There was no shortage of female escorts in Washington, D.C. In fact there was even a demand for male escorts. Lobbyists made sure their congressional clients enjoyed whatever made them feel good, no matter the sexual preference.

Jim's idea was for me to call an escort service and tell them I was playing a joke on my boyfriend and needed somebody who looked somewhat like me to deliver a package. I would need to interview several girls until I found the right one. The girl only needed to look like me from afar while seated in a cab. She needed to look like the girl her boyfriend would expect, basically a five foot seven Caucasian woman, shoulder length auburn hair, and weighing around 120 pounds. I don't know if Bob would have recognized me 10 pounds lighter, short dark hair, and deeply tanned. Well, my tan was fading fast, especially after visiting Michigan where people didn't sunbathe in February. I would also have the escort wear big Jackie Kennedy sunglasses to mask her face.

I was to meet the girls at a coffee shop on K Street near 18th. Why was I not surprised that no matter what time of day or night, holidays included the escort services could always provide attractive women? No federal holidays for these babes. It seemed like Congress was always on break, but the working women of Washington, D.C. never got a day off.

There was one girl I thought could fit the bill. She introduced herself as Candy. She told me she was working her way through pre-law at Georgetown University. A prostitute working as a lawyer reminded me of a joke. Anyway, I thought she could pull it off if she brushed out her teased up rat nest hair and parted it on the left. My grandfather worked hard to build up my trust fund. Wouldn't he be proud to know his money was going to pay for a hooker?

I gave Candy cab fare, her pimp (the escort service manager) the payment and a grocery bag full of old newspapers. I wrote out directions for the cabbie and told Candy to show up close to 10.

Jim and I rushed to Fort Marcy. We drove around until we found what we believed to be the second cannon. By nine o'clock we were hidden in bushes about 100 yards from the cannon. We parked in a small lot about a half mile away. There were numerous joggers and dog walkers on the paths. We were wearing dark clothing. At 9:30 a.m., two black Ford sedans drove past the cannon. One stopped, turned around and went back the way he'd come. The other continued. They disappeared from sight.

At a quarter to 10 a.m. Bob drove up in his big Mercedes. How could I have fallen for such an egotistical, self-centered creep?

At five after 10 a.m., the cab drove up. Before Candy could open the door, the two black Fords blocked in the cab. I was impressed how fast they appeared out of nowhere. Bob walked over as four men wearing dark suits with dark glasses set a perimeter around the cab. Bob leaned into the window. Jim and I could tell there was a heated exchange. Candy got out and shoved the bag at Bob. He threw the newspapers in the air. There were more heated words from Bob. Candy barked back. Good for her. She would make a fine attorney. We could hear their voices, but couldn't make out what they were saying. I looked at Jim. He was laughing. Bob started walking away waving his arms, then he turned back pointing at Candy yelling something. She gave him the finger and got back in the cab. The four black suited goons moved their cars so the cab could leave. The cab screeched off. Bob and the men talked awhile. They started looking around.

"Let's get out of here. They'll see us," I whispered.

"Don't move. Any movement will be detected. They can't see us. We'll wait until they leave. They'll probably copy the license plates of the cars in the park. We'll get another rental as soon as we get back to

235

Maryland," Jim said. I couldn't believe how calm he was. My heart was beating 1000 times a minute. I guess compared to sitting in the bush in Vietnam waiting to shoot someone to death or be shot, this was nothing.

When we were sure the coast was clear Jim drove out of the park while I hid on the floor in the back. He said one of the Fords was parked on a side road, but it didn't follow. "So you think he still loves you?" Jim mocked me.

"Screw you. What do we do now?" I asked.

"I'm convinced Bob isn't interested in getting you your old job back or anything else he promised, except getting you into bed." Jim just wouldn't let it go.

I was thinking bigger thoughts, "You think the President could be involved? Why would he risk his whole political career on a stunt like this?"

"Politicians are good at four things, raising money, getting elected, getting rich, and covering their ass. Integrity, sincerity, and honesty aren't part of their genetic code." Jim answered. "I think lover boy deserves an explanation. We'll call him this evening."

If he keeps calling Bob 'lover boy,' I'm going to hand Jim his teeth. We turned in the rental car in Maryland and took a cab to a different agency in Virginia. Jim used his driver's license. Whoever was after us probably had Jim's information along with mine. We were trying to make it as difficult as possible for them to locate us.

That evening I called from a payphone in D.C., "Hello, Bobby," he hated the name Bobby. He thought it was not sophisticated enough for a gentleman of his stature.

Bob didn't return the salutation, "What was that all about this morning? Where are you? We are not playing games here, you know. This is a serious matter, a matter of national security."

"You said you were coming alone. You said you loved me." I barely got out the words when Bob started yelling back.

"So you were there. Tell me where you are right now. I tried to help you. I'm not sticking my neck out for you anymore. Every law enforcement agency in the world is hunting you down. Don't make this hard on yourself," he growled.

"I'm not telling you where I am. Tell me what's going on. I want to know I'll be safe," I demanded.

"Safe, you are putting the entire nation in jeopardy." I should mention that Bob had a tendency to exaggerate. "There is nothing going on that concerns you, but you may have knowledge of matters that concern national security. We need to sit down and have a discussion of where you have been and who you have talked to since you left D.C. And I need to understand what you think Randy was talking about. I want to meet with you now, young lady." Oh, now I'm a young lady. "We know you don't have the MPC or anything else. Now get your butt in here and let's get this over with so you can return to work, and a normal life."

"Bobby boy I never said anything about MPC. Are you talking about military payment certificates that are used in the black market in Vietnam? What made you say MPC? Now let me tell you something, you never loved me, you were sleeping with my roommate, and you were making money on the black market in Vietnam off of the men and women serving their country in this savage war. I'm going to see they string you up by your eyelashes and beat your balls until you blink." Jim had a horrified look on his face. Okay, I lost my composure. I learned the eyelash thing from Chief Henderson in Rach Gia. I slammed down the phone.

"I guess that concludes your negotiations with Mr. Williams?"

"I thought I handled myself rather well considering the circumstances," I acknowledged.

Jim sighed, "Okay, I guess it's the FBI. Do you know anybody over there in your years working in D.C.?"

We got in the car and started heading back to Bethesda. "Well actually, remember I said I was dating someone before I met Bob?" I demurred.

"You were sleeping with an FBI agent?" I thought Jim was going to kick me out of the car.

"Yes, if you must know." What was so terrible about that?

"Would it be easier to ask who you haven't slept with in this town and the surrounding counties?" Jim was getting all worked up over nothing.

"I'm not going to discuss my personal life with you. Listen, I'm sure you have had your fair share of brain dead teeny boppers so don't go judging me. At least the men I've dated could read and write." It was okay for a man to have multiple partners, but never the woman.

"Okay, okay, I'm sorry. I have no right to pry. It's just that......" Jim didn't finish his thought.

"Just what?" I asked. "I'm twenty-six years old. You think I was going to hold out my entire life hoping a frogman would come along?"

"Never mind, let's get the next lover on the horn." Now I was going to get the treatment about Eric.

Back in our room I found Eric's card with his home number written on the back. I hoped that girl didn't answer, "Eric, guess who?"

"Susan, where the hell are you?" Eric recognized my voice.

"I'm right here in town." Jim was listening to every word.

"I told you to call if anything came up. Now what's going on?" Eric asked.

"I did call the morning I left, but a girl answered the phone. I thought I had the wrong number," I lied.

"That was probably Becky. She could have called me to the phone." Eric was casual about a woman answering his phone.

"Becky, is this something serious?" Why did I care? Why did I ask?

"We're engaged. Actually just this past Valentine's Day." Eric sounded excited.

"How romantic. Well congratulations, I'm sure she's wonderful." Damn him.

Eric hurried, "We need to get together. You are involved in a federal investigation. The executive branch is making inquiries. Can you be in my office tomorrow morning?"

"You sure Becky won't mind?" Why was I acting this way?

"Susan, get serious. Why would she care?" That hurt. "You are in a lot of trouble unless you come up with some good explanations about where you have been. How about nine?" Eric asked.

"Okay, I'll see you then." I hung up.

Jim sat there giving me the look. "What? He's an old friend."

"It sounded like you are still interested," Jim said.

"I'm not interested. It was over years ago. I just hope he's happy." Which deep down was the truth. Eric deserved somebody better than me.

Chapter 31

We arrived at the Department of Justice building around 8:30 a.m. A separate building was being built for the FBI, but for the time being they were still housed in the Department of Justice building. After signing in and getting a visitor's pass we were escorted to Special Agent Eric Stutter's office. "Well I see it is special agent now." I greeted Eric.

At first Eric looked at me as if he had never seen me before, "Susan?"

"Yes, don't you recognize me?"

"I don't remember you wearing glasses. I like the short hair." He got up, came around his desk, and gave me a peck on the cheek. I don't know if Jim appreciated that, but I did. Maybe I wasn't going to prison just yet. I introduced Jim to Eric which was awkward. Jim turned over the MPC.

There was another man in the room who Eric introduced as the assistant director, Mr. Frank Fitzgerald. Both Eric and Mr. Fitzgerald worked in the national security branch of the FBI.

After the usual catching up chitchat and coffee service, Eric got down to business. He informed me our conversation was being tape recorded. I told him everything. I figured it was my best chance of clearing my name. From the time I escaped from TJ up to Jim handing over the remaining MPC to Eric, I covered every step. "And it is my belief the President is using the black market in Vietnam to help finance his re-election campaign."

There was no emotion from either Eric or Mr. Fitzgerald. Not even a flinch when I mentioned I shot a Viet Cong. I got the impression this was not the story they heard from the administration. Or didn't they believe me? Did they think I was making this up? I think they yawned when I described the prisoner enhanced interrogation technique using a helicopter. I skipped the part about me and Dr. Morgan with Jim kicking him in the nuts. I didn't think that was pertinent to the black market. Also I neglected to tell them that Bob Williams and I had a personal relationship. What purpose would that have served?

The MPC was sitting on Eric's desk. What other conclusion could they come to? Finally, Mr. Fitzgerald rose, picked up the MPC and said, "Alright Eric I'm going to check out the MPC with what we just heard. I think you can handle the rest. Go ahead and proceed with what we talked about. We'll meet later today and go over everything. This puts a different spin on our investigation." And he left.

"Proceed on what? What's happening?" I asked.

"We'll get to that in a minute, but first I want to be clear about your conversation with Mary Jo," Eric inquired. "You told her about Mr. Williams' involvement in the MPC black market?"

"Yes, do you think that was wrong?" I asked.

"It's not a matter of being right or wrong. We need to know what everybody else knows," Eric explained.

"What do you think will happen?" I asked.

"Well there are several scenarios." Eric started, "I have no doubt Mary Jo will make sure the junior Senator from New York knows about this. What he does is up to speculation. Everybody plays for leverage in this town. The Senator may do nothing, but I wouldn't bet on that. This is an election year and there is no secret the Senator has plans to oust the President and claim their party's presidential nomination for himself. The Senator could blackmail the President and force him to quit his campaign. The President would most likely serve out his term and retire to his ranch. Or the Senator could go public. If that were the case the President would deny any knowledge of a black market and claim the Senator was stooping to a new political low. The press would drool over a scandal which may give the Senator an edge in securing the nomination."

I asked, "Where would the scandal go, what would it lead to?"

"I don't know," Eric answered, "If it goes public, and the President wins the nomination he may be able to obstruct the investigation until after the election. Remember, the President appointed the Attorney General, the FBI's boss, so essentially the FBI would be investigating their own boss. You see how sticky this can get? Everything is political, everything is calculated."

241

"Do you think that's possible about the Senator using blackmail and the President resigning?" I reasoned. "The President, the most powerful man in the world giving up, I don't think he can be intimidated. I think he considers himself politically impregnable. Politics is all this clown knows. He'll fight this to the end."

"I'll tell you this; if the President quits his campaign then Mary Jo has signed her own death warrant. The President will have the Senator eliminated. Oh, the assassination of the Senator will be carried out by some untraceable nobody without any ties to the President. Just like the Senator's brother, the President, being assassinated in 1963. The Senator's family will eventually figure out the common denominator is Mary Jo, and then it's good riddance Mary Jo." Eric looked like he'd made a huge mistake. "Forget what I just said."

"You know this President had the former President assassinated in 1963, don't you?" I blurted.

"Don't be ridiculous," Eric explained, "I was just expounding on your conversation with Mary Jo."

"You know what happened on that November day in Dallas?" I prodded.

"There are a lot of theories. The Vice President being involved is one of many, but it's pretty farfetched. The Warren Commission report is the official findings in that case and that's all I'm saying." Eric reverted to being stoic and professional.

I knew he knew, but he wasn't going to confide in neither Jim nor me. I changed the subject. "So you are getting married?"

"Yes, I'm taking the plunge." Eric blushed.

"Well tell me about her. Did you pick her up at a Rugby party, get her drunk, and take her back to your place?" Women have a right to know these things. Jim gave me an inquisitive look.

Eric laughed, "No, actually we met on the job. Becky works for the government accounting office. There were some defense contracts with questionable cost overruns. It appeared taxpayers' money was being siphoned off to banks in Bermuda under numbered accounts. Becky has a great sense of humor and is super smart. I liked her the first day we met. Eventually I got up enough nerve to ask her out."

Okay, he didn't have to add all that about Superwoman. "She sounds perfect, not like some of your former girlfriends."

"Come on Susan, you know what I mean. We had a good relationship until you dumped me for a married man." How did he know that? "And she's not perfect. She's a buckeye."

"What do you mean, 'I dumped you for a married man?'" I asked.

"Mr. Williams has been on our radar for quite a while. We've been watching him since 1961. Don't think I didn't take major harassing around here when it was found out my girlfriend left me for that creep," Eric explained.

"Isn't anything sacred in this town?" I asked.

"Nope, you would not believe some of the things going on," Eric answered. "Have you seen your ex-lover?"

"Actually I have, but from a distance. I may have left that part out. I called Mr. Williams when we got to D.C. I wanted to make sure he was the dirt bag I thought he was. We arranged to meet at Fort Marcy alone. He had agents there to capture me. Jim and I observed from a distance. I called him again last night to let him know what I thought. Did you know he was sleeping with my roommate?"

"Yes, we knew."

I felt ashamed, "I'm sorry. I made a mistake, but I'm glad you are happy." I don't think that made Jim feel good.

"Forget it; I've been over it for a long time." He didn't have to be so flippant about it.

"So what's this about being a buckeye?" I inquired.

"A buckeye, she went to Ohio State. Oh excuse me, The Ohio State University," Eric corrected himself.

"So?" I quizzed.

"So, don't you remember I went to Michigan?" Eric answered.

"Oh yes, now I remember. Wasn't it you who said the best way to get an Ohio State grad to come to your front door was to order pizza?" We did have a good time.

"Yes, and I stand by that statement. Alright, enough about Becky. We have some more business to wrap up." Eric got back to being serious. I could sense he was anxious to conclude the meeting. "You are going back to St. Louis."

"What?" I was stunned.

"You will be escorted by a federal agent and there will be a federal agent with you at all times. There is still a lot going on. Mr. Crotty you are staying here under protective custody," Eric stated.

Jim spoke for the first time, "You mean I'm being arrested."

"You have not been formally charged with a crime at the moment, but your movements will be restricted." Eric added, "We are moving you to a location where we have more control." It sounded like Jim was going to jail.

Eric stood, Jim and I rose. We all shook hands, there was no kissing or hugging. I thanked Eric for his help. We left the Department of Justice building together with two federal agents in tow. One drove with Jim in the rental car and I rode with the other agent in a black Chevy sedan. We first went to return the rental car. Then we returned to our motel in Bethesda to gather our belongings. I asked the agents if they could step outside for a moment.

"So that was your FBI friend? You still love him, don't you?" Jim asked.

"Don't start with that. I'm going to be frank and honest with you. Yes, that was my FBI friend. Up until a few months ago he was the only man I ever loved, but I was too self-absorbed to realize that at the time. It was my upbringing to look at a man's pedigree and not look at the man. Yes I was in love with him, and I still love him, but I'm not in love with him now, if that makes any sense. I'll never make that mistake again." My voice cracked, "I may never see you again." I started crying, I couldn't go on.

244

Jim took me in his arms, "I'll see you again. You aren't that lucky. It may take a while, but we are going to be together. This war can't go on forever. I was thinking of you and I settling down in Rach Gia, you know, a hut on the beach, salamander hors d'oeuvre at sunset with Black Label beer."

How could he joke at a time like this? The agents knocked on the door. We kissed. Unlike our kiss on Valentine's, this one had feeling. I opened the door. The federal agent took my luggage. I couldn't look back.

Chapter 32

We arrived in St. Louis during the evening rush hour. I was loaded into a black Ford sedan and driven home. Driving up to my house I was apprehensive. I didn't want to see my mother with all of her hysterics, drama, and all this being about her, and what she'd been through. Luckily my father met me at the door. I fell into his arms, and of course I started crying. At first I could tell he was hesitant. He probably didn't recognize me. "I'm glad you are safe. Come into the study." Our dog Barney, a German Shepard, recognized me. He sniffed all the new scents. An FBI agent brought in my luggage and left us alone.

"Do you want something to drink? When did you last eat?" my father asked.

"I'm fine. I'm not hungry. I ate on the plane. They have taken good care of me." I felt uneasy being home.

"We have been so worried. We want to know everything, but I understand if you are tired and don't want to talk right now. You're safe now. We've talked to the local FBI office and they are leaving a detail of men here until they feel you're safe. One agent is staying in the guest room. I'm sorry, but your movements are going to be restricted. Somebody will be with you at all times. You may drive, but one of the agents must go with you. And for your own safety the phone, TV and radio have been removed from your room." How is that going to make me safe? "I know this sounds draconian, but they have convinced us it is for your own good." Did they tell you why people were trying to kill me? Once Mr. Williams learned the FBI possessed the MPC it would seem he had bigger problems on his hands than trying to eliminate me.

"Well, how are you? You've changed your hair." My father noticed.

"Yes, a lot has changed. I'm sorry this has caused you and Mom so much trouble. I didn't intentionally do this to hurt you."

"We know. We're just glad you are finally home."

Then there was the awkward silence when nobody had anything to say. "Where's Mom?"

"The news of you coming home has overwhelmed her. Doctor Purcell gave her a sedative. She may be asleep until morning." my father answered.

"And David, where is he?" I asked about my younger brother.

"He's flying in from Chicago tomorrow. He said he can only get away for a couple of days, but he really wants to see you. Janice won't be coming." Janice was David's wife. She had a one month old to take care of. "I guess you haven't heard that you became an aunt last month," my father added.

"I can't believe I forgot. Janice was only a few months along when I left. Is it a boy or girl?" Men never think of a baby as being a boy or girl, or birth weight or anything."

"Oh, it's a boy. Janice did great. The baby is healthy and has a full complement of equipment. Your mother is ecstatic being a grandmother for the first time. She has already been to Chicago twice in addition to the time when the baby was born. She can't stop talking about him. I think she already has him slotted to be Country Day's football captain."

I bet she does. "Can I see my room?" I asked.

"Of course, you must be tired. There's one more thing I want to mention. Your mother, I mean your mother and I, want to make sure everything is alright, you know, health wise. We are scheduling appointments with your doctors. And your mother thought you would like to get your hair and nails done. So we are going to keep you busy."

My room looked the same, depressing. I took a shower and went to bed.

The next morning I got up and started to get unpacked. How was I going to communicate with anyone? I found a clean running outfit and headed downstairs. Jim's physical fitness obsession had become ingrained in me. The agent was having coffee in the kitchen, "Whoa, wait a minute ma'am, where do you think you are going?"

"I'm going for a run," I stated as I reached for the kitchen door.

"I'm sorry, but somebody has to be with you at all times outside of the house," he stated. "We weren't briefed that you exercised. We'll be ready tomorrow if you can hold off for a day."

"Alright, but I must warn you I used to work out with the Navy SEALs."

"Ooh, we'll keep that in mind. One of the men on our detail was an Army airborne ranger in Vietnam. I think he'll be able to keep up," the agent said with a wry grin. What was the ditty Jim said they sang while running at Army airborne school in Fort Benning, Georgia? The Army version was, 'I want to be an airborne ranger, live the life of love and danger.' The SEAL version was, 'I want to be an airborne ranger, full of shit and scared of danger.' I went back upstairs to shower and dress.

When I returned, Lilly Mae was in the kitchen doing the FBI agent's breakfast dishes. Lilly Mae had been our maid since my childhood. She gave me a genuine hug. "Oh, Miss Susan, you have had us so worried. I'm so glad you are alright." Lilly Mae was part of the family. She fixed the two of us breakfast. "I must say li'l girl, you have changed. I like the hair Child."

"Yeah I know, I didn't want people recognizing me. Supposedly they are still after me."

We sat at the kitchen table and talked for an hour. She filled me in on the neighborhood gossip. Lilly Mae loved to talk. I wished I could ride the bus to and from work with Lilly Mae and her friends. Lawyers should ride those busses. It would make their job so much easier to find out what was really going on in a divorce case or corporate fraud case. The women on those buses saw the soiled telltale sheets when the master was on a business trip. And they saw the corporation's cooked books that should not have been left out in the open. Lilly Mae set her own schedule and got done what she felt necessary. She helped me through a lot of my growing hormonal problems as a teenager.

Speaking of problems while growing up, I heard my mother approaching. She walked into the kitchen as if she'd undergone a heart transplant the previous day. She wore a terry cloth bath robe, fluffy

slippers, hair rollers, and for full effect to convey that she was the victim
of this ordeal, she wore sunglasses. "Hello Mother."

"You're home, how delightful. We are so grateful," she slurred as she
stumbled to the coffee. "What on earth have you done to your hair? It
looks atrocious."

Lilly Mae started to tiptoe out of the kitchen. "Before you go, I want
the beds changed in the guest room. It seems we have an uninvited guest
staying with us. And we'll need extra towels in the guest bath. Don't
forget to dust in the solarium. It was filthy in there last week. I was
mortified when I took Mrs. Orthwein in there for coffee. And I suppose
we'll have to give up the den or some other family room so these men can
work. We'll be prisoners in our own home until this matter is resolved.
God knows when that will be."

"Yesum," Lilly May said as she scampered out.

I felt uneasy. I went back to my room. What was I going to do? When
was this going to be over? At noon, there was a knock on my door, "Yes."

"It's your father. I have somebody here to see you. Do you want to
grab lunch?"

"Yes, of course." I opened the door to see my brother standing there.
We hugged while exchanging greetings. I congratulated him on the new
arrival. There was my younger brother who I teased unmercifully, now all
grown up and a family man. I'm surprised he got married after the
emasculating childhood I put him through.

"You look great," My brother commented. "Different but great."

"Where did you get that skirt? You look cute." My father could
always make me feel good.

"Hong Kong," I mentioned.

My father lowered his voice, "Let's go to the club. I want to be out of
listening range of you know who."

"Okay," I whispered back.

My father called out, "Margaret, this is your last chance, do you want
to join us?" My father waited a moment. There was no reply from their

room down the hall. My father pumped his fist in the air and mouthed, 'YES.' "Okay we're leaving."

I wanted to know, "What's wrong with Mom?"

"Oh, you know how she is. She's going to play this to the hilt," my father deadpanned. And I thought I was the one who'd been kidnapped. How come my mother got to be the martyr?

As we made our way to the front door, one of the men asked us where we were going. "I'm taking my son and daughter to the club for lunch."

"Sir, we need to go with you," the agent ordered.

"It's a private club, members only. I'll take full responsibility. It's right across the street. The number is in the index by the phone." We kept walking. My father had a tone to his voice and a way of saying things that most people didn't challenge.

My father scanned the dining room looking for a table away from the cackling herd of women, excuse me, lady diners. My father knew, as well as I did, that ladies were a subspecies of the female gender. Four ladies could be sitting at a table all speaking at the same time and understand every word each was saying, not only at their table, but at the adjacent table. And they could do this while playing bridge, and eating, always eating. An amazing physiological feat evolved over millenniums by those who flourished in the snob world. The draw back was that after lunch the enormous pile of gossip accumulated and assimilated in their multi-emotional brains brought on excruciating headaches that rendered them incapable of cooking, cleaning, or having sex.

My brother asked, "Where have you been?" I went through my travels. I think my father was impressed, especially with Vietnam.

"Do you know why the FBI is keeping an eye on you?" my father asked. "The government won't tell us anything."

I wasn't going to hold back, "Yes, there are people trying to kill me. They won't tell you because it's the President's administration."

My father and brother both rolled their eyes at each other, and then they leaned in with an incredulous look. My father said, "You are making a serious accusation."

"I learned of a black market in Vietnam that was run by the administration to finance the President's re-election campaign. And now they are trying to kill me. They have already killed scores of people who have found out about it. I told you months ago how it began when I was home for Mother's birthday." I didn't want to beat around the bush. I felt my time was short. Something was going to happen soon once Mary Jo blabbed her big mouth to the junior Senator from New York. My father and brother gave an incredulous look to one another. "What, you don't believe me?"

"I know you've been through a lot. You were held captive for over four months," my father stated.

He probably doubted I was in Vietnam or Hong Kong. "I haven't been held captive. I've traveled on my own volition." That was the nonsense I'd heard at Busch's when I was in town incognito Thanksgiving weekend. Supposedly I was being held captive by a native in the Caribbean, or a sex slave in Massachusetts, or some other ridiculous thing.

"We were talking to Dr. Flemming at a party. He knows about your situation and approached us. I don't think you know him. He's a psychiatrist at Washington University School of Medicine and worked with returning prisoners of war after the Korean conflict. He said the human mind can be manipulated to believe anything. Would you like to meet him?"

"No, I know what I'm talking about," I started to feel trapped.

"I'm going to give him a call none the less. It can't hurt to talk," my father said.

That annoyed me. Something else that annoyed me, "Can I use the phone?"

"Of course you can. Somebody has to be with you," my dad answered.

"Don't you find that strange? What harm is there in me making a personal call?" I asked.

"Nothing, but the FBI wants to monitor your calls just in case you have forgotten to tell them something. You might say something in one of your conversations. Personally we think whoever you have been traveling with may have brainwashed you and may try to contact you," my father accused.

"Whatever gave you that idea? The person I was traveling with is in FBI custody." If I ever got a hold of Bob Williams I was going to brainwash him with a baseball bat.

David chipped in, "You mean like the Stockholm syndrome?"

I wished I was in Stockholm, "This is preposterous." I knew they were not going to believe a word I said. They believed the gossip mongers who said I was held against my will and fell in love with my captor. Well, I did fall in love and I hoped I'd gotten that point across to Jim when we said goodbye. I figured I might as well play along with my dad. I resigned to enjoy a pleasant lunch and reverted to worthless small talk about worthless people or in other words, gossip.

I could feel a few of the lady diners giving me the eye. Nobody came over to say hello though I recognized many of my parents' friends. Maybe they didn't recognize me, or maybe they thought it was my brother's wife. Either way, I didn't want to talk to them anyway.

When we returned home I needed to call my best friend Franci. As I recalled, I was to be her maid of honor in June. I called from the den where the FBI hooked up a second phone with a tape recorder so they could document every word I said or heard. "Franci, guess who?"

"Susan, where have you been? You had us all worried sick. I heard you were rescued." It was good to hear Franci's voice. Rescued would not be the word I would use.

"I've been traveling." I couldn't talk freely with the FBI listening. "We should have lunch."

"Of course, I'm pretty busy this week."

She's too busy to have lunch with her best friend who has been gone for over four months? "Maybe we could get together for a drink."

"That sounds wonderful, but I really don't have time right now. We'll get together soon, I promise," was her reply.

"What about the wedding? I want to know when I'm to be fitted for my maid of honor dress. This is so exciting." That was what I really wanted to talk about.

"I don't know how to tell you, but there's been a slight change of plans. We didn't anticipate you coming back so soon. So we went ahead and completed the wedding party without you. Cathy Wagner is going to be my maid of honor." Was she telling me I was out of the wedding?

"Cathy Wagner, you can't be serious! We still have over two months. I'm sure I can get fitted for a dress in that amount of time and things can be worked out with Cathy. She will understand." I really wanted to be in Franci's wedding. I feared what she was about to say.

"It's not that. My parents felt it would be better to move on," Franci replied.

"Okay, Franci, we've been friends since kindergarten. Tell me what moving on means," I demanded.

"It's just that it's a big day. We didn't want my wedding to be overshadowed by any distractions," Franci said.

"What distractions?" I asked.

"You know, you living with another man. Everybody is talking about it," is all that Franci offered.

"Who told you that?"

"It's been on the news practically every day since you were kidnapped." So that's where the speculation started. I was kidnapped and of course that meant a man, and if I was being kept by a man that meant sex.

"I wasn't living with another man in the context you're thinking. It's a complicated story. But I understand your predicament. I'll bow out gracefully." This was what passed for friends around here. Once somebody stepped out of line, whether imagined or real, they were persona non grata. Now I understood my mother's consternation about me coming home. She wasn't going to be invited to the big-to-do wedding. Some loyalty these people possessed, even toward their own children. "Don't let the drummer get a piece before your husband." I slammed down the phone.

That evening we ate as a family dinner at home. I noticed there was a new cook. The life expectancy of a cook in our household was about five months. One use of an incorrect ladle or a misplaced piece of china was cause for dismissal. How Lilly Mae survived all those years I have no idea. She must have had something on my mother. To think that anyone but my father ever touched my mother made my skin crawl. It crawled a little even thinking of my father touching her. It was a miracle I was ever conceived, but how? Did my father resort to self-inflicting himself with drugs, or get drunk out of his mind? My mother made a dramatic entrance, of course. She was dressed nicely in an outdated, old matron sort of way. With her at the table the conversation was stilted and muted.

Monday my mother and I had appointments for the beauty parlor. When I came downstairs my mother gasped, "Are you wearing denim?"

"Yes, do you like them?" I knew what was coming.

"I most certainly do not. Young lady you march right back upstairs and change into something acceptable," my mother ordered. I'd bought a new pair of jeans in Bethesda. I knew my mother wouldn't approve. Maybe I wore them to be spiteful, but more importantly I was demonstrating my independence.

At the beauty parlor my mother was demanding as per her usual demeanor. The other ladies avoided us. They must have known who I was. I'm sure the rumors had spread that I was back in town. I really was a pariah in Ladue. I could tell that their avoidance upset my mother. On the way home my mother asked, "I noticed you don't smoke anymore. And your skin is darker but, I must admit, looks healthier. Have you been in the sun? And I also noticed you have not taken care of your nails." Anything else you noticed?

"I quit smoking along with taking vitamins, using lotions and all the other artificial crutches you people cling to. I'm not much into hair and nails anymore." I might as well get it over with and tell her what I thought. She'd been storing up her frustration for months and couldn't wait to unload on me. This was going to be embarrassing. The FBI agent driving us would get an ear full. My mother insisted the agents drive. She enjoyed being chauffeured at the taxpayers' expense. My mother didn't think waiters, hairdressers, manicurists, maids, retail clerks, or anyone would dare eavesdrop on her conversations. They were there to serve, not to listen.

"Evidently you don't care much about anything anymore, especially your family." She had me trapped in the car. I couldn't run to my room. So I braced myself for the scolding. "Let me tell you something, young lady. As if you coming home unannounced weren't inconsiderate enough, you drag home these men you need for protection. And your gallivanting all over the globe with that man has ruined our lives. Now I hear you were fired from your job by the President of the United States, how disgraceful. This is our home, and now we have to face people who used to be our friends. Because of your vulgar behavior nobody will speak to us, we will never be invited anywhere." Mother you don't have any real friends like ones who would wash you when you were sick, risk their lives, even give their life to help save yours.

"Whatever you think you have been through, it has been 100 times worse here." Oh yeah, is somebody trying to kill you, do you live with the memory of taking someone's life, have you ever feared for your life while being mortared like I was during the Tet Offensive, did you almost die from food poisoning, did you ever hold the hand of a friend as he died? Tell me Mother how bad it has been!

"You had an obligation to society, a responsibility to be a lady in this community, and you squandered it like you have squandered every other opportunity we've ever provided for you. We worked our fingers to the bone to raise you in a nice home, send you to the best schools, and this is the thanks we get. After all we've done for you, you ungrateful little girl. Never have I been so disappointed in a person. I can't believe you are the daughter I raised." Lilly Mae raised me and I can't believe you are my mother.

"You have left us with no alternative, but to have you treated by a psychiatrist for brainwashing." Was brainwashing a disease? "Next week you are going to be deprogrammed." You mean reprogrammed, don't you? "Also you are going to have a thorough examination by my gynecologist to see what other diseases you are carrying." What other diseases I'm carrying? As if she knew I was infected with some venereal disease. "After that, we are going to try and rehabilitate our standing in this community. It won't be easy. We'll have to entertain a lot more than usual." For God's sake shut up! I was about to scream.

I did see Dr. Flemming, the psychiatrist at Barnes Hospital. He was very nice. His office was a mess with journals, scientific articles, and books scattered about, and it smelled of pipe tobacco. He appeared overweight with a touch of dandruff in his mussed graying hair, and he wore an untrimmed beard. The tweed jacket had the leather elbow patches to further enhance the professorial look. And of course he spoke with the obligatory aloof British accent required of all Washington University professors. He took notes for the first 10 or 15 minutes, but as we got into my story he stopped writing and we just talked. He was most interested in my experiences in Vietnam and my observations of the men and women serving there. "So you lived with this man for months, slept in the same bed, ate with him, shared a bathroom with him, and you never had sex?"

"That's right. It was a strange relationship. At first we hated each other, but as time passed we developed a respect for each other, and it's my impression a love for one another. Jim and I talked about relationships. I don't think Jim has a problem with sex as long as he doesn't care about the woman. He has a problem committing to someone. But on a few occasions I felt we were connecting on a personal level. I believe with time we would become intimate."

256

"Is that something you would want?" the doctor asked.

"Yes, I'm not going to kid myself anymore. I believe we need each other. I know he needs me," I answered.

"So, by your argument, Jim cares for you and for that reason he didn't want to have sex with you," the doctor concluded.

"I guess so. Is this the weirdest relationship you have ever heard of?"

"I would like to meet Mr. Crotty. Your situation is not unusual for combat veterans, and I consider you a veteran of combat stress. But with time most combat veterans return to some level of normalcy and can function in the real world. There is always some residual effect. Of course there are the exceptions that go off the deep end. That's where I come in," the doctor stated. "If you do have a problem committing to someone I want you to contact me. Agreed?"

"Yes of course, I would welcome the help. I don't know if I will ever see Jim again." I felt a tear forming, but I got myself under control. "He is in a lot of trouble. Not just from what we did together, but something about killing innocent Vietnamese on his previous deployment."

"Well, I hope things work out for you. I'm going to have to cut this off, but I would like to speak with you in an informal setting. I've devoted much of my career to combat stress and find it enthralling. Your story is fascinating. Men and women engaged in armed combat I believe goes to the very essence of the human experience." Dr. Flemming made a few notes. I imagined he wrote, 'the daughter is sane, the mother is crazy.'

A few weeks went by. I worried about Jim and what was going on. I was cut off from the media. The television in the den was never turned to the news. I did have a gynecological exam and passed with flying colors which irked my mother. It gave Mrs. Know-It-All one less thing to whine about to her friends. I spent most of my time in my room reading.

I was able to run every morning with Greg, an FBI agent stationed in St. Louis. He was a lot like Jim and the other SEALs in how they spoke of combat. Jim said over 90 percent of the people sent to Vietnam never experienced combat. It took nearly 10 people in the rear to support one soldier in the field. With all the administrative, medical, mechanical support, air operations, disbursing, public relations, armory, food service, supplies, base security, and a slew of other things it was no wonder. Just to put one aircraft in the air required many man-hours.

I could tell a combat veteran from a REMF or Rear Echelon Mother Fucker as Jim called them. The combat veterans were usually self-effacing and talked more of mishaps than being like John Wayne. Whereas the non-combatants, like the jeep driver in Saigon, spoke in bravado terms like, 'there I was staring death in the face.' Serving in Vietnam was no picnic for anyone. Being away from home, the threat of a terrorist attack, contracting gonorrhea were all hardships. But if one worked in disbursing, then say you worked in disbursing. The Tet Offensive was a wakeup call for a lot of REMFs. I got the impression while running with Greg that the Rangers were a pretty tough bunch of guys.

At dinner one Saturday night in late March my mother blurted, "Susan, as you know, tomorrow is your birthday. We feel obligated to act as normal as possible under the circumstances. You have put our family in a most undesirable position. Your father insists on having a small dinner party in your honor at the club. Personally I feel we should wait until you are fully deprogrammed before venturing out into the public. But since your father never listens to me and insists, I have taken the liberty of inviting Walker Knolton as your escort. He's eligible and quite possibly the only gentleman who would be seen with you. Please try to behave like a lady even if you must fake it. And please don't further damage your reputation." 'Don't count on it Mother.' With that my mother excused herself from the table without eating a bite to go lie down. She was just too distraught and it was all my fault.

Walker Knolton was a class A twerp. Knowing somebody was trying to kill me was bad enough, but the idea of an evening with Walker was worse. He was two years my senior. As I recalled, he was divorced after a year of marriage to a celebrated socialite. The story I heard was that he came home early from work one day to find the club's golf pro in their bed teeing off in his wife's rough with his big wood.

So this was the man my mother arranged for me. She probably thought this was the best I could do, a divorced loser. Was I really going to live the rest of my life in Ladue, live in some big tomb of a house, have spoiled brat kids, belong to that country club, and play golf and bridge with those shallow ladies? The idea of worrying about being invited to the 'right' parties, and what to wear, and having dinner with the same drab people night after night, and making the same conversation made me want to puke. I would rather live in a trailer with someone I loved than in a mansion with somebody I didn't know.

Sunday evening I started getting ready for my big twenty-seventh birthday bash. Dinner was to be at eight. I think Walker was already downstairs. I could hear chatter and strained laughter. I wasn't going down until the last moment. My mother already chirped a couple of times reminding me that company had arrived and we were going to be late to the club. I couldn't wait to act like a lady in front of all my loyal friends.

I was in my panties and bra when I heard a tapping on my window. My room was on the second floor. The tapping came from the window that overlooked the garage roof. I looked out and couldn't believe what I saw. It was that incorrigible Petty Officer Jim Crotty and the unfaithful FBI Special Agent Eric Stutter. They were grinning and laughing having the best time watching me scramble for a robe. How long had they been out there? I yelled, "Get in here you assholes." I wondered what Eric told Jim about me. Jim probably thought I was a horrible tramp.

I struggled with the window. Finally after some banging and with their help we got the window opened. Jim came in first and grabbed me, "I've missed you."

"I've missed you too," he squeezed me so hard I could hardly breathe. We kissed.

Eric came in next. He also squeezed me hard and whispered, "You and I both made mistakes." He kissed me affectionately.

I was confused, "Tell me right now, what's going on?" I grabbed Eric's arm to get his attention. "Is the public execution taking place in St. Louis?"

"No execution," Eric offered. "But there is some big news. At eight o'clock the President is addressing the nation."

"About what?"

"I'm not positive, but I have a pretty good idea. We thought we'd drop by and watch it with you," Eric stated.

As Jim put his arm around my shoulder I pressed to his side. I asked, "Just like that you two pop into my bedroom to watch television?"

"You started all this and dragged this poor sailor into this mess. We've come to an understanding. We both love you. I can't understand why," Eric revealed. "But whatever the President says tonight will determine your fate."

At that moment my mother burst through the door. "Don't you ever knock?" I screamed.

"What is all the commotion in here?" My mother gasped, "What is the meaning of this?" My mother was beet red and I think frothing at the mouth at the sight of a man with his arm around me while I was holding the arm or another man only dressed in my bathrobe.

"Oh, these are my friends. They dropped by to watch television," I answered.

"Is that what you have come to, receiving your gentlemen callers through your bedroom window?" My mother couldn't control herself. "And you aren't dressed!"

"That's alright. They've both seen me nude." My mother's jaw dropped to the floor. "Let me introduce you, this is Navy Petty Officer Jim Crotty an enlisted sailor. He is the gentleman I've spent the past few months with. You may remember him attending my 16th birthday party. He became ill at our front door. And this is FBI Special Agent Eric Stutter. We lived together and were lovers once. I love both of them."

My mother went screaming down the hall, "Menage a trois, ménage a trois."

"We better get downstairs." Eric informed us, "The speech is about to start."

As we got to the head of the stairs my father was rushing up. "What's going on up here?"

"Nothing, a couple of friends dropped in. The President is speaking in a few minutes and they think we should listen," I told my dad as we started down. He retreated. Walker was standing at the foot of the stairs.

Eric had informed the FBI detail he was coming. Everyone greeted each other and as we retired to the den. I sat on the couch in my bathrobe between Eric and Jim. I held hands with each of them. I really did love these men. I didn't care what anybody thought.

My dad took his easy chair. The two FBI agents stood. Walker was in the doorway. I think any hopes he may have had of getting lucky on my birthday quickly faded when he saw me walk down the stairs with two men who could have been mistaken for Steve McQueen and Paul Newman.

My mother appeared out of nowhere, "We have company waiting for us at the club. We are already late."

My father replied, "I'm listening to this. Go ahead without us. Walker would you mind driving Mrs. England to the club?"

My mother retorted, "You make up your mind right here and now. It's either me or your daughter. If you stay you can kiss your airplane goodbye. It was my family money that bought you that God damn contraption."

"We'll catch up with you later," was all my father said as he waved her off.

The President began his speech. He looked tired, but he always looked tired with his droopy ears, half closed eyes, and that annoying slow forced speaking style. The speech went on and on and I was beginning to wonder why Eric thought this was so important for us to hear until the end when the President said a few words that I will never forget, and most Americans living at that time will never forget.

"With America's sons in the fields far away, with America's future under challenge right here at home, with our hopes and the world's hopes for peace in the balance every day, I do not believe that I should devote an hour or a day of my time to any personal partisan causes or to any duties other than the awesome duties of this office—the Presidency of your country.

Accordingly, I shall not seek, and I will not accept, the nomination of my party for another term as your President."

Author's note: several of my friends, who were kind enough to proof read Question Authority, have suggested the story ended too abruptly. I suggested they re-read the first few paragraphs.

Acknowledgements

I would like to acknowledge my cousin Cathy Weidle who worked with me throughout the writing of <u>Question Authority</u>, also, my office manager Roz Choen who edited the text. A special thanks goes to Joyce Ulrich, a high school friend, who made significant suggestions about the story line.

36059277R00147

Made in the USA
Middletown, DE
23 October 2016